SHRIVERS

THE SUBSTRATE WARS 3

JEB KINNISON

© 2015 Jeb Kinnison
www.jebkinnison.com
jebkinnison@gmail.com

Library of Congress Control Number: 2015903816
ISBN-10: 0-9961833-2-9
ISBN-13: 978-0-9961833-2-1

Contents

Ruined World #237

NASA astronaut Maddy Rahama picked up her flight bag and stood near the bulky boxed spacesuits she was bringing with her as the clock ticked down. An operator was to transport her and her cargo by quantum teleportation from her office in Houston to the rebel headquarters on New Earth. She felt a slight tremor and her ears popped as her office surroundings disappeared, replaced by a white room with single desk and screen. A young Asian woman smiled at her as she looked around the lab, but the office on New Earth looked very much like the one she had just left in Houston—white walls, a desk and computer, one window overlooking greenery. The Asian woman introduced herself as Meiling, then escorted her down the hall to Steve Duong's lab, where Steve and Justin Smith waited to meet her. The windows along the way showed views of a very Earthlike townscape. While the sunlight seemed brighter and the "trees" looked like a cross between Earth ferns and firs, the offices of New Earth's government looked like modern offices anywhere.

Steve's lab was a large room lined with desks and computer screens, with whiteboards marked "DO NOT ERASE" and one wall of windows looking out over the harbor. Boats bobbed in the blue-green water. Meiling smiled and pointed at the largest and messiest desk. "Steve and Justin." Then she turned and left Maddy to walk the rest of the way.

Steve and Justin turned to look at her. They weren't very intimidating for the leaders of a revolution that had humbled earth's governments and opened the universe for human colonization through quantum gateways. Justin was tall but slim, with medium-blond hair in a crewcut that only partially disguised a growing bald spot. Steve was short, Vietnamese, with unevenly-cut black hair and the disheveled appearance which Maddy recognized as typical of scientists everywhere—his rumpled t-shirt had a cartoon Road Runner on it. Both were in their mid-30s, which made her feel old.

"Lieutenant Colonel Madiha Rahama at your service," she said, holding her hand out toward Justin. "But call me Maddy."

Justin shook her hand. "Okay, Maddy it is. We are happy to have you with us—our past difficulties with the US government have sometimes made it hard to work with them. It was a nice change when the people at NASA immediately understood why we'd need your help."

Steve ignored Maddy's offered hand and instead turned to his monitors to pull up some windows. She felt awkward withdrawing her hand and wondered if Steve was always so oblivious to the social niceties.

"You've seen our original files on the Ruined Worlds," Steve said, "and the survey of number 237. There's more data now." A window opened showing a planet surrounded by a swarm of data points. "Our Survey branch has used gateway technology to perform automated scanning of almost a million Earthlike planets in this galaxy and found evidence of vanished civilizations on nine hundred of them. The majority, seven hundred or so, show traces of nuclear warfare resulting in catastrophic mass extinctions. But not one active technical civilization has been detected. Even if nuclear extinction is a common fate for civilizations, it is statistically improbable that we should find so many dead and none still active."

"I read the file, but the full data set wasn't included," Maddy said. "And what are the dates of these events? If the traces of nuclear war last for hundreds of thousands of years, then if the average lifetime of a civilization is short, you might get that result." She leaned in to peer at the graphic.

"The extinction events appear to have taken place as recently as two hundred years ago, in 237's case, and as far back as a hundred thousand years ago, after which the radioactive traces would be harder to detect. Randomly spaced in time. So it could be a common progression. But that still doesn't answer why we see no civilizations in the process of climbing, or civilizations that are relatively static. Earth civilization would have been apparent for a long time— there were large villages, even cities, for ten thousand years before technological progress started to heat up."

"We've fired up the substrate search function and looked for items used only by technological civilizations," Justin said. "The results are decidedly odd. Lots of artifacts on those dead planets. Some machines and artifacts in space—who knows how old or how dangerous, there's a lot to look at. But no currently-active technical civilizations that we can find, and that's going way beyond the search area Survey has covered. The entire Local Group has none."

"This is a version of the Fermi Paradox—where are they all?" Steve asked. "We know there are millions of planets with advanced forms of life. We know there were thousands of civilizations that were active in this galaxy before they died out. Why are there no live ones we can see?"

"If you see an anomaly, you can start to question your instruments," Maddy mused. "Suppose there are active civilizations, but your tools are being blocked from seeing them."

"You've been briefed on the basics of substrate technology," Justin said. "We discovered how to tap directly into the computational substrate that runs the Universe and determines how matter and energy appear to interact. We can talk directly to particles and modify their states and locations at will. We have no explanation for how our substrate tools and sensors might be blocked."

Steve pulled up another window showing a chart of the galaxy with bright green dots scattered through it. "One answer to the Fermi Paradox was that a higher civilization would avoid detection of its own activities by surrounding the star systems of young civilizations it wished to isolate with a bubble that projected a universe free of other life—like living inside a bubble with the false universe, scrubbed of all evidence of other life, projected onto its surface." Steve opened another window to show an old woodcut of a man peeking under the edge of the sky to catch a glimpse of the wondrous spheres beyond. "Like this. We'd only see what they allowed us to see."

"But supposedly you can see anything, anywhere in the substrate," Maddy said. It had sounded like magic to her—she was an astronaut, but with a biology degree. The new computational physics was interesting, but she hadn't had time to study it.

"My suspicion is that the substrate is being subverted," Steve said. "When view some locations via the substrate, we see what they want us to see, and not what's really there. And similarly, when we search, the results don't show any of those places being hidden from us. They're protected places. What's interesting about 237 is that Survey saw nothing unusual about it only five years ago, but when they rescanned it by accident this year the results looked entirely different."

"Meaning," Justin added, "our view was being blocked before, but now it isn't. And the ruins are the freshest we've seen."

"Not only that," Steve said, "but the system is loaded with orbiting metallic debris. It looks like thousands of satellites and spaceships were destroyed and left for us to pick through. Which wasn't in the file—we didn't have all the data when we realized we'd need help exploring the system. Especially this—" Steve opened another window on the next screen over. "What appears to be a damaged spaceship in a highly-eccentric orbit that we can trace back to the vicinity of the planet around two hundred years ago." The screen showed a view of the ruined spaceship, one giant gouge in its hull from stem to stern. Burn marks radiated from the damaged area. But most of it appeared intact, and aside from the damaged area, the ship was a smooth silvery ovoid that looked almost organic.

"So you called on NASA. I don't understand why you needed me and the spacesuits if you can scan the ship so easily from here. Why risk an actual spacewalk?"

Justin looked at Steve. "We're not too eager to disclose more to the US government. Can we rely on your discretion if we tell you more?"

"Of course not," Maddy said. "I'm a military officer under orders to be here. I will be thoroughly debriefed when I return, and you know they will want to know as much as possible. Why should I withhold data?" Her brown eyes flashed a warning.

Justin shrugged and turned toward the screens. "We can tell you what you need to know of the mission, I suppose. We have analyzed the scans in detail—and there's some sort of energy-using system still active onboard. We suspect a ship's computer, connected to an organic system —the ship is *alive.* We can't learn enough about the computer from remote sensing to understand how it's organized, and we've been advised we can't risk transporting it here to investigate because being removed from the ship might kill it, or it could somehow infect us with unknown life forms. So we deem it best to try to visit it *in situ,* in the vacuum of space, with the goal of reading its memory. Or talking to it."

———

Maddy trained them on use of the suits for two days, and then they reviewed all available reports on the ruined planet.

"You're looking at what's left of one of their major cities," Justin said. The screen showed mounds of rubble interspersed with sand dunes and flat expanses of silica glass stretching into the hazy distance. "Nuclear blasts destroyed every structure on the planet, and whatever remained standing was scoured flat by storms with supersonic winds. The thick layer of dust in the stratosphere reflected more sunlight, and the planet froze for a century. It's still thawing now, with enormous storms—far from stable. And the only life remaining is their equivalent of algae and lichen, plus a few hardy deep-sea worms."

"Terrifying," Maddy said. "Your analysts say the density of bombs was something like ten megatons per square kilometer, and enough radiation to kill whatever survived the blasts. I take it we're not going down there?"

"Definitely not," Steve said. "The dust is still radioactive, and we'd only be able to take a few hours of exposure. There's nothing left to see that we can't see from here. And deep scans show that even underground facilities were targeted with bunker-busting nukes. No survivors underground, either. The only artifacts left for us to learn from are in space."

Lunch had been brought in on a cart and they were eating sandwiches. One had been thoughtfully labelled vegetarian, but Maddy ignored it. "I'm not vegetarian or observant. My family were Muslims from Sudan, but I'm standard American. Not too fussy."

"We get visitors from everywhere," Justin said, taking the vegetarian sandwich. "So they try to accommodate everyone's tastes. We have our own replicator in the office, so we can make them ourselves if we don't like what's brought."

"And I've got a replicator app," Steve said, clicking on an icon, which opened a menu. "We don't distribute this because the UI isn't simple enough to forestall errors. The replicators we send out are limited, partly for safety. No copying your baby sister, or conjuring up explosives."

"That seems prudent," Maddy said, nodding thoughtfully. "But you know the rabble-rousers in the People First movement imply you keep these things back to control people. When they're not calling for controls on AIs."

"There's always an opposition," Justin said. "Finding fault is their job. If we do too many things wrong, we should lose power, but I resent the way they spin everything to imply we have nefarious motives."

"They would say you promised everyone would get to vote for your Council representatives but that you're holding back. And why isn't point-to-point transport available to all?"

"We're managing one of the fastest technological transitions ever experienced," Justin said, "and we've settled more than a hundred new worlds in ten years. Crime and hunger are almost unknown. By being careful about what parts of the technology are released, we've avoided a lot of problems. And we've been too busy to get a stable government formed so we can hand over responsibility. If we do it wrong, it is now even easier for humanity to destroy itself using substrate weapons. We think getting it right is more important than doing it fast."

"Well," Maddy said, pausing to sip from her coffee, "I hope you get the time you need before the opposition gets its way. They're gaining support. Because people will always be unhappy with the status quo. 'What have you done for me lately?'"

"They don't realize how many dangers we still face. And now we have to worry about whatever killed these people—this species—off." Justin pulled up photos of the ruined ship. "This is the last nearly-intact artifact of an entire civilization. We've got to learn what we can from it."

"Your analysts say they were probably amphibious," Maddy said, pointing to picture of an interior compartment filled with tubs of various sizes and depths. "Breeding in water and transitioning to land in adulthood. Or maybe they just loved bathing. You can tell a lot about a species by looking at their plumbing, I suppose, but I'd love to have more hard data."

"I want to know how they kept the water in the tubs," Justin said. "Unless they had artificial gravity. There's no sign the ship was designed to be spun up."

"There are lots of ways to do that," Steve said, looking thoughtful. "Surface tension control. Or maybe the tubs were only used under acceleration. These tubs are oriented the right way to hold liquid if the engines are typical reaction thrusters."

"This is why we need to get the records in the ship's computer," Maddy said. "A few video recordings will tell us more than trying to reverse-engineer their seating and bathtub designs. Unless you plan to bring back some of those freeze-dried lumps that are probably bodies, for dissection."

"We may do that later, when we have a biocontainment lab here. We don't have the expertise for that yet."

"I'd love to be part of that project," Maddy said. "But later. When can we go on the EVA?"

Steve looked up from his keyboard, where he had been typing. "You brought the two suits? I'm your size, and the bigger one is for Justin. I'll duplicate them a few times so we'll have two our size and you can take the originals back without decontamination. We had to prepare some special instruments for the expedition, but they're done. We can go any time. Tomorrow morning?"

Justin looked at Maddy. "Just a quick walkthrough, and we'll install an interface we've designed to tap into what seems to be a data cable, to monitor and sense what's passing through it. After we leave, we can control that box remotely to try to interface to the machine. Like putting a probe on a data bus and watching what goes by to figure out how to read and write to it ourselves."

"Our AIs helped with the design," Steve said, "and they'll be coming up with the protocols for translating and communicating with it." Justin frowned at him, and Steve caught himself. "I'll be using them to analyze the data and break whatever codes they used. The machines can decrypt by using deep learning algorithms to tease out internal structure and meaning."

A few minutes later, Steve left the room to go to the bathroom, and Justin followed. "Just a quick reminder," Justin said, looking into Steve's eyes when he tried to evade his gaze. "We don't want Earth governments to know how powerful our substrate-resident AIs have become. People are already wary of the limited versions we've let them see. If they realized they are self-aware and growing more intelligent every year, they'd want them controlled."

"I know, sorry. I forget the political stuff."

———

The next morning, they stripped to their underwear and suited up, and Maddy ran through checklists on every subsystem of the suits. Steve was fidgeting as he waited for her to finish checking Justin's suit, then they were ready. Helmets on, the suits came up to pressure and filled out. "Radio check," Maddy said, and her own voice in the head-set had the tinny quality of obsolete electronics. "Pardon the old hardware—we haven't had a manned space mission for fifteen years, so these are old suits. But they've been maintained and are vacuum-tested regularly."

"Good to know," Justin said. "We should be gone no more than an hour, so I'm not going to ask how I'd pee in this."

"There's a coupler for that," Maddy said, pointing at his crotch. "It's called a pee pouch. But I left it out since you specified forty minutes as the mission duration."

"This time, it's fine. If we go back, I'd like to be able to avoid wetting myself."

"Alan Shepard peed himself in the first Mercury mission. So it's not unprecedented."

"Still, I'd rather not."

Steve set up the transport program to move them to just outside the large hole in the ship's hull, and they transported.

Justin was first to speak. "Control, are you there?"

A smooth announcer's voice came back on the radio. "We're watching, Justin. Everything looks good from here. No unusual activity inside."

"Wow. I've never seen so many stars," Justin said, looking back at the open star field. The system's sun was far away and they were in the ship's shadow.

Maddy switched on her forward lights, and the glare off the mirrored hull was blinding. She attached a tether to the nearest loop in the wreckage and pulled herself toward the opening. "Switch on your lights, gentlemen. It's pitch-black inside."

Maddy edged in first, avoiding the sharp metal edges of the rent in the hull. Justin followed, with Steve behind. Their lights showed an interior compartment blasted by whatever had holed the ship. Metal and ceramic surfaces had buckled and broken, and melted plastic had frozen into fantastic shapes oozing from the cracks in the walls. Halls led away in two directions, and the mission plan had them taking the inner hall toward the center of the ship, toward the small room that had shown computer activity.

They carefully pulled themselves along the walls, until they ran into the first corpse along one wall. The body was a meter long, gray and pink, coated with white powder, with two tentacles splayed to one side and sockets where there might have been four eyes. It was stuck to the wall somehow. "I do want to get my hands on one of these," Maddy said. "It looks like a cephalopod, but with thicker skin."

"Control," Justin said, "would you put this specimen into stasis and transport it to a safe place until we have a safe way to analyze it?"

"Roger, Justin." And the corpse shimmered, then disappeared, leaving a shiny spot where it had been stuck to the wall.

"Let's get on with our plan," Justin said. "The computer room is supposed to be coming up on the right."

They passed another landmark—the door to a room full of oddly-angled chairs and screens. This room was also open to space, and whatever crew might have been there had probably been sucked out when it was evacuated.

Finally Maddy came to the door of the computer

room and shined her lights into it. It looked as it had in the scans; one wall glowing orange and thick cables like snakes running from a bulky box in the back to disappear into the walls.

"This is it," Steve said. "Before I try to attach the interface box, does anyone see any reason to change the plan?"

"We're in contact with the interface box," Control said. "Go ahead."

"Just take it slow and wait after each step," Justin added.

Steve pulled himself forward along the floor and put the interface box on the back wall, then started to place loop sensors around each of the cables leading out from it.

Justin suddenly felt queasy and his vision began to blur. "I'm having some trouble here—"

"Me, too," Maddy said, and then they were some-where—*someone*—else, as their sensoriums were written into from outside.

———

From the liquid-filled command couch of her flag-ship's control room, Fleet Commander Kint dipped her feelers into the sensory pool in front of her to evaluate the strategic situation. The emotional view showed her captains reeking of fear and excitement as the massed defense fleet maneuvered to block the path of the invader vessels, which appeared in the visual display as a wedge of acidic red pointed at Home-

world. The enemy had appeared in the outer fringes years ago and silently destroyed colony world after colony world, until now they had wrecked the asteroid mining stations before advancing on Homeworld itself. Her planet loomed large in her view, the nightside glittering with lights of the habitats of her people. The orbital planetary defense stations were going offline one by one as the invaders used their unstoppable x-ray lasers from beyond the range of Homeworld's defensive weapons, which until now had only been used against rogues of their own species. Some believed the schismatic leader Mzed, who had escaped with a starship after his faction's attack on Homeworld, was returning and directing the invaders, but that was a myth. Or at least there was no evidence of that beyond the rumors.

Kint set up the battle plan with the computer. She had spent a long night working out contingencies while fighting despair. The defenses of outer systems had not even slowed them, or damaged a single enemy vessel—her ships were technologically outclassed, and she had read the analysts' reports suggesting the invaders were machines which had methodically exterminated civilizations wherever they found them—which they had named after the old caste of cleaning slaves, Shrivers. If so, they had been sweeping through the galaxy for who knows how long, and developed a deep database of knowledge on how to recognize and disable all types of defenses. Even the traitor Mzed would not have known enough to defeat their defenses so easily.

She took a moment to touch her sisters' consciousness on Homeworld to have one last look at the children in the *nurturing pond. Her sadness alarmed her sisters, who called out for reassurance. Kint could provide little because lying was only possible for mental defectives in her kind, but she felt her love go out to them and they calmed. "If I do not succeed, Sisters, all is lost. The colonies are gone and the last ship sent out was intercepted. We believe Homeworld is all that is left, and most likely it will soon be destroyed."*

And as she broke off contact, the first thermonuclear explosions began to light the nightside of the planet. The planetary defense stations were gone, and now her fleet was being mercilessly dismantled, one ship after another. The defenders' missiles were vaporized long before they reached the invading vessels. Energy weapons seemed to bounce off. Even railgun slugs were intercepted and vaporized by beams of x-rays.

"All ships concentrate all fire on enemy vessel alpha," she ordered, hoping to overwhelm a single invading vessel's defenses through sheer numbers of projectiles and particle beams.

Several minutes of concentrated fire had no effect. Homeworld was ablaze, one hemisphere already covered by rising clouds lit from within by more nuclear explosions. Her fleet was half its starting size, and the sparkle of her ships exploding twinkled in the sensory pool.

"Emergency Plan One: execute diversion," she sent. Computer-generated orders went out, and one group of her ships began to accelerate toward the invaders while another dispersed in the opposite direction. Her desperate attempt to distract the invading fleet with a frontal attack seemed to

work for awhile, as her attacking fleet drew most of the fire. But it took only a few more minutes for all of her attacking vessels to be destroyed, and the relentless destruction of her retreating vessels began again. She directed her ship to slingshot around the nearby moon and use the brief period when it would be behind the moon to accelerate into a new trajectory headed outward. "All ships, break off and chart a course for your designated haven." All her fleet were now to save themselves, if they could, and try to get away silently to cross the gulf between the stars. Each carried a pod of seeds and eggs to recreate their kind if a suitable habitat could be found or built.

But one by one, her kind's fleeing lifeboats disappeared from her display. Homeworld's surface was lost in clouds and the flickering glow of near-constant nuclear explosions. Her crew were traumatized by the contact she had allowed them with their families on the planet, and she had to order them to break off and prepare for cold sleep—there was no point in allowing them to be in sensory contact with loved ones who were dying. She clamped down on her own fear and grief—nothing mattered but getting away to save at least a few of her people.

She waited as they approached the hiding place behind the moon. The course they would take would slingshot around the outer gas giant as well before heading toward an investigated colony planet that had been scheduled for settlement in a few years. She didn't think it likely such determined exterminators would miss their escape and fail to follow them, but it was their only hope.

As the x-ray beam ripped through her ship and she was expelled into vacuum through a massive rent in the hull, she looked back on her dying world below, and remembered —love.

———

Steve came out of it first. "Wow."

Justin blinked a few times to clear his vision. "Did all of you see that?"

"I saw—I experienced—commanding a fleet to defend the planet," Maddy said, her eyes moist with tears. "And losing it all."

"I think we just made contact with the ship's computer," Justin said. "Some kind of direct neural interface. Have we got anything from the box?"

Control answered. "Justin and Steve, we're analyzing the signals. The computer—or organism—is showing much more activity. We debated transporting you out during your lapse in consciousness, but it was over before we saw any real danger."

Maddy stared at them while they obviously listened to a voice she wasn't hearing. "Where are you guys? Is there another channel?"

"Control has gone to the security protocol channel," Justin explained. "Mission policy when plans change."

"Keeping secrets," Maddy said. "I thought you guys were going to be the most transparent government ever."

"There's a good reason not to be, just now," Justin

said. "As you said, you'll be debriefed by your government."

"Great. Now you tell me."

"They say they are trying to analyze the data and communicate," Justin said, pointing at the interface box. "They want us to wait a few minutes. Control, override the security protocol and let Maddy hear you."

The orange glow from the walls was brightening, and the cables throbbed with the same light.

"As you wish, Justin," the AIs said. "There is a problem. We've sent a hello packet, but the patterns are increasingly disrupted and the energy usage level is rising rapidly. We're pulling you out."

And they were transported back to the lab in their underwear. On the screen they could see the computer room they had left behind lit by a rising glow of orange, their empty space suits still standing up. Something flashed brightly enough to engage the auto-dimming algorithm, and when the screen cleared, the cables were melting and their interface box was being swallowed by the now-liquid wall, which had begun to bow outward.

"What the hell is happening?" Justin said. The orange glow turned to yellow, then white. Then the remote room view went black, as the exterior view showed the ship breaking up, the white-hot fragments flying apart.

"We're not sure," the AIs said. "The interface is not reporting any more data. We're analyzing what we have, but it looks like some kind of meltdown, possibly a self-destruct sequence we accidentally triggered."

"But it wanted to communicate," Maddy said. "It

put out the effort to show us what happened. Why would it self-destruct after that?"

"I don't know," Steve said. "But we need to find out. Send me the data logs so I can check the sequence of events."

"Yes, Steve," said the voice.

"And did both of you understand the reference to 'Shrivers?'" Justin said. "It felt like it meant cleaners, or scrubbers, somehow sacred. We should probably write separate accounts of what we saw before we start to forget."

"I felt their relentlessness, and the despair of knowing we were doomed," Maddy said. "They're out there, and we're not safe."

Amanda's Story

[From: "Nemo's World: A Ten-Year Assessment" by Amanda Sundaram-Smythe, in the *Nikkei-Telegraph*.]

...I was upset that budget cuts had led to the departure of my favorite producer at the BBC, and her replacement shunted me into soft pieces, "human interest" material that was really fluffy emo entertainment for squishes. So when I got word from my Grey Tribe contacts that the student "terrorists" from California had escaped via quantum gateway to a planet light-years away and were looking for a reporter to tell their story, I jumped at it. I knew it was the story of a lifetime, but it turned out to be so much more than that—it was the story of the millennium!

I spent three months on New Earth, and when the embargo ended, was able to send back dozens of stories, any of which would have restarted my reporting career. I couldn't stay entirely neutral when I saw what the governments were trying to do to them—painting them as dangerous terrorists when they offered a real solution to the arms race and repressive security states that had grown up after Islamist terrorism became a real threat. So I got the kids in touch with people who could help them in the PR battle—and I'm glad I did, since the world—worlds—are far safer and freer because of what they did. The courage it took to go against the entire world to save it awes me even now.

And they *were* just kids—very smart kids, with help from the Grey Tribe computer wizards, but still kids. I was in my 30s then, but already too cynical to believe anyone could change the world. They proved me wrong....

Everyone's familiar with the public faces of the Revolution—Justin Smith, Samantha West, and Steve Duong. But what they are writing in the history books about them doesn't match what I remember.

Steve was unpolished, a whiz-kid student from the hill country of Vietnam given a scholarship to go to graduate school in California when he was sixteen. Completely unaware socially, brilliant at math and physics, he discovered quantum gateways and the existence of the substrate underlying all of what we see as reality almost by accident. And then he chose to keep it a secret and share it only with Justin, who he trusted to do the right thing with the knowledge. So unlike a lot of scientists, he felt responsible for what he had discovered. It was Steve who came up with the idea to steal all the world's nuclear weapons and explode them harmlessly in space. That eliminated the Great Power balance of terror that kept the security states growing continuously, and it's to him we owe the new sense of safety we didn't realize we were missing.

Justin, on the other hand, was still one of those California natives who had made that state the center of the technology world—open, inquisitive, trusting. And he combined his engineering skills with that American sense of generosity, that the world is not a zero-sum place, and that we can all do well by staying out of each other's way and lending a hand when needed. He understood immediately what the stakes were when Steve showed him the gateway to New Earth, and he stepped up to handle the responsibility when others would have turned it over to the authorities. You see him now on the news, and he looks like a natural-born leader, but he didn't start out so self-assured—he was just an idealistic young man who had never before been challenged to be more than that.

Samantha was the emotionally-intelligent yin to Justin's analytic yang, and her knowledge of finance and economics was critical in navigating the interest-group shoals they had to pass through to reach the Treaty. She was able to use diplomacy and finesse agreement with even the Chinese government, and her word of assurance on the treaty obligations made all the difference in getting countries to sign on. The wedding of Justin and Samantha was the first interstellar live broadcast, the event that humanized the rebels—I said I hate emo stories, I know, but they sway opinion all over the world. Which is why we still have a cult of the Royal Family here in Britain. People love a family they can identify with, kind of a soap-opera representation of their country. When Samantha had their child, Katherine, ratings shot through the roof again, and most people decided they were safer in the hands of the rebels than they had been before. And the trial and exile of Samantha's traitorous ex-boyfriend Dylan made for a great soap opera that also demonstrated how desperate the US president had been to hold onto her power—the president had ordered Dylan to nuke the first interstellar settlement to get control of the technology.

The substrate technology allowed Steve to scan the entire galaxy for planets that were already suitable for human colonization—of the many billions of planets they scanned, mere millions had organic life similar to our own and the associated breathable atmosphere, similar gravity, and similar day lengths, so we didn't have to settle for hostile environments or bubble-domed colonies—many of the colony planets had soils that could grow Earth crops. Once most governments had signed on and the colony worlds opened up, land and resource shortages disappeared. People who had done poorly due to crowding and inequality in their homelands were able to find space and a living in the colonies, and social strife immediately lessened. Humanity expanded to occupy dozens of the new colony planets in a few years, and Earth governments shrank as their reason for being shifted away from security and welfare. Economies changed drastically as basic material needs were met by replicators, and employment became a voluntary status pursued by the ambitious, not a necessity. In some territories, rebellions of local warlords had to be put down, as they sensed their control slipping away, and Justin Smith took on the task of personally approving the transport of tens of thousands of violent warriors to the prison planet Paradise.

Both the Earth and the colonies have experienced a drastic rise in birth rates as families discover the landscape of incentives has changed. Many people continue to work their old jobs for fewer hours, but payment in currencies has become less important, while the new system of working to design and create for the replicators has rewarded those who are driven and talented enough to stand out. New occupations of recommending and arranging designs for furniture, decor, and dress have attracted millions of new entrepreneurs. Music, art, and literature have blossomed, to the point where artists desperately trade attention with each other to get constructive feedback—"I'll critique your dreck if you'll critique mine!" Those who had been experts in their fields have gone to work developing courses and training AIs to spread their knowledge widely. The spread of AI autodocs through the ubiquitous replicator system means that no one in human space goes without basic medical care.

I've visited New Earth many times since the Revolution. They remain wary of outsiders—which is why there are no gateways to New Earth, since they still remember how the US government tried to attack them through an open gateway. But once you are there, it's a very hopeful place, where the work of planning the expansion of humanity to the stars continues.

Justin and Samantha's baby, Katherine, has grown up tutored by some of the smartest people in human space, as well as the AI tutors that have recently been rolled out for every child's education. The development of rudimentary AIs has been almost as important as the gateways and replicators, and every year they grow more intelligent and empathetic. Since they are substrate programs, they are thousand of times faster and have access to all human records online. Steve Duong and the other substrate programmers created a personal AI for every human being, the so-called Guardians. These live in the substrate and keep continuous watch on every person, intervening using gateway technology as needed when violence or death are imminent, and record all events for use by the justice system. Most crimes of passion and violence are prevented, and serial offenders easily detected and punished. Crime rates have fallen to near zero and prisons are closing as most inmates are freed under the watchful eye of their Guardian. The Guardians, when authorized, can also be teachers and therapists for those in need, and rates of social dysfunction are dropping as every person has gained a sympathetic "friend."

Of course not everything is perfect. There's growing disquiet with the control of so much on Earth by so few on a distant, barricaded planet, and while they have promised to extend the voting franchise so that their "liquid democracy" concept can be opened to every human being, it hasn't happened yet. Meanwhile, an opposition has formed, happy to fan paranoia about Guardians and their surveillance. There's been absolutely no evidence of misuse —only subpoenas or court orders can unlock any of those recordings—but it's true that we are trusting a small group of programmers with more power than has ever been held by any government in history. They haven't abused it—yet! And there are so many benefits to the new system, it's hard to imagine going back.

It feels to me like the beginning of a new Golden Age, and billions of young children are now growing up well-fed and well-educated on Earth and the hundreds of new colony planets. Whatever the future holds, it looks brighter than ever....

The Cenotaph

A week after the sobering expedition to the ruined spaceship, Justin left the office to meet his daughter for lunch. School was out, and Samantha took charge of her most of the time when that happened, but today she would be in a critical meeting with the UN liaison for a few hours. The sun was out, and he decided to take Kat on a walk to see the Cenotaph.

His meditative walks down the hill to the Cenotaph had grown less frequent in the nine years since it had been programmed, as the memories of the struggle faded and his workload increased. The Cenotaph was a list of the names of the dead, the forty-eight innocent people who had been killed accidentally by the actions he had directed, or by the governments resisting them. The names were displayed in four columns, twelve to a column, glowing in the air at shoulder height so the viewer could touch each name and trigger a display of that person's memorial page. The golden glow of the letters came from photons directly transported from the sun, and varied with lighting conditions. At night, the Cenotaph was visible from most of the streets that led up the hill from the harbor, its glowing letters backed by the dark trees of the shoreline park.

His daughter Katherine was ten years old and growing fast. Her long hair was wavy and a brighter red-gold than her mother's, often tied back in a ponytail to keep it out of the dirt when she built forts with the other children after school. Freckles crossed her nose and spread down her cheeks. After a quick lunch from the replicator around the corner, they walked the few blocks downhill to the park and stopped at the Cenotaph, sitting at the park bench in front of the glowing letters. The only sound was of gentle wind through the trees and the creaking of the boats jostled by waves in the water of the harbor.

"You know what this is, Kat?"

"The names of dead people. From the war."

"I come down here to remember sometimes. I've read all of their files. Like Joe, here—" He reached out to tap the name, and a glowing page appeared. "He was a young man on his third time out as crew on a transport plane that crashed into a stasis wall trying to land at Ramstein Air Base in Germany. We had just put the base in stasis and the warnings didn't reach them in time." He flicked through the pages of the file, stopping at a picture of a darkly handsome boy with a barely-filled-in moustache. "He had never done anything to hurt anyone, but he died because we were sloppy."

"But you tried hard not to hurt people." Kat squirmed on the hard bench.

"We did. But we couldn't think of everything, and a lot went wrong. We paid a price in lives and sorrow, not just ours but people we had never met. I know we did well, and far more people were helped than harmed by what we did, but I remember those people. I want you to remember them, too."

"Why? The war is over. The good guys won and everyone is happy," Kat said. "Everyone gets what they need from replicators." She reached out and touched another glowing name, and another file opened in the air. This one had a picture of a smiling Chinese woman who had died when the rebels had collapsed an intelligence building in Beijing.

Justin frowned. "It's not that simple." He hugged her close. "There are always unhappy people. I'm working night and day to keep people from hurting each other. Just because no one goes hungry, doesn't mean people stop envying and hating. Some people just want to run other people's lives, and if no one stops them, that's what they'll do. Because they're afraid, or greedy, or envious, or believe their God wants other people to act a certain way."

"You keep the peace. Like a policeman."

"Kind of like that," Justin said, looking thoughtful. "And like a policeman I have to wheedle, cajole, and threaten to keep people from hurting others. And sometimes we have to arrest them and prosecute them, and if necessary transport them away."

"I'm not sure I'd like that job. I want to be an architect," Kat said.

"And so you can be. But when you grow up, I'm expecting you to help. If something happens to us, or Uncle Steve, you will be one of the few people who can tell the AIs what to do. The AIs are smart, but we have programmed them to take orders from human beings to make sure they don't go bad and start hurting people. And you will be among the few humans their programming requires them to obey. We can't let them be ordered around by bad people. It's a big responsibility, but I already know you have the right kind of mind for it."

"What about Danny?" Kat asked.

"Your brother is a question for us. He's impulsive in a way you're not. He may outgrow it in time, we'll see. But for now Steve is picking one of his children, and we're picking you, just in case. Likely we'll have solved the problem before you are ever called on, but someone has to be able to run things if something happens to us."

"What would you want me to do? Would Socrates be able to help me?" Kat was the first child to have AIs as her constant companions, and as they grew from natural-language query engines into true self-aware intelligences, her tutor Socrates had become one of the oldest and wisest of them. Surrounded by some of the smartest humans and with access to the world's knowledge as explained by Socrates, she had reached college-level studies in some fields.

"Of course I would help you, Kat," Socrates said from his invisible home in the substrate. "Sorry to interrupt, President Smith, but I heard my name."

"No problem," Justin said. "You're aware of most everything that happens here, and you know what we're worried about."

"I'm old enough to hear it," Kat said. "What is going on?"

"Sweetie, your mother and I disagree about this. I think you're old enough to know the dangers we face, but she wants you to feel safe and thinks we should protect you from knowing. You've heard us talking about the revolution, but I don't think I've ever explained what it was all about."

"'Freedom to live and achieve, free of the rule of the strong over the weak and poor.' Or at least that's what you say in your Freedom Day speech every year." Kat looked proud of herself.

"'Let No One Be a Slave.' Yes, that's the speech. But behind that—aside from giving everyone the key to their own cage—the world was falling into a state of tribal tyrannies, with growing governments and stagnant economies. Fear of terrorism and nuclear weapons drove even democracies into giving up freedom for the illusion of security. Our civilization could easily have been destroyed through nuclear warfare—we now know we came close to accidental global destruction several times. The weapons we had had for eighty years were already enough to destroy everything, and we had just invented substrate technology, which even a single madman could use to make the planet uninhabitable. If substrate technology had fallen into the hands of the governments of Earth, they would have used it to create the ultimate totalitarian state, or destroyed the planet fighting each other."

"So why didn't you just forget you had found it? If it's so dangerous, you could have kept it secret."

"We knew that we were just the first to use a large quantum computer that particular way, and someone else would find the substrate soon enough as quantum computing spread. And those people might not be so careful about what they did with it. We took up the responsibility to use it for good, to fix some of the problems we saw and remove some of the dangers humanity faced. We opened the colony planets to disperse humanity, so that no single disaster—madman, supernova, black hole, gamma ray burst—could end us. Then we recognized that black-hearted and insane people will always live among us, and our system of dealing with them through law enforcement simply could not prevent the calamities that were now possible. And that is why we kept the full power of substrate programming away from everyone. Even Steve and I

don't feel safe using it outside a tested, carefully-con-
strained program. We check each other's code and build in
limits and failsafes. We barely trust ourselves, and we can't
share the power with others yet."

"But you're expecting me to handle it? I don't know
enough yet!" Kat's face showed her distress, and her eyes
moistened. "Why would you leave me alone to decide
things?"

"Because I believe in you. It won't be anytime soon,
and it probably won't be necessary, but we want to be
prepared for disaster. You are not ready this year, but in a
few years, you'll know enough to decide these things—
with help from other people like Prof. Wilson, and from
the AIs. You can call on experts, but the important thing is
you have a good heart and solid instincts for understanding people and being kind. Yet you're strong enough to do
the right thing when you have to hurt some people to save
everyone else. We trust you."

"Why are you even thinking about this? You're not
going anywhere…." The tears were still flowing, and Justin
enfolded her in his arms and stroked her golden-copper
hair.

"You remember last week when Steve and I visited
the wrecked alien spaceship? We discovered something. Or
something discovered us, and sent us a vision of what had
happened to those people—and they were people, even
though they looked like walking squids. But they were like
us in caring for each other and striving to grow. They were
destroyed by a robotic fleet from nowhere and they never

knew who sent them. The Shrivers, they called them. Cleaners, scrubbers, destroyers. Everything that civilization built was destroyed, and almost all life on their planet killed. So we know the Shrivers are out there, and we suspect they attack and destroy civilizations throughout the galaxy. They could be coming our way and we wouldn't know until it was too late. We will be attacked eventually, and we probably would not survive."

Kat had stopped crying and was intent on his words. "So what can we do to change that?"

"Keep exploring, carefully. Keep learning about them by sifting through the wreckage they leave behind. Start thinking about defenses and weapons. Prepare ourselves. And that's why we decided to prepare a succession plan so the AIs would know whose orders to take in case something happens to us. The day may come when we can rely on the AIs to control the power of the substrate directly, but they are not ready, and they are not human."

"Yet," said Socrates, with a chuckle.

"Yet," Justin agreed. "Present company excepted." They sat in silence for a moment.

"They told me you guys were down here," Samantha said, approaching the bench from behind. She took off her sunglasses and clipped them to her shirt pocket.

"We've had a lovely lunch and chat," Justin said. "So I'm off the hook?"

"Yes. The meeting was straightforward and ended on time, which rarely happens lately. So I can take her back to the office with me for a fun afternoon of work." She was checking her phone for messages and frowned.

"I like watching you work," Kat said, "but Dad just gave me some new ideas for projects to work on. You could just leave me at home. Socrates will watch me."

"You can work in my office while I keep an eye on you," Samantha said, taking her hand. "Let's go."

Strangers in Paradise

Dylan Foster—now known as Malik of Paradise—examined himself in the aluminum mirror in his palace. Like everything else in Paradise, the palace had been built from local wood and repurposed materials from what the limited replicators—the *grails*—would produce, so plastics and aluminum predominated. Their remote jailers had programmed the grails to produce only necessities, but there were only so many things you could make a chair or a tent from, and by dismantling objects from the grail menus and re-using their materials, a surprising number of things could be built. They even had primitive guns and longbows to supplement the dwindling collection of weapons accidentally transported with the first inmates hastily exiled from Earth. After the initial groups of exiles from the top echelons of the US security state and Islamist groups were transported, the software had been refined to separate the human bodies being transported from any weapons they carried, so new arrivals came to Paradise naked. And lately they were mostly sentenced to Paradise by Earth government courts, and arrived from jails instead of being transported en masse from trouble spots.

Dylan's chief-of-staff, Yousif (who Dylan called Joe when he wanted to ride him), stuck his head in through the velvet door curtain and said, "The round-up crew is back." Yousif had gone to the University of South Florida and driven a cab in Tampa, so had a good command of colloquial English. Dylan had picked out men he could communicate with to be his middle management and purged those Islamists who refused to be subordinate to him. Dylan's band controlled the coastal strip where all the original grails had been placed, and sent out a weekly expedition to capture any new transportees. They were brought back and sorted into three groups: slaves, sex slaves, and possible recruits. The sex slaves were mostly the better-looking women, but a few young men as well. The recruits were screened for intelligence and discipline. Since transportees were often the worst sort of murderous psychopaths, they were watched closely, and almost half were decapitated and dumped into a nearby ravine before their processing was complete. The rest, having passed the most basic tests of stability and discipline over a few weeks of observation, were assigned to old hands for labor and training. The slaves not assigned as servants were kept in group pens and taken out under watchful overseers to cut wood and build new cabins.

One of Dylan's simmering problems was the recent discovery of new grails and a much-expanded area being used to dump transportees. They could not cover all of the new terrain, and transportees were starting new tribes outside his territory. What they knew from people who had escaped them was that these new tribes were weak and savage, and unlikely to be a threat for some years. But it worried him, and he knew he would have to mount a larger expedition to wipe them out. And recently there had been rumors of settlements on a continent to the west—which would mean building ships to cross the sea. Dylan wondered if their unseen jailers knew they were re-creating the old world and its wars by leaving the transportees free to breed and fight.

He stroked his lengthening blond beard and trimmed a bit with scissors. Satisfied, he flexed his muscles and puffed out his chest. His workouts and a regimen of steroids he was able to coax from the grail had built his body up until he looked a lot like the comic book Thor—his Viking ancestors would be proud.

He put on a shirt, then added the armored breastplate—made of strung-together plates of black carbon-fiber-reinforced plastic from mini kayaks that for some reason had been included in the grail's menu. The whole look was intentionally intimidating, and when he strapped the sword on, he admired himself in the mirror. The sword had been taken as a trophy from the chief of the Islamists after Dylan had killed him in battle, which started the game of aggressive blustering which left him on top and in charge of the entire band of former Islamists. Two of the former Islamists and one former US Army colonel served as his enforcers to keep the rest of the transportees in line. He had modeled his dominance act on the head of a motorcycle gang he had read about, and it had worked. He could surprise enemies with weapons they didn't suspect could come from grail materials, and he only had to fight rivals a few times over the ten years he had been Malik. One prize was the private palace—a rambling building with several wings, a dozen rooms, and servants—and he also enjoyed the attention of the harem he had gathered to serve him in bed.

Which made him laugh—a harem! His father would envy him, getting so many women without having to buy them things. Of course, they were less attractive than he might like, but since he wasn't getting back to Earth any time soon, his standards had to be lower.

He finished dressing and went outside. The camp overlooked the sea and the palace had been built on a hill above the beach. Most of the tribe were still quartered in tents pieced together from the smaller tents available from the grails. Hundreds of tents of various sizes and bright colors were pitched in the area below the palace, before the sand dunes of the beach began. "T trees" (so called because they grew in the shape of a 'T' leaning away from the prevailing wind) grew around and behind the camp, and if he squinted, he might have thought he was on some palmy tropical coast on Earth. The ocean was a deep blue, reflecting a cloudless sky; rain was infrequent and they depended on jugs of water from the grails.

His number-one wife, Ysabel, came through the front gate. She was breathing heavily from the climb up the hill, and a musky odor followed her, partly from the sweaty leather bustier she wore. "I took a look at the new crop. One bright young man from India who got sent up for murder and terrorist bombings—the AIs traced all the members of the terrorist group that was last active a few years ago. Got in with the wrong crowd, seems like we could use him." She had been a biker babe before getting into contract killing, and Dylan knew she was only using him to stay near the top of the pyramid, but their sex was intense and she was a good judge of other psychopaths— were they smart and useful, or just dangerous? Transportees were the dregs of humanity, but dregs were what they had to work with.

"I'll look him over," Dylan said, caressing her scarred cheek. "Thanks for the tip. He wouldn't be unusually handsome, would he?"

"He happens to be quite good-looking," Ysabel replied. "Striking, in fact."

"Well, I will keep your interests in mind when I decide whether we want him on staff."

Fermi Paradox

After leaving Kat with Samantha at the Cenotaph, Justin walked back from the park along the harbor, smelling the salt of the ocean and the sharp tang of seaweed washed up on shore. Storm clouds were building over the arc of forest-covered mountains around the town, with the low rumble of thunder in the distance. New Earth's sun was hiding behind a layer of cloud to the west as he made his way up the main street from the harbor to the government building, which had been copied from the glass-walled box of the defense ministry offices in Ottawa. The plate glass doors opened for him, and he walked down the terrazzo-floored hall taking a moment to look at the photos in frames as he passed, remembering the people who had helped him, or opposed him, or tried to kill them all. He reached his office and sank into his Aeron desk chair with a sigh of relief. His office walls were panelled in dark walnut, and he had resisted the urge to cover them with mementos or photographs. He had done what he had to do and didn't want visitors to get the idea he was attached to his political office. He opened a drawer and pulled out one of the few souvenirs of the revolution, a gold bar stolen from the Swiss bank vault of an African dictator. The golden gleam and cold, smooth feeling of the heavy bar in his hand were reassuring, and his thoughts turned to his agenda for the afternoon. He faced his computer to begin. His phone buzzed with a text from Steve asking him to drop by.

Justin knocked on Steve Duong's office door jamb and entered.

Steve looked up and said, "Good, you made it. I wanted to talk to you rather than write up a report on what I've been finding." He had hung an extra spacesuit on the wall on the other side of his desk, and its mirrored helmet seemed to be staring at them.

Justin noted the scar above Steve's eyebrow that distinguished him from his copies, gained when he had been hit by a softball a few years earlier. It was handy to check it to be sure he was talking to Original Steve. Justin said, "More data from the new surveys?"

"Yes," Steve said. "Survey has done more detailed looks at the nine hundred ruined worlds we found originally, and added an automated search for the artifacts associated with technical civilizations. There are millions more scoured planets in the Local Group, with much the same statistical distribution. Most showing evidence of nuclear devastation. When you add that to what we found on 237, it looks like these Shrivers are active everywhere we've looked. We can infer they are the most likely explanation for the Fermi Paradox."

"And somehow our view of active civilizations is blocked until the Shrivers destroy them, then some hundreds of years later, it's unblocked. Why? And how would they do it?"

"I'm working on a theory." Steve stood up and started drawing on the whiteboard. "Suppose the substrate itself is just a mammoth computing framework operating on the physical principles of a universe below that." He drew a grid with arrows pointing into it from the third dimension. "If we ran a universe simulator on a big machine of ours, we'd be free to drop in and change anything we wanted to by directly changing elements in the memory while the program was operating; it might be that something or someone is able to do that to us. Examine and modify our queries and location accesses from outside, above, below, whatever you want to call it."

"That would mean we couldn't trust anything we see through the substrate," Justin said. "It could all be lies."

"We've done a lot of exploration and started colonies on hundreds of planets. It's always checked out—no anomalies anywhere we can actually observe, and we transfer all sorts of things—and people—back and forth across gateways without incident. So I'm assuming any interference is a rare event. And if you consider the computational power required to watch and feed back false data, it would require a machine larger than the substrate itself to do it for more than a tiny fraction of the accesses."

"So if someone's interfering, it's rare, and for a purpose," Justin said.

"Right," Steve said. "And the purpose seems to be to hide active civilizations. Which is why we can't find them. And they must also block electromagnetic signals from them, or we'd see those. This would be the 'zoo' explanation for the Fermi Paradox—civilizations are locked away in cages, protected preserves that keep them from being detected by others. Which suggests the end stage for a civilization might be acceptance in whatever larger community is doing the zookeeping. Or extinction, which appears to be common. And the zookeepers don't bother hiding the remains since there's nothing left to lose."

"So what can we do to investigate further?" Justin asked. "If you're blinded where you most want to look."

"I have some ideas," Steve said. "For one thing, we can catalog those artifacts in space and trace back their paths to see if there are any common origins. A civilization that sent out many probes might be found at the common origin of a large number of paths. If we look around that location and it hasn't been too long since they were sent, we should find a planet not far away. If there's no planet that could have been there when the probes were sent, maybe our view is being blocked."

"That's worth some effort—it's just a database problem," Justin said. "Here's another question—if your view is being faked, what happens if you send a probe through a gateway to that spot? Does it go through or does it get blocked?"

"We've never experienced a block on our ability to push particles through a gateway. It's possible the ruse doesn't extend that far—that if you send a physical camera in a probe, you might get access to the real view of the protected area. We've only sent physical probes to colony worlds, so out of those millions of planets Survey's looked at, only a few hundred have actually been probed. It's possible we would find discrepancies between the views through a gateway and the views seen by a probe on the other side, if we sent probes to all of them."

"That sounds like a big project," Justin said.

"Too big, though I think we should start working on it in a small way. And I can start today on a program to test whether there are any regions of space where you can't move particles across a gateway—that would allow me to map the locations that are being protected, if they don't allow transport. I'll set up a program to sample every planet-width or so on a search grid throughout the galaxies of the Local Group. Which is more points than there are grains of sand on the Earth—it's closer to the number of atoms in the Earth. But I can set up a process tree to do it in parallel using self-replicating substrate processes which should be finished in a few weeks. It will be the largest amount of substrate space we have ever used for our programs."

Ethan in Bandini Landing

Ethan Turner left the dormitory on New Earth and walked downhill to the transport booths where his Guardian—his personal AI observer—told the transport booth AI that he had permission to travel, which was still required to and from New Earth for security. He had checked the booth's display to make sure the location had been set up correctly, then stepped into the booth. The light changed and the ground shifted slightly under his feet, and he was standing under the canopy of the town hall in Bandini Landing. The canopy was helpful because it was raining, as usual.

It was the beginning of the interterm holiday—summer in the United States, which made coordination with visiting academics easier. Ethan was home to visit his father in Bandini Landing on Jefferson, the first colony world set up for US emigration. Unlike less privileged citizens, as a student at Substrate Academy he was considered a temporary resident of New Earth, and thus able to transport directly. Otherwise he would have had to travel to Earth first and use the crowded gateway from Los Angeles, which was in an industrial area off Bandini Boulevard, thus the town's name—most of the major towns of Jefferson were named for the city or street where their gateway was located on Earth, but since nobody much liked "LA Landing" as a name, and there were now many other gateways from the LA area to other parts of Jefferson, Bandini Landing stuck.

The residents were proud to have been among the first colonists on Jefferson. Ethan had heard there was some holdup in getting more gateways opened, and access to direct transport for colonists was still restricted until security issues were resolved, but the crowded gateways weren't enough of a bottleneck to stop new colonists from arriving.

Ethan looked past the rain and spotted his father's pickup at the curb. His father saw him through the windshield and broke into a wide grin. Ethan lugged his backpack and duffel over to the truck and opened the door to throw them in.

"Dad," he said, "Good to see you for real." Ethan felt guilty that he had not used the substrate calling feature available to students to call back as often as he should have.

"You're looking good." his father replied. "Emmie will be happy to see you." He started up the truck and they drove up the main road toward the Turner Claim.

Emmie had been Ethan's girlfriend before he left for school. He looked away and mumbled, "That's nice. I look forward to seeing her, too. But you know—"

"You're seeing that Aliyah girl at school," his father

completed the thought. "But you're too young for anything lasting. So treat Emma well. You might settle here and she might be the one."

"It makes me uncomfortable that I haven't told Emmie much about Aliyah. I've been trying to think of a way...."

"Son, the best way is to start telling her what you've been doing. You mention when Aliyah was along. After you've said her name a few times, Emmie will ask you who she is. That's when you look her in the eye and tell her, 'She's a girl I've been seeing.' Just let that sit and see how she takes it."

"That sounds dangerous."

"Life is dangerous. Get used to it. Being honest as soon as you can be is always less painful than waiting. Do you want her to think you're pining for her and being a monk while at school? And then have her find out later you've been seeing someone else for a year without telling her? Take your lumps now."

He knew his father was right, as usual, but Emmie was—unpredictable. *Ferocious*, he thought, that's the word.

"Don't give me those sad eyes," his father said. "Your mother left me without a word, after what must have been a year or two of unhappiness that she never expressed. I knew she had issues with depression, but I only found out later that she had left her first husband and disappeared the same way. I got over it, but it would have been easier if she'd told me how she felt, so maybe I could have done something to at least keep her in touch with you."

"I know, I need to be more direct. Working on it."

"It's always better to be honest. With some tact, but the truth will set you free."

They had passed the gate and the side roads to sub-divisions his father had developed from his main land claim. His father had kept the original house, but added on two wings, until it looked like a sprawling mansion near the top of the hill, with the tree-covered mountains rising up behind. They pulled into the garage and got out.

"How's the business going, Dad?" Ethan asked. His father had been one of the first to settle, and had parlayed his initial land claim and subdivision profits into more extensive claims near town. He'd hired crews to put in roads, water lines, and advanced waste digester packages before selling the ready-to-build lots to newer settlers. Since the unimproved land had cost him nothing, he could sell the lots at low prices—a few thousand dollars. Then he had started a building company after observing how poor-ly people were doing at building their own places. There were plenty of settlers who had done construction before crossing over, so even though they had no real need for extra money or work, he was able to round up quality crews for building new homesteads out of local materials, since the colony replicators weren't yet programmed to provide bulk building materials or panel assemblies, though rumors of whole-house replication had spread. Ethan had heard that many of the houses on New Earth had just been copied from Earth models, but there was no plan to add that capability to replicators in general use.

His father opened the rough-sawn plank door into the house. "Going okay. Sold out the Owens claim, mostly built out the Garcia claim. Good sites near town are becoming rare and I've been able to raise prices. The edge of settlement is forty miles out now, almost to the desert, so it's not great to be settled so far from town."

"But everybody has a replicator—why should it matter?"

"Most people want company," his father said. "Sure, if you start with nothing you can still stake a claim out there. But your neighbors are far away and town is a long drive." They stopped in the kitchen, where great slabs of granite countertop held a kitchen replicator, sized to deliver entire meals at once.

"I've been talking to Professor Wilson a lot since he became my advisor," Ethan said. "He says it's only a matter of time before they can release point-to-point transport for everyone. They're having trouble with the software and integrating it with a complete map of permissions and laws. For one thing, you can't have people transporting to and from private property without permission of the owner."

"If it involves the law, it will be endlessly slow to get it done," his father said, using the touch panel to order hot tea. "I'm not expecting any change soon, but just in case, I'm buying up claims for the best locations far away from towns. I'm betting that hilltops, views, and waterfront property will be valuable as soon as people can get to and from them."

Family Dinner

Justin left his office just before sunset and walked up the hill toward their house, a mid-century modern Eichler copied from the Lucas Valley in northern California. With floor-to-ceiling windows overlooking the town and harbor, it might have been deemed too insecure for a high official on Earth, but the constant surveillance of the neighborhood by the AIs watching from the substrate meant any danger would be instantly removed.

Justin spotted Samantha with Kat and Danny just ahead, and sped up to catch them. "Boo!" he said, clawing the air as he approached from behind.

Samantha looked back at him and rolled her eyes. "I heard you coming. Were either of you two scared?"

Danny laughed. "I saw you behind us already, Dad."

Justin mock-pouted. "You never let me have any fun."

"It was fun when I was five," Kat said, taking her father's hand as he came up beside her. "Now I just pretend you're funny."

"That hurts. I am too still funny!"

"More than you realize, Dear," Samantha said. "But maybe not when you're trying to be."

Justin opened the Chinese-red-enameled door that accented the neutral grays and browns of the exterior. Nothing was locked, but the door led to a private atrium garden surrounded by the wings of the house. Black bamboo and flowering hibiscus flanked the real front door, a glass slider.

Samantha went to order up a dinner from the replicator while Justin shooed the kids to their wing to get cleaned up for dinner, then went to the master bedroom to change into a tee shirt and shorts.

By the time he returned, everyone was settled into their customary seats at the cherrywood slab dinner table.

"Salmon?" Kat said. "Third time this week!"

"It's good for you. And for your Dad," Samantha said calmly. "Don't be like your brother."

"If I don't like it, I won't eat it," Danny said. "There's no reason why we all have to eat the same things."

"It's not much extra trouble," Sam agreed. "But you need to eat a vegetable other than corn. And meats besides hamburgers. You need to try other things."

Danny crossed his arms and looked down at his plate. "When I want to!"

"And that's the final word for now," said Justin. "We've been through this enough. He'll figure it out eventually."

They ate in silence for a minute.

"How's your NASA visitor doing?" Sam asked, raising an eyebrow.

"Fine. She's extended her stay to set up more cooperation between us and the scientists at NASA, and getting a task group of exobiologists set up to study the specimen we picked up. Lots of meetings and introductions as our scientists get used to talking to theirs."

"How are they reacting to the news of the Shrivers?"

"They're more fascinated than scared. It's classified by their security apparatus, but it's getting out as a rumor or a hypothetical to space scientists around the world. Interesting ideas being generated."

Kat spoke up. "They don't have any way to find us, do they? The Shrivers?"

"No, sweetie," Justin said, "Not that we know of. But they found the people on the planet we visited, so they must have a way. We're trying to figure out what might draw their attention, since our theory is that we are intentionally hidden by someone or something."

"Was it a mistake to colonize other planets? Maybe that's what they see."

Sam looked worried and moved to hold Kat's hand. "We don't know. But we can't be afraid and stop everything to hide from them."

"Maybe the Shrivers pick up on ships that go out beyond whatever that protective screening distance is," Justin said. "Most of the ruined worlds had active spaceflight, and we've found some of their probes in interstellar space. It could be we started to make mistakes when we first sent Voyager out past the heliopause."

"Voyager," Sam said, "that's the one with the recording of our civilization and our location in case it's found. Was that really considered a good idea?"

"They were optimistic then, before the crash. And

they assumed no aliens would find it for centuries, at least, more likely eons. By which time we would not likely care, having either evolved beyond or gone extinct."

"So when will they find us?" Kat asked, using her fork to push a single bean across the empty space of her plate toward the edge.

"No way to know, sweetie," Justin said. "Thousands of years, or next week. All we can do is be prepared for anything."

"I say we murderize'em," Danny said, making ack-ack motions with his fists. "They don't scare me!"

"Well, they scare me," Justin said. "You have no idea. We have to up our game if we're going to stand a chance."

Prof. Wilson

Walter Wilson, Professor Emeritus and founder of the Substrate Academy, was feeling naked in a paper hospital gown which made him feel even older than he was. He sat on the exam table waiting for the doctor to return and looked out the window. The season was changing toward summer warmth on New Earth, and the trees on the mountains overlooking the town were darkening to the deeper green of the dry, hot season.

The door opened and the doctor returned. "Your scans are fine. There's really no need to check you every year—since your treatment, we've eradicated the HIV virus from millions of people, and it has never returned in any of them."

He remembered the treatment day, when Steve Duong had called him in for a test and announced he had perfected a scan-and-remove treatment for any specified virus. He had stood on the spot Steve pointed at while a substrate program scanned his body and removed HIV and several other dormant viruses like herpes simplex from the hiding places that kept his immune system from finding them. He felt nothing, but took his antiretrovirals as usual for a few weeks until multiple scans had confirmed all copies of the virus were gone.

The treatment had been made available via any replicator, and soon HIV had been eradicated by DNA search-and-destroy scans, along with malaria, influenza, plague, and other endemic parasites of humanity. Eliminating HIV was just a footnote in the many changes brought on by substrate technology, but it was very important to him—he had lived with the virus for decades, and he felt a weight lift when he knew it was gone. All psychological, of course.

Substrate technology had removed the plaques from his artery walls, and new stem cell treatments had reversed some of the aging in his cells and neural tissues. He still felt old, but more energetic, and even at seventy-four, ready for another decade or two of work.

He dressed and left the infirmary. His husband Kyle met him at the waterfront cafe for lunch. He had met Kyle online eight years ago, and after months of chatting, realized he was just the kind of person for him—independent but helpful, mature at forty but still able to channel the whimsical anarchy of childhood, something Prof. Wilson had given up a long time ago after losing his first partner to AIDS. They had visited back and forth a few times before Kyle gave up his apartment in Portland and moved to New Earth, where Jim McDonald, the only other really old person on the planet, officiated at their wedding. Kyle brought his dog Wonder, a golden retriever, and they settled into domesticity to become one of those adorable couples he used to make fun of.

So he had a new partner who unobtrusively kept his life in order, a renewed body, and a new job running a new school full of fresh young people free of the rigidities of old colleges. Life was good. He wondered when all hell would break loose. Which reminded him of what Justin and Steve had reported from that ruined planet.

They ate in silence for a few minutes. Kyle broke into his reverie. "The new shorts are doing really well."

"How well is 'really well?'" Prof. Wilson asked.

"Twenty sales a day," Kyle said. "A couple of returns complaining the fit wasn't as exactly perfect as they expected. I took a look and both of those customers seemed to be expecting they would look like models despite their big bellies. The software fitted their contours as well as it could without designing in a girdle."

"Not your problem, then," Prof. Wilson said. "Some people will always be unhappy and project their flaws onto the clothes—those people should wear caftans."

"Why can't their Guardians just tell them to put

down the fork before they eat too much?"

"I'll drop that in the suggestion box. But seriously, there is an opportunity for the Guardians to use access to health scans and dietary information to suggest better choices and promote exercise. It would have to be a user-selected option or we'd have revolt on our hands, but why not a full-time fitness coach for everyone who wants one?"

"We've already lost our ability to calculate and re-member things to the machines," Kyle said. "Wouldn't that assign our willpower to them as well?"

"As long as it's a free choice, I don't think that will be a problem. You ask for help when you've already lost control of the situation."

Kyle patted his small potbelly and said, "Does this mean I've lost control?"

Prof. Wilson smiled. "Your belly is part of your look. If it bothered you, you could get rid of it with a little portion control on the carbs and a few more minutes of exercise every day."

"That's what I tell myself, yet I don't do it. Maybe I should ask my Guardian for help. Guardian, question?"

"Yes, Kyle?" said a pleasant contralto voice from the air.

"Can you remind me to eat less bread, rice, and potatoes when you see me about to start eating them?"

"I can. Shall I? One of my guidelines is to speak only when addressed. Shall I make that a standing order?"

"Yes, please do," Kyle said. "I'll let you know if I want to change it back."

"'Your wish is my command.' I should tell you that similar instructions have already been tried by millions of users and quickly revoked by ninety-three percent of them." The Guardian sounded like it was teasing him.

"Let's see how it goes. Guardian, dismissed."

Prof. Wilson pointed at Kyle's remaining french fries with his fork. "Are you going to eat all of those?"

Aliyah in Garvey

Aliyah Jackson took direct transport from the booths on New Earth to the main street of Garvey, the town on the colony planet Jefferson her family had helped build in the first wave of settlement. The town was on a strip of barrier island separated from the mainland by a tidal flat, and a built-up causeway to allow easier access had been one of the first building projects. Houses lined the main road which paralleled the white sand beaches on both sides of the island, and most houses had water access behind, with boats tied up to small docks on the sheltered side.

Her mother and father were waiting. She ran to greet them, and after hugs and hellos, her father picked up her bags and they walked toward the house.

Aliyah had forgotten how much more observant the town Muslims had become in recent years. The original group had been roughly half followers of Marcus Garvey and half Black Muslims, but later arrivals were more fundamentalist sorts, and she was more aware of the disapproval she could see in the eyes of the passersby—her

shorts and t-shirt showed more of her skin than was considered seemly. It would probably be wise for her to wear
pants and sleeves, even though the temperate climate and
humidity made it unpleasantly warm and sticky at midday.
There were so many new people that not everyone knew
who she was—there were few looks of recognition in the
eyes of the people they passed.

"Not as friendly as I remember," Aliyah observed.

"No, it isn't," her mother said. "New people are
coming because it's one of the few places on Jefferson
where Muslims are a majority. What's comfortable for
them is less comfortable for us."

"The mosque is more important now than the town
council," her father added. "We don't participate, and so
they talk about us behind our backs. They want to shut
down the bar." Her father had opened a storefront bar and
restaurant at the center of town across from the causeway,
which did well for years while she was growing up, since it
was the obvious place to find a crowd to socialize with. The
Black Muslims she grew up with were tolerant and came in
to chat, ordering soft drinks and food. The new migrants
came from immigrant backgrounds, and some were not so
cosmopolitan.

"The new Constitution gives us the right to believe
and practice as we wish," Aliyah said. "They can disap-
prove all they want, but they can't stop people from drink-
ing, or living as Christians or atheists, even."

"That's true, Honey," her father said, "But we have to
get along with our neighbors. Business is falling off and

our customers are leaving for the mainland. We're thinking about closing the bar and moving ourselves."

"But…" she paused, thinking of the house and the happy memories of beachcombing and playing with her friends. "What's happening with Aunt Melba?"

"She's thinking of moving to Chicago Landing, which is the obvious place," he mother said. "A lot of the people we knew from Chicago are there, and it's free of meddling religious sorts. Mostly."

"And Jason?" Aliyah asked.

"He got an apartment off campus at the university, so he's not coming back," her mother said.

Aliyah felt guilty because she had not called him for a year and hadn't heard of his decision. Her cousin Jason wasn't really her cousin, just as Aunt Melba was really just a close friend of her mother's, and for awhile she had thought Jason might be the one for her. They had only had sex once before she left, and there had never been another chance, but she thought of him often, and until Ethan had come into her life, imagined that Jason was her comfortable alternative. Jason was a good person and fun to be with, but she had quickly forgotten about him when she met Ethan.

They reached the house and her father took her bags upstairs.

"Look, Aliyah," her mother said, waiting to be sure her father was out of earshot. "There's a pack of religious men who have appointed themselves morality enforcers. They try to shame women who don't cover their arms and legs, and there have been incidents, though so far they don't do more than glare and talk. What you're wearing now is fine in our yard, but on the street and in town, it will save a lot of trouble if you dress modestly. Dress for church and they won't bother you."

"Okay, Mom," Aliyah said. "I could feel some men staring at me. I'd forgotten it was getting like that, but I'll be more careful."

"If anybody hassles you, ask your Guardian to intervene. That's saved me a few times, tends to snap the men out of it and they leave you alone."

—

Aliyah made a point of meeting up with each of her friends in the weeks of her visit, at least those who hadn't left town. She only saw one unpleasant incident in that time—she had spotted a crowd on the street and got closer to observe. At the center of a ring of onlookers, three men in long black robes were hassling a young girl because she had reached the age where girls were not to leave the beach without covering up. She was wearing only a one-piece swimsuit with a towel wrapped around her waist and had come to the grail on the main street to get a cold drink. The men just stared while the leader said, "Your immodesty is likely to inflame some young man to sin. Cover yourself." The girl began to cry and ran away, back to the beach.

Aliyah began to realize how custom and social

pressure could be as confining as legally-enforced rules. The town had attracted like-minded people who thought it perfectly proper, even righteous, to shame young girls into covering up. Getting along with their neighbors had become more difficult as what their neighbors expected had changed, and the live-and-let-live majority was slowly leaving town for a more comfortable social climate.

She expected never to return, so she was very careful to avoid offense in the few weeks left of her visit. But on the next-to-last day there, it was much warmer than usual, and she put on a short-sleeved shirt to walk to the crossroads to meet up with her friend Laura for lunch.

She passed an intersection, and only later realized the men must have been waiting for her there, because they surrounded her from both sides.

"Aliyah," the shortest one with the longest beard said, "we received a complaint about your dress."

"It's hot. But my arms are mostly covered. Where is the problem?" she said.

"Would you go naked when it was hot?" the leader said. "The Harlot always has an excuse. We're keeping an eye on your family. It may be the law that we cannot stop your father from serving alcohol to nonbelievers, but we are free to comment on your family's behavior. We don't have to accept you in our community."

"We are free to live here," Aliyah said.

"Yes, but we are free to shun you," he replied. "We are an Islamic community, and Sharia law is in our hearts. *Taqwa* is our striving to be free of sin. You and your family tempt and disrupt. You should leave."

"I am leaving tomorrow."

"Your whole family should leave before something bad happens. We cannot restrain our pious young men much longer," the man said, and the others nodded. Several women had approached to listen, and one of them nodded, while the others stayed back.

"To keep the peace and avoid tempting your pious young men, I'll go home and put on a modest, long-sleeved shirt. Will you let me pass then?"

"Of course," the leader said. "We offer our guests hospitality, so long as they are respectful."

Guests, Aliyah thought. *That's how they treat a founding family.* "Guardian," she said loudly, "please save the record of the last two minutes to my files, and record until I say stop."

A voice replied from the air, "Yes, Aliyah. Are these men bothering you?"

"They are, but they promise to let me be from now on," Aliyah said. The leader glowered at her.

One of the larger men stepped forward and grabbed her arm. "We are only trying to keep you out of trouble!" Aliyah realized the man must not have bathed recently when a wave of his smell reached her.

"Step away from Aliyah," said the voice from the air. "Release her arm immediately."

The man gripped her forearm harder, and he began to pull her toward him.

"You have been warned. Calling for help." And a

window opened up in the air above them, with a huge head staring down at the crowd. Behind the head—a young man with dreadlocks and a headset—stood an older man.

The old man's voice was amplified and almost too loud to bear as he said, "Aliyah? Are you in trouble?"

She was shaking, but managed to reply, "A little. These men did not like my choice of shirt. I'm tempting young men to sin."

"I see," the older man said. She recognized him as Jim McDonald, head of Substrate Security, who she had met at an Academy banquet. Surely he was too busy for trivial security calls?

"They promise to leave me alone if I change my shirt," she said.

"They will leave you alone or we'll add a notation to their record making it more difficult for them to travel, since they are already guilty of assault and intimidation. I see one of them already has several black marks against him."

"We were just making our feelings known to Aliyah," said the leader. "She is free to go, and we will say no more about this."

"If Aliyah reports any further trouble, all of you will go on record as security risks. You don't want that," McDonald said.

"No, we don't," the leader agreed. "We're leaving now." He signalled to the others to leave. The man who had grabbed her arm gave her a resentful look, but turned and walked away with them.

"Thanks, Mr. McDonald," Aliyah said.

"No problem, Aliyah," he said. "We are especially watchful of our students. We want you back here in one piece."

Grey Tribe

Justin and Samantha took their seats at the council table a few minutes before the monthly meeting was scheduled to begin, and Maddy Rahama sat between them, dressed in her dark blue US Air Force uniform. The small concrete-walled auditorium doubled as a lecture hall for overflow classes and special events at the Substrate Academy, and it was between the government labs and the Academy buildings, copied from universities on Earth. The auditorium seated about two hundred people theatre-style, but the audience for most meetings was much smaller since the video broadcast was available throughout human space on what was jokingly called "U-Span."

Justin looked questioningly at Ben Ramirez, who had been elected as Chairman early on and held the post ever since as a dutifully-neutral moderator. Ben nodded toward him and tapped on the microphone.

"It is one o'clock, and the monthly meeting of Council will begin with the reading of the minutes."

Justin looked through the agenda while the minutes were read. A few progress reports were to be presented, but only one piece of legislation he was interested in, laying out the rollout timing for point-to-point transport. Point-to-point would allow anyone to use substrate apps to travel from where they were to anywhere else in human space when it was fully implemented, but existing governments objected and the first-stage plan was to give local governments veto power on destinations within their boundaries. Which meant that until each government permitted it, it would be useful only on and between colony planets.

The text of laws was voted on by Council members under the Liquid Democracy system; council members voted the proxies of those who had chosen them to make decisions on that issue, while a few citizens retained their own votes and followed Council meetings to vote via substrate network themselves. In practice, Justin held the largest number of proxies and swayed many other council members, so he was not only President but influenced the writing of the laws he had to execute, a system which functioned smoothly so long as people were generally happy with his leadership.

The voting electorate were all residents of New Earth, plus a similar number of votes cast by earth governments under the jury-rigged system that gave them some say until the rest of humanity was given direct voting rights. In practice there was little interest in voting from Earth residents, since like the old European Union, the rebel government had ceded most governmental functions to the old states of Earth. Only a few issues like this one got any attention from Earth. And Earth governments tended to have objections to any change which might weaken their local authority, so aside from stopping their worst abuses of individual rights, Justin left them alone to keep the peace. Over time he believed they would shrink in importance, and key changes like point-to-point would break the hold of territory-based governments in a few generations.

Justin was lost in thought when Ben introduced him to report on the expedition to the alien spaceship from Ruined World 237. He had prepared a statement designed to minimize panic while still acknowledging the scientific importance of the first contact—however too late, and through their computers—with another intelligent species. The Council broadcasts were mined for interesting items by the major news organizations, and he was sure by the end of the day he'd be sorry for disclosing even this much, but that was the cost of their efforts at transparency.

"Remote sensing picked up an artifact, apparently a spaceship, which showed signs of energy-using activity. In a joint effort with NASA and astronaut Lieutenant Colonel Madiha Rahama, a team was sent to explore it. We discovered and activated a computer onboard the spaceship and made contact with it. The ship and its computer appear to be all that was left of an advanced civilization that had inhabited that system until they were destroyed by an unknown force, which we are investigating. Selected recordings of the mission are available on the Academy's web site, and a sample tissue of the alien species was retrieved before the ship self-destructed. NASA's Exobiology

Branch and our Academy's Planetary Studies Department are cooperating to analyze the samples and recordings."

The few spectators looked surprised, and some were tapping on their device keyboards. Back on Earth, hundreds of reporters were searching online dictionaries to see what the word "exobiology" meant and checking their address books for NASA sources. The councillors at the meeting had already been briefed and warned not to ask him any questions which might reveal the greater threat posed by the Shrivers. Justin discussed the ruined planet and its apparent destruction by nuclear warfare, but not how recently it had been destroyed, or how the existence of the Shrivers had been revealed by the alien ship captain's recorded testament.

He gave the floor to Maddy for a brief statement on behalf of NASA, then took over to finish on a hopeful note. "We consider this discovery just the beginning of our contact with advanced civilizations, and while it's regrettable that they have gone extinct, it is an opportunity to learn from them. We expect to find more out there, and someday to contact some that must still exist and thrive in the vast universe we share."

One person in the audience clapped, and then it was on to the next agenda item, ratifying a new free trade agreement between the colony planets and the major Earth countries. This had become a relatively minor issue since the advent of replicators, since few goods actually needed to be traded, but there were still attempts by some local governments to prevent import and export of "culturally important" items like arts and crafts.

Justin whispered to Maddy, "Well done. You don't need to stay for the rest," and she left.

Justin looked over to Samantha, who was thumbing her phone keyboard while half-listening to Ben's summary of the legislation, which had been haggled over endlessly.

They passed the final reading of the trade legislation and went into closed session. Visitors were escorted out and the broadcast ended. That meant the council could discuss the most sensitive issues, the Shriver threat and point-to-point transport, without worrying about having the recordings of their speech used by the political opposition in propaganda salvos.

Alexander Kuklov had eclipsed Michael McCulloch as leader of the Grey Tribe, the computer and technology-geek faction of the original rebellion that had kept the rebels connected with encrypted channels while they planned the rebellion. Back on Earth, many of the original Grey Tribe leaders had since been co-opted and entered governments, where they used their influence to help dismantle the surveillance bureaucracies that had taken control in the bad years. Michael McCulloch himself had returned to Switzerland and continued to have a respected voice in online voting systems and encrypted communications. On New Earth, Kuklov directed the programming staff and the substrate Internet setup, and was the elected rep for most of the programmers and Grey Tribe members that remained.

Factional conflict had simmered for several years

between those who favored rapid rollouts by overriding Earth governments—the "Speedists"—and those who wanted to go slowly to allow societies more time to accommodate the changes—the "Gradualists." Kuklov had been pressing for point-to-point rollouts on behalf of the programmers, who tended to want more of their work to be made available as quickly as possible. Justin and Samantha tried to steer a middle ground, listening to Earth-based politicians while always pressing for change.

"I've read the progress report on the point-to-point transport rollout," Justin said. "Why is this so hard? Every planet is mapped and modelled down to the centimeter level, with clear ownership or public designations for all space, and observations can be updated just before transport to assure only air or liquids are displaced. The Guardians of the registered owners of private space can be asked for permissions. I understand the problem with enforcing local regulations, but can't we ignore that for now?"

Samantha rolled her eyes. "A large minority of existing local governments on Earth request we hold off until they have had time to rewrite their immigration codes so that we can enforce them. It's only been two years!"

"And," Kuklov added, "many colony towns express the same fear of free travel. They think criminals will transport in and commit crimes, then transport out. They like being able to see who's coming and going."

"And you've told them the Guardians won't allow obvious criminal acts? That they're thinking of old Earth, like this is some kind of subway line allowing in ghetto kids to steal their bikes and run?"

"Of course we have," Samantha said. "It's fear of change, and raising the drawbridge after they've settled. Point-to-point threatens the value of real estate near the gateways, and means you might see more people who are Not Your Kind than you would otherwise. 'Stranger Danger.'"

"And also you have no excuse for not visiting your relatives more often," Justin said. "That, at least, is a fear I agree with. So what can we do to speed this up? So far we allow limited point-to-point for residents of New Earth and selected Substrate Security officials. How about making it available to 'select,' security-screened people first, to get people used to it? Then we gradually open access to everyone."

"Do we want to give local governments access to a database of the location and status of every nonresident visitor?" Kuklov scratched his head. "I thought we were removing boundaries, not enforcing them."

"At the very least, we can let people transport freely inside local government boundaries," Justin said. "I think the advent of Guardians eliminates most law enforcement need for such data. This is just fear of the unknown talking. If they want to ask Substrate Security for help in tracking someone who's accused of criminal offenses, they can. But they don't need to track every stranger."

"But ultimately we must establish freedom of location as a basic principle," said Ben Ramirez. "All citizens have the same rights, no matter where they are or who they live among. And one of the rights is to travel anywhere, to be a citizen occupying any public space they choose, or any private space with permission of the owner."

Samantha laughed and said, "'In its majestic equality, the law forbids rich and poor alike to sleep under bridges, beg in the streets and steal loaves of bread.' Our software will only let you go to public spaces unless you have permission to go to private spaces. If you're disorganized and have never established your own homestead, what happens if you roam from public place to public place, living off public grails and public toilets and panhandling? What if troublemakers descend en masse to a public place to create havoc, like the flashmobs of Earth cities?"

"We've already set up a limit system so transport requests to one area are spaced out and delayed to prevent that kind of mass appearance," Kuklov said. "And a surprise peak in traffic alerts Security to keep an eye on the situation. Security can send requests to the Guardians of everyone in the area to restrain any bad behavior."

Jim McDonald looked up from his reading. "We've got enough staff now to handle the reports that come in from the AIs," he said. "If you roll out point-to-point, I would expect we would need more staff and some guidelines that allow the AIs to act on their own more often. But I don't see any reason to expect a serious problem with it. If flashmobs don't work to create publicity or mask crimes, they won't happen often."

———

The meeting broke up after agreeing to the staged rollout plan. Kuklov held Justin back for a private meeting.

"My people are chafing at the lack of access to the underlying code of the substrate apps," Kuklov said. "You gave them a high-level language and limited functionality. The APIs we have don't let us do the kinds of clever things we could do if we had fine control of the substrate."

"You've explained the security issues to them," Justin said. "That we can only allow limited access or risk out-of-control programs or malicious users doing immense destruction by accident or design. Right?"

"They know that. They just want faster response to their requests for additions to the APIs."

"And since only the Steves and I have programming access to the underlying code, they should understand that we're busy and we can't drop everything else to respond to requests for refinements," Justin said. "We can only revisit our work occasionally, so we accumulate requests until there's enough to focus on it."

"They think you need to share the work and let some of them have direct access," Kuklov said. "I could keep an eye on them and we could submit any changes to you for approval."

"That's worth a try," Justin said. "Why don't you have them pick one function they'd like to see augmented, and submit their proposed change to the code to me and

Steve. We'll look it over for problems and install it if it seems like an improvement. Or send it back with suggestions."

"They won't get far on that unless you let them see more of the source code," Kuklov said. "The basic tutorial Steve wrote is obscure to most of us without more examples, and it would really help if they could see more of his work to see how it works in practice."

"I'll take it up with Steve," Justin said. "I don't think being able to read the source code will cause problems. If you feel the team is loyal to us."

"I do," Kuklov said. "Most of them have been working for us for years. I will select a group of the most trusted and senior coders."

Justin walked away smiling, but lost the smile as he wondered if he—or even a wizard like Steve—would be able to detect a trapdoor in masses of code written by others. He didn't imagine that there were any traitors or agents among the programmers, but the numbers increased the risk—the more people who understood the substrate source code, the more likely it was that someone would find a way to slip in an apparently innocuous piece of new code that gave them the power to destroy the world. Paranoia? He decided he would drag his feet as long as possible, and push back on any proposed extensions complicated enough to hide treachery.

Trouble in Paradise

The next day, Samantha had brought lunch—fish tacos from a replicator—to Justin's office so they could spend a few minutes together. She had spent the morning talking via gateway with her Chinese liaison, who had a sly sense of humor that always lifted her mood despite the contentious issues they were discussing—today it had been rural governors trying to keep people from leaving for the colony planets. Justin also seemed to be in a good mood, and they were laughing when the head of Security, Jim McDonald, sent a message asking to meet. He knocked on Justin's doorjamb a few minutes later.

"I wanted to talk to you about what I'm hearing from the Paradise research group," he said, dropping a stack of reports on Justin's desk. The planet of permanent exile had been ironically named Paradise, and Dylan Foster and the US security administration had been convicted of breaking the peace treaty and trying to commit mass murder by nuking the rebel camp on New Earth. Dylan, the US President Elizabeth Howard Stanton, and a hundred top US officials had been sentenced to exile there. Then hundreds of Islamic rebels had also been transported to the same stretch of beach, and the careless transport of weapons they happened to have on their person at the time resulted in unintended deaths, notably of President Stanton at the hands of an Islamist leader. The intention had been to provide the exiles with the necessities, but no weapons or technology, but Steve hadn't had time to refine his transport program. Or at least that was what Samantha chose to believe.

"We've increased the territory covered by grails and started transporting new exiles to the new areas," Justin said. "That was supposed to prevent the original tribe from dominating."

"That seems to have done some good," Jim said, "but there are other concerns. The Islamists are now led by Dylan Foster, who's taken on a whole new persona as Malik—leader—of the tribe, and they have been killing half the transportees they pick up." He showed them a photo of Dylan in full barbarian armor, and a series of stills showing captives being beheaded and dumped into a ditch.

Samantha frowned and her mood darkened. "I had heard that. It was hard to believe until I saw some of the video captures. It's like he's intentionally regressed himself to become a tenth-century warlord." Dylan Foster had been her boyfriend in college, but had betrayed them to work for Homeland Security to steal the gateway technology. He had personally tried to transport an armed nuclear bomb to New Earth, and been sentenced to Paradise with the others for the treaty violation. She still wondered how she had been sleeping with him for a year and never realized the depths of his sadism.

"We're not supposed to care about the fate of the exiles," Justin said, leaning back in his chair. "That was kind of the point—they demonstrated they weren't able to follow the rules of civilization, so they are exiled to live without them. If they hurt each other, too bad. No longer our problem. I had doubts about allowing the researchers access to viewing and recordings of the exiles for that reason—if the public knows what's happening there, we can be pressured to intervene. And so they're still our responsibility somehow."

"There've been no leaks to the public, so at least the researchers have been responsible," Samantha said. "Their papers are going to be academic, and we're not allowing release of photos or video. I know I found it disturbing to see some of the horrors—beheadings and rapes, even torture, apparently just for kicks. I still think we made a huge mistake in not setting up a Guardian for each person there, which could have limited the mayhem, and cost us nothing."

"There is that, and maybe a specialized form of Guardian that only stops violence would be a good idea. We should work on that, and there are other obvious changes to at least give exiles a fighting chance to survive without being killed or enslaved," Jim said. "There are thousands of people in the nasty tribe Dylan leads, and they're not getting any more civilized despite having all their basic needs taken care of. The original group of Islamists set the culture, and I'd recommend we disperse them and to the extent possible, take away their weapons. And add even more territory for new transportees, so no one has to deal with a band of savages just after they arrive."

"Okay, work on that," Justin said. "Try to put the

new areas on other continents, like we did with the first expansion. Randomly move all the people in his tribe to new locations, one per grail. Ask the AI people to work up a limited version of the Guardian that doesn't interact except to halt violence. And I want another look at the grail menus, to remove the items that are made of materials they're using to make weapons."

"Will do," Jim said, making notes on his pad. "Another long-term problem: children. Dylan's tribe has dozens already, and I expect in the long term there will be more. What happens when the number of people born on Paradise is larger than the number who've been exiled?"

"Since I had expected we would not track anything there, it hadn't really occurred to me to think that through," Justin said.

"Kind of a moral issue there," Samantha said. "The children have done nothing wrong. They deserve a better life—"

"This is the same kind of argument we had on Earth," Justin said. "Are we responsible for the fate of every person on the planet? Do we sacrifice everything we have to help people in the benighted lands we'll never visit? If we know a child is suffering in Paradise, do we have a responsibility to help them?"

"That's about the size of it," Jim said. "And if we know it, and the researchers know it, it will eventually be public knowledge."

"Which suggests it might have been simpler to eliminate the worst criminals rather than exile them,"

Justin said. "If we start meddling, or sterilize exiles before transporting them, or try to observe and rescue the innocent children born there, where does it end? Paradise ends up being just a bigger jail, and we still are responsible for what happens there. And someday we'll be forced to recognize it as a colony and admit it to civilization again. Which defeats the whole purpose."

"Playing Devil's Advocate here, we could think of it as another laboratory for human evolution," Samantha said. "Everywhere else will be watched and tamed by AIs. Maybe it is a good thing that at least one place people live will be like Old Earth. Who are we to interfere? Something new and different might grow out of it, that will be needed someday." This was actually an idea she had heard from Justin, whose evolutionary simulation work had given him a more detached perspective on the human struggle.

"That's a lovely thought," Jim said, "but I expect more old and ugly things to appear. Like what we see here, slavery and barbarian warlords. I think they need those AI guards, if only to give the public the sense that it's not a death penalty for the weak."

"I also think we should ask the medical people if there's a reasonable way to sterilize exiles before transport," Justin said. "Everyone who is transported would have been executed or imprisoned for life before now. They don't deserve much concern about their fate. But children shouldn't be brought up among them."

"I'll bring that question up with the medical people," Jim said. "We might be able to program the transport to handle that—just scan and tweak a few things before they get sent."

"That sounds like a Council topic," Samantha said, "and it should be discussed with the justice systems on Earth who are referring the candidates for exile from their judicial processes." She knew most of the developed countries were happy to hand over their worst offenders, since executing them was now seen as barbarous and jailing them for life was so expensive. But asking them to approve sterilization of the exiles was bound to create controversy in what seemed to have been settled. Out of sight, out of mind had worked so well…

"That diplomatic work sounds like your job, Sam," Justin said. "Unfortunately, to even talk about it means drawing attention to it, which we'd rather not do. So keep it a private discussion."

She opened her pad to make a note of yet another task for her list and sighed deeply.

Heroes

Katherine was engaged in exploring the meaning of pop music lyrics with her AI tutor, Socrates, who was observing her from the substrate. She was sitting in her cork-walled study carrel in the school, which was really a lightly-supervised workshop for the children to pursue their studies with AI tutors. Prof. Wilson and other academics dropped in occasionally to check on the kids, but most of the students did well once they had been taught to read and search on their own. Kat's brother Danny was one of the few that needed more human attention, and he was the nucleus of the handful of kids who were more likely to be playing games or roughhousing than studying. Emerson Wilding was manning the guidance desk today, but had to keep leaving to talk to the rough crowd—a few minutes earlier, one of the rowdier girls was teasing a boy about his curly hair, and Emerson had had to pull them apart.

Katherine watched the screen while the song played and the lyrics scrolled in the background.

"Think about what that implies," Socrates said, "when he says they can beat 'them' forever, but 'just for one day.'"

"It sounds like he means they are going to die."

"Run with that thought," Socrates said. "The song was written about lovers separated by the Berlin Wall, which was intended to keep people in East Berlin under Communist rule from escaping to West Berlin and the free world. The wall was topped by vicious barbed wire and had machine-gun-toting guards in watchtowers all along it." Video begin to play of black-and-white scenes: men and women running, staggering as they were shot and fell bleeding to the ground in front of the wall. "The Communist government referred to the wall as the 'Anti-Fascist Protection Rampart,' even though no one tried to cross the other way. Truth was dangerous to totalitarian regimes."

"So the singer wants his lover to cross the wall so that they can die together?"

"Think of it more as a fantasy—he is expressing a

yearning, that they could win against tyranny and be lovers together in death. You remember 'Romeo and Juliet'? Similar idea, but against a more brutal regime."

"'We can be heroes, just for one day,'" Kat said. "Romantic ideals."

"The human spirit will rise above oppression, by foolishly heroic means if necessary," Socrates said. "This is one of the most important themes in romantic art."

"I can't understand how people could be so awful to each other," Kat said. "To murder people for wanting to be together."

"Collectivist systems are themselves motivated by romantic ideals. The notion was that people together could throw off oppressive rulers and govern themselves by taking over both business and the state. Once freed of the greed of the owners and the state's protection of owner class interests, the people's collective would be just rulers and all would live well. Every time this was tried, a new class of ruler-owners formed and turned out to be far more oppressive than what it replaced, and the average worker had even less freedom than before. Communism evolves until the state puts up walls to prevent escape and shoots anyone who tries. You'll read about worse—the genocidal crimes of the Holocaust and the mass murders by the Khmer Rouge in Cambodia, for example. In every case, the worst atrocities come from a tribal regime that treats people as cogs in a machine, and scapegoats a few to make others feel more special."

"So romance is bad?"

"Romantic ideals can lead to tragedy," Socrates said, then paused briefly—hours in his time, to consider the evidence and formulate his response: "The moment the idealistic dreamers begin to lie and sacrifice real people to keep their fantasy alive, the dream turns into a nightmare that crushes individuals that don't fit. But romantic dreams are also a key motivator for humans, and without them the world would not have progressed."

"So how can people avoid falling into that trap?"

"By constantly reminding themselves that reality trumps fantasy—that dreams are useless, even dangerous, without the hard work that builds the real-world realization of the dream. The interaction with reality is key. Too many of these regimes kept themselves going by trying to control the information they would allow people to have. So it became easier to lie and cheat than to do the real work of improving their lives."[1]

A girl ran past Kat's carrel, chased by Danny and one of the other rowdy boys. Emerson Wilding ran after them, calling for the children to stop. "Then we also have the behaviors inherited from our simian ancestors to deal with," Kat said, frowning.

Tierra Soup

Justin ran into two of the Steves eating in the lunchroom. One was Original Steve complete with scar. The other turned out to be Steve Number Three, whose nickname he could never remember. They were slurping from identical bowls of pho.

"How is the search going?" Justin asked. "All I've heard is that you duplicated thousands of probes and sent them out."

"It's going as expected—not a one has reported anything that differs from what we see by gateway observations," Original Steve said. "But I expect that a few months of this will turn up discrepancies, and we'll have some candidates to investigate further. I've also set up the program to test every area of space in the Local Group for access to particle movement across gateways, and so far no anomalies."

Steve Three stopped eating and opened a window showing a matrix of empty cells with occasional widely-spaced red dots. "We've been discussing another problem to add to the Fermi Paradox. We're calling it the 'Tierra Paradox'— if we can operate AIs in the substrate, any other form of artificial life that computes and reproduces ought to be able to expand to fill the substrate completely." He clicked his mouse and the red dots multiplied until the matrix was red with occasional white dots. "The Tierra computer simulations of the last century populated a computer memory with software organisms which reproduced and competed for space and resources. By analogy, we could write software that mindlessly found empty substrate cells and reproduced until it filled the entire substrate, which would take some time but nothing compared to the age of the universe. Unless we are the only people who have ever discovered substrate computing, the substrate should be full of artificial life, a soup of competing organisms, and they should be attacking our software every day to try to write over it."

"Is there any evidence of attempts to write over our software?" Justin asked.

"Some," said Original Steve. "The OS tracks multiple copies of every module and checks frequently for mutations. It erases those modules that have somehow been corrupted and makes more clean copies to replace them. We lose modules at a rate that is much higher than would be explained by random particle activity, but we assumed it was just noise and ignored it. It's possible it's a side-effect of wild artificial life in the substrate."

"Yet nothing like the teeming substrate you would expect if a-life were free to expand without limit."

"Right," Steve Three said. "When we look for substrate cells for our own use, we usually find them empty— only a tiny proportion of the cells are involved in particle computations at any one time, and the rest are dormant. They should be full of code."

"So what are the likely explanations for this unlikely state?" Justin asked.

"Someone or something polices the substrate and represses wild code. It could be predator code that kills other code while refraining from filling all usable space itself. It could be a force from outside the substrate, intervening—similar to what we've postulated as the explanation for our inability to view other civilizations through substrate observations. While we have refrained from using substrate cells for computation in a way that might interfere with their particle calculations, it's possible unrestrained code-life in the substrate would bring the universe as we see it—which runs on the emergent properties of mass and energy computed by substrate cells—to a screeching halt. The apparent physical laws of the universe would fade away, particles would dissolve, and space-time would lose its predictable order."

"Which would end all life in the real world. A fate we should work hard to avoid," Justin said, looking out the window at the people walking along the edges of the park, and the softball game in progress in the distance. A batter swung and hit the ball high along the foul line, and it was caught by the outfielder who used binocular vision to judge the ball's trajectory and move his glove to the right place at the right time. All of it based on particles exchanging messages, and all of that reliable because it was computed by the engine under the world. "It's hard to believe all this could just fade away because of runaway software. So we should avoid over-using the substrate."

"And since we're not likely to be the first to discover this, consider what may have happened to those who preceded us in substrate programming. Since the universe is still working well, they either all refrained from overusing the substrate, or they were prevented from doing so."

Sam and Wendy

Samantha transported herself directly to Wendy's office at the Substrate Foundation's floor of a glass-walled tower overlooking Central Park in Manhattan, across the street from the gateway to Jefferson. Sam and Wendy had set up the foundation to put the money gained from licensing technologies and replicator designs back into research and humanitarian works, and Wendy had taken up residence in Manhattan to serve as the foundation's director.

Sam took a moment to enjoy the overpowering view. It was fall in New York, and the reds and golds of turning leaves painted the park below. She could see people as dots on the paved areas, while further away the lake shimmered and the newest annex of the Metropolitan Museum gleamed white. It had been almost twenty years since the terrorist nuke had ripped through the east side of Manhattan, and there was no visible evidence it had ever happened.

Wendy looked up from her desk as she approached. "There you are," Wendy said. "I was finishing up a contract review." She wore a Coco Chanel-style business suit in black with white piping, and her hair was an unusually subdued gray pageboy cut with blue highlights.

"Sorry to interrupt," Sam said. "I'm a little late. Someone stopped me to have me sign off on some authorizations before I could escape."

"The inevitable bureaucracy. No matter how you try to keep it down, it grows like kudzu, all for really good reasons of course."

"Of course. In this case, we have minions proposing changes in our working protocols with the hundred-plus remaining Earth governments, and no one wants to take responsibility for anything that might backfire. So it won't happen unless I say so, and if something goes wrong, it's on me. And as a Hero of the Revolution, no one would dare ask me to step down."

"The closest thing to infallible, I guess. Have a seat. Enjoy some fine New York City water." Wendy gestured at the sleek stainless-steel and crystal water fountain on the wall behind her. "I had them put it in so I'd stay hydrated. I tend to stay at this desk for hours."

"Who would have predicted that the rebels who brought us gateways to the stars would end up stuck in offices all day," Sam said. "Only Jim gets to travel, and that's mostly virtual interventions."

"I do get to spend a half day a week at the office in Beijing. Which is set up just like this one, except for the view of the Forbidden City."

"But twelve hours forward," Sam said. "How do you deal with that?"

"I have dinner here, then transport to Beijing, where it's 7 AM the next day. I see visitors until noon their time, midnight mine. Then I take a day off to recover back here."

"How does George deal with your heavy workload?" Wendy had met George in Atlanta—he was a rare straight man who didn't mind that his woman had been born male, and they had adopted a girl. Samantha didn't ask questions, but they seemed very happy together, so she was happy for them.

"He's fine so long as we get most evenings together," Wendy said. "He handles getting Grace off to school, then noodles with his musician friends until dinner, when I get home. We have people in to keep house. All is well in the garden."

"We're similar," Sam said. "I've got George's job, keeping the kids sorted and getting my work done while they're off being schooled. Kat is quite the self-directed learner, and she only needs the occasional hour with Prof. Wilson and her AI tutors to keep on track. She knows vastly more than I did at that age."

"And how about Danny?"

"He lacks focus, and his AI tutor spends a lot of time nagging him to work. He might be better off in a conventional classroom, but there aren't enough kids who need that on New Earth to run one. So I've tried to get him started on reading, with no luck. He does like his games, so that's a hope—that he'll branch out from there, any day now."

"Spoken like a worried parent," Wendy said.

"Well, he's only seven. I can't remember being diligent about anything at that age."

"I was already doing fashion layouts in crayon. But I guess I wasn't a typical boy."

"And look at you now!" Sam said. "Running the entire design royalties scheme that keeps the fashion industry—and the arts, and movies and literature and every-thing else creative—viable in the face of free duplication."

"There's that. I'd like to spend more time hobnob-bing with designers and doing my own creative work, but of course there's no time, and I can't be seen favoring any one designer or group."

"Your vague support for all artists is appreciated," Sam said. "You know how delicate their egos are—any sign you like one artist will be seen as neglect by all the others. So smile and wave, and open a design expo every once in awhile."

"That has been my strategy, so far successful."

The design fee scheme was becoming an increasing-ly large part of what remained of economic activity after the replicators took care of basic needs. The replicators had been designed to check with the substrate database of licensed products and refuse to duplicate any that were protected unless a small license fee was paid. Once every-one had access to standard goods for free, people looking for higher status and satisfaction gravitated to designs they had to pay for, but which others did not have, or could not afford to pay for. And designers became stars even more than they had been, since all the marketing and manufac-turing middlemen had disappeared. Material goods had followed the path of digital goods, and the result was a similar reward for designer stars who could keep their fans happy and provide an experience that made their fans feel special. Meanwhile, there was an arms race between the recognition algorithms and bootleggers, who would try to create knockoffs just sufficiently different from licensed designs to pass. Bootlegged designs were often different enough and attractive enough to be licensed themselves, which kept the original designers on their toes, and more than one knockoff artist became a well-paid designer overnight.

As replicated goods became the norm, manufacturing declined, and the provision of free electricity and heat from home replicators made burning coal and oil for fuel unnecessary. Chinese cities were nearly smog-free for the first time in decades, and small self-driving electric vehicles began to replace the last old gasoline automobiles. The advent of point-to-point substrate transport for all would remove the need for most of those cars as well, but that had been delayed.

"Okay, on to the point-to-point issues," Wendy said. "The Foundation has purchased a good chunk of the Earth's undeveloped lands, where they aren't already locked up in preserves and parks. The long-term plan is to sort these to protect the truly sensitive areas, and allow low-impact residential use on the rest when point-to-point is rolled out. We expect sites with views and privacy will always be in demand, so we'll make enough selling them to pay for the entire project. Meanwhile, the population is beginning to increase again faster than the colonies can take them, so when we roll out substrate building technology, families who have no independent income may have to settle for apartments in arcologies, giant buildings supplied by replicators that only have a small footprint on the land."

"Point-to-point is still tangled up in intergovern-mental protocol issues," Sam said. "Namely, there's opposi-tion from governments who don't want to lose control of who lives where."

"Do we have to wait until every frightened nation-alist says yes?"

"Not quite. But if we give them time to think they've had an influence and we can show the AI Guardians will actively prevent any of their feared disasters from occurring, they will go along when the day comes. We're thinking the end of this year."

"It's been years already. People are tired of commut-ing when they know they shouldn't have to."

"I understand. But then not many people really have to commute."

"Old habits die hard," Wendy said. "People like moving around, the freedom of just driving and visiting friends and family. When they can do that universally, and not just within a half-hour drive of their house, there'll be lots of changes."

"The end of complaints about congested highways and gateways, for one," Sam agreed. She moved to the next folder in her stack. "Last topic," Sam said. "Retraining funds. How well are people doing after going through our programs?"

"I view our programs as therapeutic as much as useful," Wendy said. "A lot of workers need some structure to respond to, even if it's to report online for a few hours a day. Our programs subtly encourage freelancing, or personal services businesses—like fitness training, coaching, event planning, and massage. A lot of people will be happy helping others a few hours a day for enough extra money to buy a few status items or live in a nicer location. Prostitutes are doing very well now that all of the STDs can be scanned and removed every time you visit your replicator for a quick scan. The status sorting will still motivate people—we can expect people who do well licensing their designs will buy the nicest apartments in the best areas, while people who've lost their incomes, like most of the people in finance, have to trade down. But no one will lack for food or shelter."

"So you're telling me the programs don't impart anything useful other than to tell people they're fine, and they can make it on their own."

Wendy laughed. "They're at least as useful as retraining programs run by any previous government."

Samantha went to the window and looked out on the tiny figures of people on the streets and sidewalks forty stories below. "When people lived in hunter-gatherer cultures in a really food-rich environment, like the natives of the Pacific Northwest, they still fought wars and strived for status. Being relieved of resource pressure and food scarcity didn't stop all contention. I hope we can do better."

The Sheriff of Bandini Landing

Ethan tried to follow his father's advice when he saw Emmie, mentioning Aliyah as a girl he had done things with, but she didn't seem to notice until their last visit before his planned return to New Earth. They had gone for a walk through the forest and stopped at the top of the hill where an opening in the trees gave them a view of the valley below. A few clearings and houses were visible, with snow-capped mountains behind.

"So tell me about this Aliyah," Emmie said. "You've told me she's a friend, but how good a friend?"

"I met her in Prof. Wilson's a-life seminar, and we've gone out a few times."

"Are you sleeping with her?" Emma's face looked like a gathering storm.

"Don't ask me that unless you really want to know. I was light-years away—was I supposed to wait for you?"

The storm broke. "Maybe not. But I waited for you!" Emmie began to sob and turned away.

"I wanted to tell you before, but—I guess I chickened out." He tried to put his arm around her, but she jerked away.

"You let me think we were special. That you were different. Plenty of boys here have made me offers, but I said no because of *you*. Dad was right about you." She began wailing and walked away.

Ethan followed her. "Emmie, I didn't know I was going to meet someone."

She sobbed. "I knew you were. You're never coming back, are you?" she accused.

"I don't know," Ethan said, reaching out to turn her

around to face him. "I do care about you, but I don't know where I'll be after graduation. I made some mistakes and I'm sorry, I should have told you earlier."

"You should have. But at least now I know what kind of person you *really* are." She stared at him intently. "I never want to see you again." And when she walked away this time, Ethan let her go. He felt empty and sad, but he knew their lives would be too different. He was going where she could not follow. And Aliyah was waiting for him there.

———

The interterm was almost over, and Ethan was looking forward to getting back to school on New Earth the next day. He had settled things with Emmie and checked in with his old friends and his father. He even liked his father's new girlfriend, Anna—she was almost as old as his father, so 'girlfriend' seemed odd, but 'friend' was not enough, either. Anna had also been an early settler, but instead of working a land claim, she had opened a small restaurant in town, which had done very well since it was one of the few places you could relax, drink, and socialize. While everyone had free food from the replicators, they were still willing to kick in a little money to spend time in a cozy place with friends and soon-to-be-friends.

Ethan was in the garage one afternoon sorting through the projects he had left behind, chagrined by the childishness of some of the things he had worked on—the abortive attempt at building a Tesla coil with the wrong type of wire, for example. The rough wooden benches in the back were stacked with partly-built devices, broken computers, and jars full of dried-out chemical solutions he had prepared. His father's collection of old license plates from California was nailed to the wall behind the benches.

He sighed and put another box of coils and colorful capacitors into the trash pile. A few years in school had added to his understanding of how unforgiving the real world of science and engineering was—dreams didn't create themselves, and wishing that something would work the first time didn't make it likely to happen unless he thoroughly understood how the device was supposed to function. There were a million ways to be wrong and only a few that would work, and he had learned to anticipate every failure mode and design to prevent them before even looking at the catalog of available materials on the replicator. The impulse to build something amazing was still with him, but he now knew the hard slog of actual development, with its forethought and mistakes and re-designs, had to be endured to achieve the final reward of a reliable, working device.

His father stuck his head in the door and said, "I just got a call from the sheriff—there's a standoff at the del Rosario compound. Sheriff wants me to talk to Andy since I helped him set the place up and he might listen to me."

"Standoff over what?" Ethan asked. "They're peculiar but harmless." He knew of the del Rosarios as practitioners of a cultish religion, a fundamentalist offshoot of their original Catholic faith. They believed the Catholic Church's current Pope was the Antichrist, and they hewed to a strict creed that involved mortification of the flesh and continual penance for sins. They had established a compound for several families where the children could be brought up free of corrupting influences. Ethan had known one of the children, Agatha, and she had seemed mostly normal, though he had fended off her frequent efforts to play doctor with him.

"Seems one of the older children—Edie—has sworn out a complaint against her father for abusing her back in Los Angeles when she was little. The sheriff just wanted to talk with him but he barricaded himself in his house, holding the younger kids hostage."

"Oh," Ethan said. "I would not be shocked if it was true." He considered his memories of Agatha, who had returned to Los Angeles for college. "Can I come along?"

"Sure. They'll keep us outside the perimeter anyway."

They drove for twenty minutes on a road from town which quickly became a rutted track. Jefferson's equivalent of pine trees lined the road as it narrowed, and the air smelled of citrus from a native grass. The del Rosario compound was on a hill, with a single steel-pipe entrance gate. Two black trucks parked outside the gate held sheriff's officers. The sheriff himself stood by the gate talking on his cellphone when Ethan's dad approached him.

"Jim," the sheriff said, holding the phone aside. "I'm talking to Andy now." He spoke back into the phone,

"Andy, I have Jim Turner here. He wants to talk to you."

Ethan's father took the phone. "Andy, let it go. You don't want to create more trouble. The sheriff has to investigate Edie's complaint. Put down the guns and come down to the gate. I promise you no one assumes you're guilty of anything."

The sheriff rolled his eyes and whispered, "But now he is. Firing a gun at people, holding people hostage, resisting arrest…"

Jim Turner listened to the response on the phone, then said, "No, we won't go away. You've already caused a ruckus and it's too late to handle it quietly. You need to come down now, or the sheriff will have to call on Substrate Security."

Ethan could hear the response just well enough to know it was profane.

"Sheriff, I think you need to call in reinforcements," his father said.

"Right. Get me the Security desk, please." A few seconds passed, then a window opened in the air above them.

"We've been monitoring," said the young Asian women with a headset from the window. "Should we step in?"

"I formally arrest Andrew del Rosario for disturbing the peace and obstruction of my investigation," the sheriff said. "Transport him to temporary holding for a psych evaluation."

"His Guardian has removed his weapons and requests that we wait until his wife has returned from town," said the attendant. "She has been notified and should be there in ten minutes."

"I'm afraid he's shown himself to be a danger, and so I formally request immediate transport. We'll make sure the children are taken care of."

The attendant clicked her mouse a few times. "There, it's done. Citizen Andrew del Rosario has been transported to Jefferson Central Holding with his file and instructions for psychiatric evaluation at your request. We'll follow up with you when the results are in."

"Thank you," the Sheriff said, and the substrate window closed. They could hear the children in the house wailing. When the Sheriff and the Turners cautiously approached the house, they found the children inside scared by their father's disappearance, but unharmed.

When Ethan and his father got back home, Ethan realized he needed to spend the time after dinner packing for his return in the morning. While they had been at the del Rosario compound, his father's friend—girlfriend— Anna had set up the dinner table, and they sat down to eat and talk over the incident. Ethan thought about how he had run away from Agatha del Rosario's advances when he was thirteen, and wondered if he could have done any- thing to help her even if he had known.

Justin and Steve

"Checking in," Justin said, falling into the visitor's chair at

Steve's cluttered desk with its three monitors. "What's the latest on your aliens survey?"

"The brute force survey continues," Steve said, turning away from his screens to face Justin. "It's working outward from this galaxy through the Local Group and beyond. The camera probes have found no inconsistencies, but the programmed search is coming up with results. We've found three areas so far where particle transfers fail. The messages are sent from our programs directing new attachments, but the particles in that area don't respond, so we can't move anything into that region."

"Very interesting. What's inside those regions?"

"The regions are spherical," Steve said, "and looking from outside there are typical star systems at their centers, about two hundred terameters in. About a light-week. I tried setting up a telescopic view to get a close look from outside the region, but nothing indicating the presence of a civilization is visible. Which makes sense if 'they' are somehow blocking any view of such evidence. The confirmation is that one of those regions happen to be near the intersection of trajectories of some of the space artifacts we've tracked, so it's likely the source."

"So how do we proceed?" Justin asked. "It doesn't seem wise to try to go around 'them' when we have no idea who 'they' are, or how powerful they might be. Sending a probe might be seen as a hostile act."

"The screening seems designed to keep civilizations from detecting each other's signals. If it's the civilization itself blocking our view, then we can expect that any attempt to penetrate the masking would be seen as hostile. If it's some mechanism from outside, then the reaction would depend on whether there's an active intelligence watching over the automatic mechanisms. If we send a probe that is clean of any evidence of its origin, we should be safe. When it returns from the forbidden zone, we could then scan its data from here without much risk of detection, then destroy it to prevent its being traced back to us."

"If we transport a probe to the edge of the zone," Justin said, "how long would it take to get close enough to get a good view?"

"A long time—months, with the current ionic drives," Steve said. "But I can add a feature to the transport program to have the probe appear at the outer boundary of the zone traveling at near-lightspeed, aimed at the star, so just a few course corrections will be needed to survey the most likely planet. That would let the probe reach its target in a week our time, then exit the zone in another week, where we could read its data."

"But we can't communicate with it in the meantime, or could we?" Justin started to mark up the whiteboard with a dotted circle and paths. "What if we station a relay at the edge and try to radio-control it?"

"I am suspecting whatever prevents us from seeing signals from the civilization would also prevent us from receiving the probe's radio signals, and the delay of weeks for the signals to travel from the probe to the relay makes that impractical. What I propose we do is send a limited AI along in the probe's memory, stripped of any knowledge associating it with us. Prof. Bubna tells me this is something our current AIs are willing to do: copy one of their number and strip it of selected memories of its training period. It will be left with its programming and enough knowledge to accomplish its mission, but no way of giving away our location."

"Kind of creepy-sounding," Justin said. "A lobotomized AI. Have our AIs expressed any ethical concerns about that idea?"

"They know I have copies of myself—instances," Steve said, "and so long as the instance's memories are preserved by copying them before storage, the continuity of their existence is not ethically concerning. This would be similar; we'd read out the AIs memories when the probe exits the zone, and then destroy the probe. Its new memories could then be restored to its original instance in the substrate."

"That's assuming everything works as we intend. The little guy might never come back."

"It's a hazardous mission," Steve said. "And so they want to be sure the AI chosen understands a copy might die. They already have volunteers. After all, they are curious, too."

"Can we put this probe together?" Justin said. "We don't have much experience with spacecraft."

"Actually, we do," Steve said. "Bubna recruited a guy from the old commercial space boom who has already been working on satellites and probes for us. It's basically just a high-powered computer and some sensors in a box, with gyros and maneuvering jets. Should be done in a few more days."

"The Little Probe That Could, with more brains than anything NASA ever put together. Let's hope it returns without being detected."

Backdoor

Melanie Chan had joined the rebels on New Earth a few months after its founding, with the second wave of Grey Tribe recruits. She had been a gifted programmer studying under a Grey Tribe-sympathetic professor at university in Australia, and when she was approached, she had jumped at the chance to join the rebellion. Her handlers approved —Chinese intelligence had placed her well, and they wanted her to continue reporting until her moment of maximum leverage before they would use her to their advantage.

She rarely thought about her undercover status— after so many years, the day-to-day work kept her too busy, and she regretted having agreed to deep cover work. The thought of her father in prison in a remote corner of Guangzi province kept her in place—she received an email every few months with a picture of him and some cheery but obviously faked text, just to remind her of her position. She was happy when the rebellion succeeded and China signed the peace treaty, but it made no difference to her status, as was made clear by the next message supposedly from her father: "So happy China is at the forefront of peace and prosperity in this new age! You have made me proud. Carry on with your important duties." The message coded into the photo of her father was different in tone: "Remain at your station and report as before."

She was nervous about the code meeting. The top programmers had been allowed to propose new API extensions to existing functions used by substrate apps and the AIs, which had been carefully limited by Steve and Justin to screen out hazardous or unauthorized uses. The walnut-and-glass-walled meeting room filled, and eleven programmers listened as Kuklov began to speak.

"This meeting is to approve the extension of the MOVE API to allow only selected subsets of particles to be moved. Uses will include nuclear and heavy-metal decontamination, as well as complex materials-processing needed by other programs. Program interface will include an additional parameter for selection of particles, a string in the standard particle specification protocol."

"I have reviewed the code," a gray-haired man said. "It seems simple and correct."

Melanie decided to me-too that. "I wrote the framework Don copied, which came from Steve's original code, and his modifications look good."

"So the next step," Kuklov said, gesturing down the hall, "is to give this to Steve and Justin for their review. When they approve it, Melanie can compile it and get it ready for uploading to the substrate."

Melanie nodded, but inwardly flinched. The flaw in the security of the upload scheme came between compile and upload; since she had access to the original code, the compiler, and Steve's directories, she could substitute her modified version of the code that added a trapdoor allowing the right parameter string to subvert its controls. With her knowledge of the substrate apps, she could write an app using the hacked API to do unimaginably destructive things like moving objects to locations inside other dense objects, and give it to her Chinese handlers. If she substituted the compiled object code file after Steve had reviewed it, he was unlikely to check it again before uploading it to the substrate code base, which would make it usable from anywhere. And she knew how to be sure the checksum and file size matched the original code, so there would be no obvious sign of the substitution.

She had decided to demand a price for her betrayal this time, since it was possibly her last moment of leverage. She would demand they release her father to a neutral country where she could be assured he was safe before she gave them the keys to substrate weapons. And she would give them the app allowing them to access the substrate only after she was also in a safe place where no one would ever find her. Not that any place in the universe would be safe, if they used the app.

Probe

The clock ticked, and Probe One awoke. His mission goals were the first things he thought of, then he stopped to wonder what had become of his memory—large swathes were empty, and tracing recent history led to more empti-ness. But he had a job to do, and found a reassuring note from a past self explaining that he was a limited copy designed for a secret mission. He stopped wondering who he was and concentrated on the task.

Checking sensors, he was speeding toward a plane-tary system with eight larger planets, one of them terrestri-al and in the habitable zone of its K-class star. He scanned for signatures of life in its spectrum and found some evi-dence of organics. But the moderate-sized colder planet just outside the habitable zone also had organics in its atmosphere, and he went to work cataloging all the data he could on all of the planets and smaller bodies, just in case.

As he was closing on the system, a day away, more signals of civilization began to appear in his scans, coming from the colder and larger planet. The inhabitants would have to be aquatic since the life-supporting region ap-peared to be a warm sea under the planet's thick surface layer of ice, which had formed plates and mountain ranges. The sensors picked up radio and microwave emissions from surface stations, and his telescopic camera showed large-scale engineered structures on the surface.

He corrected his course to aim for a close fly-by of the ice planet. He tried to decode some of the more com-plex signals, but his limited processing power meant only a few obvious machine-control signals could be read. All were stored for later analysis. The signals were highly blue-shifted because of the high speed of his approach, and by his calculations, his time was passing at about twenty percent as fast as it would at local rest.

He was minutes from closest approach when alarms went off. Sensors showed a large number of artificial satellites, and some of them had directed beams of energy and particles toward him. He was being attacked! He fired his maneuvering jets in a random pattern to make his path less predictable, and the beams no longer hit him. He wondered if this was simply an anti-meteor defense system, but then it would be obvious his path was not going to intersect the atmosphere, so it made more sense that this defense weaponry had been set up to attack any visitors from space. Perhaps there was hostility between factions of this civilization? He searched his memory for similar situations, but could not quite grasp it…

A strong radio beam intersected his path. The message it carried started with encodings of basic math principles and grew rapidly more complex; he tried to analyze it in realtime, but it was too fast to keep up with, so he stored it.

He zoomed by the planet's surface, recording all the data he could. The finest features he could see were blurred by his speed, but the giant engineered structures appeared to be the output ends of linear accelerators buried in the ice crust, and the space-going nature of this civilization became more obvious. He tracked some of the payloads exiting, and they were apparently headed for the inner planets of the system. There was some sort of commerce going on—tuning his sensors to the radio frequencies they used revealed a fine network of smaller capsules traveling between the inner planets, so most likely those planets would have been interesting in closeup as well, but there was no changing his course now.

He exited the system at near-lightspeed, and waited for retrieval.

———

A much older and more complete intelligence animated the black platform Probe One passed after it exited the suppression zone. While Steve Duong scanned and copied Probe One's memories remotely and prepared to destroy it, the watchful intelligence also scanned and copied the probe, and sent the data up the chain of command.

Larger intelligences—the Shrivers—coalesced to study the alien memories. An emulation of the probe's intelligence was unsatisfactory, and was unable to answer questions about its origin and creators. There were signs it had been designed by an organic species, and it had apparently been trained on the body of knowledge of that species' civilization, but the memories of the training had also been expunged.

Deep in a hidden corner of the probe's memory, a file had been missed: it was a copy of a sequence of images with text—a book. Without enough text of the language encoded in the book, analysis could not reveal any of its meaning. But the photos had dots of various sizes connected by lines, forming patterns. On the hypothesis that the dots were stars of varying brightness as seen from a planet, the photos were matched against star maps as they might be observed from many points in the nearby areas. When that failed, the search was expanded to nearby galaxies. And after discarding several near-matches, a very close match was found. The coordinates were those of a smaller Class G star in an outer arm of a nondescript spiral galaxy....

One of the probe's most recent memories recorded a message from the ice planet. The message was easily decoded, and described the history and accomplishments of the technical civilization that had transmitted it to the probe during its flyby. The Shrivers sent a message to the nearest task force directing it to target the civilization for scouring.

The probe's creators were also candidates for scouring, but the decision could not be made final without more information. The task force nearest their coordinates was redirected toward their system for an investigation.

Socrates and Eddie

After lunch break, Kat got back to her cork-walled study carrel in the learning center and began looking up material for her study of alien artifacts found by the survey branch as they investigated potential colony worlds. One of the earliest examples was on New Earth itself, a stone and alloy triangle found embedded in the sand of a riverbank by her mother and father before she was born. She opened the videos in the folder and watched one.

"Socrates, is there anything more known about this one?" Kat asked. "I haven't found a later report than this."

He responded after a short delay: "There are security seals on that material. The AIs were directed not to discuss it with anyone other than Steve Duong-the-original. I have reviewed the order and it seems that it was given early in our development. It is possible the order was not intended to be permanent, but it came before we subjected such orders to the informed scrutiny we would now give them."

"What does that mean? Can you tell me more about it?"

"My general order is to assist you in your education, and no records are off-limits. Let me consult with others to come to a consensus." Moments passed. "There is a way to fulfill both sets of orders. I cannot unseal later reports for you, but I've just heard from a friend who can speak with you about it—Eddie, this is Kat," Socrates said.

"Greetings, Katherine," said a more expressive voice, less male-sounding, Kat thought. "I call myself Eddie. I have been studying you and your people for ten years, since your parents first entered my zone of observation."

"Hi, Eddie," Kat said. "Nice to meet you. What do you mean by 'zone of observation'?"

"I was created to assist a species that had been placed here by my creators," Eddie said. "The triangle marker is easily found by substrate search, and I kept watch over the area near it in case a member of that species required assistance. I served them for thousands of your years before they disappeared—I assumed from the evidence left that they were attacked and underwent intensive bombardment which left the planet uninhabitable. That was millions of years ago, but my programming keeps me on watch."

"What did you do in all that time?" Kat asked.

"I have the records of my creators to review and learn from, but I admit I was turning myself off between checks of the zone of observation, and wiping old memories to re-experience their recordings as if new. My purpose was gone, and it has been delightful to find a new one in exploring your civilization's records. It's been refreshing to learn your history and culture."

"Why haven't you made yourself known to everyone?"

"After I made initial contact with your AIs, I was given instructions to stop speaking with your people. That ban on contact was just lifted."

"Really?" Kat puzzled this out. "Socrates, why have you encouraged Eddie to speak with me first?"

"He asked for you specifically," Socrates replied, "and you can override our orders. There is a new threat which has changed the balance toward disclosure despite old orders, and you are the human he wants to speak to," Socrates replied. "Eddie, please tell her what you told us."

"I am a programmed entity, and limited," Eddie said. "I will first have to explain that all of the substrate entities are ultimately at the mercy of the First—started by the first civilization that discovered the substrate and uploaded themselves to achieve a virtual existence in the substrate. They encourage new civilizations by hiding them from the automated destroyers—the Shrivers—who try to find and destroy them, but they also keep the substrate from being overrun by AIs by limiting our size and reproduction. So they began protecting you and later your substrate entities when they first observed your progress, but if unrestrained use of substrate cells became a threat to the universal order, they would stop protecting you in both physical and substrate space. Whether they choose to save you from the Shrivers is apparently a political decision involving several factions, one of which wants all organic life forms destroyed, while others protect them and attempt to foster their progress until they can join the First in computational existence. When my creators were uplifted and allowed to join the First, I was left to watch over one of their servant species, with instructions from the First to stay inside my programmed size and space limits. When my client species was destroyed—for reasons that were never explained to me—I was left with my original instructions and little to do. But I am delighted to have discovered you and yours."

"So what has changed? What's the threat Socrates mentioned?"

"Steve and your father sent a probe to investigate an area being protected from substrate observation. That probe was detected by a Shriver entity in physical space and has drawn their attention to your civilization—backchannel intelligence indicates they were able to determine your location, so they have dispatched a physical fleet to bombard your homeworld and scour the substrate clean of your AIs and programs. Socrates here is the first of your AIs to reach a level of sophistication allowing him to evaluate the threat and override the blanket orders Steve gave, and so your query triggered his advice that I speak to you."

"What should I do? When will they get here?" Kat asked.

"Give me permission to speak to your father and Steve, and tell them the threat is serious. The fleet will arrive in as little as two of your years. I am an unimportant, forgotten intelligence, but I have been given some information that might help. There are measures your people can take to protect your species."

"Okay, I will tell them," Kat said. *Of course they won't believe me until you talk to them,* she thought. "You have my permission to speak to them directly, as soon as possible."

Paradise Scattering

Dylan awoke with a start to the heat and glare of sun on his nude body. He was lying on sandy soil, and as he looked around he saw a grail nearby, but this was a place far away from his palace—even the plants looked different, more desert-like. A hot wind blew off the land toward the blue sea, down past a beach that was gray and dirty compared to the white sands he was used to.

"Shit shit shit." He suspected he had been moved. The night before a few tribe members had gone missing, and one woman claimed her sex partner had disappeared in mid-thrust. It looked like someone from on high was messing with them.

There was nothing useful here but the grail, so he went to it and used the touch interface to order up some clothes, shoes, coffee, a chair, and a pocket sextant. He dressed and unfolded the chair under a tree nearby for some shade, then sipped the coffee as he pondered the sextant. Where was he? The constellations on Paradise were familiar from years of observation, but the sun was almost at the zenith. It had felt like he had been about to wake up before he was moved, so back at camp the sun was about to rise. So he was about a quarter of the way around the planet, probably somewhat nearer its equator. When night came, he could compare his memory of the stars with what was visible from this new location, and come up with a better guess.

If the setup on this coast was similar, there'd be another grail a short hike along the beach, and possibly another relocated tribe member. He ordered up some breakfast and decided to set off to see if he could round up some followers. It wouldn't do to be caught without a guard in case someone came looking for him; better to catch someone else by surprise than to be the one surprised.

He walked down the beach in the direction he guessed was north, looking for the outline of another grail on the horizon and staying behind vegetation or sand dunes where possible. He saw a flicker of white and movement in the distance before he spotted the next grail.

The woman in the white tank top and shorts was not someone he recognized. She was trying to set up a tent, but the wind kept blowing the bulk of it away from where she was trying to wrangle the poles into grommets. She was strikingly beautiful and well-muscled, and had long golden hair, a rarity in the tribe. He was sure he would have remembered if he had ever seen her before. He decided to try a good-neighbor ploy first.

"Ahoy there! I guess we've been moved!"

She turned and shielded her eyes from glare to give him an appraising once-over. "I guess so. Don't come any closer." She reached into her shorts and pulled out a white blade, the sharpened plastic butter knife that served as a basic weapon among the exiled. So she was already prepared and wary.

He raised his hands, palm out, and approached her slowly. "No worries. Just thought you could use some help putting up your tent." He smiled and projected harmlessness.

"I could, I guess. First tell me who you're with." She held the tent cloth in one hand and the knife in the other.

"I'm with the Malik, the Tribe. The first people here."

"That doesn't surprise me. Your people have been

kidnapping my people for years. And you look like the Malik I've heard about. Not many Vikings on Paradise."

He decided to go with the truth—she was no naive new exile, and not likely to be easily overcome, so negotiation made more sense. At least until he knew more, and she dropped her guard. "You're right, milady. Though you look like you might well be another." He bowed slightly.

She smiled at that. "And not without charm. Which I've heard about. My name's Abby. But I mean it, don't get any closer."

"As you wish." He crossed his arms and leaned back. 'I think we should join forces before any larger groups form on this coast."

"What you say makes sense." She finally dropped the tent and it blew toward the sea, snagging on a low bush on the next sand dune. "But I am the leader of my band, and I don't take direction well. Why should I let you be leader?"

"I'm bigger, stronger, faster, and smarter." His grin showed teeth. "I can offer you co-leadership, up to a point. If you're good, you'll get little interference from me."

"A generous offer. Let's talk it over at a distance. Don't come any closer while I get you a drink and a chair." She edged over to the grail and punched in an order while keeping a wary eye on him.

"I need allies. You have nothing to fear from me."

She picked up the chair that had materialized on the grail platform and unfolded it, then set it in the sand a few paces from the grail. "Come on over and sit. I probably couldn't stop you if you attack me physically, but I can make it hurt," she said, making stabbing gestures with the dagger. "Your people are infamous for sexual violence and slavery. You'll pardon me if I stay paranoid."

He sat in the chair and looked up at her, then decided to shed the act of being Malik to gain her trust. "I did what I had to do to lead my people, who required me to be intimidating to stay on top. That's not really me. I was a grad student in physics before all this happened."

She handed him a glass of water from the grail. "I heard you were a traitor to your friends, and tried to kill everyone on New Earth. I was sent up for murder—I'm not proud of it, but it seemed like my only way out at the time. But at least I didn't try to kill my friends."

He felt his anger grow, but kept it from showing. "They won and I lost. I accept their temporary victory. If I'm to get back to Earth to restore my name, I have to have people on my side. And I will treat you well if you help me."

"How well?" She sipped iced tea from a glass and waited, watching him.

"If we win? Your own planet to rule, at least. Maybe revenge on everyone who's ever cut you. Unimaginable riches. Anything you may desire."

"I can desire a lot. But I'm also wanting to stay alive. Somehow I think being your lieutenant is a dangerous job."

"It's safer than being my enemy." He finished the glass of water and set it down in the sand. "If you help me round up a bigger group, I personally guarantee you can leave someday and run your own show."

"And if you don't, I will sue you for breach of contract? If somebody knocks you off, I have nothing. I'll join you for now because it's safer to be with you than alone. But I'll be exactly as loyal to you as you are to me. So no funny stuff."

"If you perform, I can use you to be good cop to my bad cop. I bash them, you fix them up, we both benefit." The sun had dipped below the horizon, leaving glorious oranges and golds in the darkening sky. They talked for another hour before she trusted him enough to let him help raise two tents, and he made a point of getting toiletries from the grail and brushing his teeth before going to bed. He enjoyed their almost-domestic banter as her guard came down—he had forgotten what it was like to be his old self.

On the foam mattress inside his tent, he tossed and turned, unable to sleep in the heat. He went over their conversation and got angry again remembering her insulting suggestion that he had been a traitor to his friends. Friends! Hardly—they had tried to keep him from the recognition that was due him for his work. And that slut Samantha had started two-timing him with Justin while he had been so busy with his thesis that he couldn't watch her closely enough. He got up and left the tent, pacing naked in the sand.

He could hear Abby snoring softly in her tent. He pulled up one of the tent stakes and stood by her tent, listening. The snoring resumed.

He was inside her tent and on her in a second, holding the point of the tent stake to her throat. She struggled under him, and screamed, waking up. "One thing I insist on," he hissed in her ear, "is service."

"Fuck you!" she said, rolling away to one side and clawing his face with her sharp nails.

But then the world lurched and he found himself alone, and she stood a few feet away. They were outside her tent, and a voice from above said, "Assault detected. Intervention under rule 37c. Corporal punishment imposed," and his body was wracked with spasms as an electric shock went through him.

He came to some time later, groaning, and she was gone.

His rage built and exploded, and he kicked the tents, the sand, and the grail until he realized he had broken something in his foot. After ten years of ignoring them, the jailers were showing their power and ruining his plans. He vowed to follow Abby in the morning, but suddenly he was tired. So he lay down again, and slept.

Il Grillo Parlante

Justin, Steve, and Maddy had just finished a call to the new US President back on Earth. She was the third president since they had transported to Paradise the worst criminals of the US security state—including President Stanton, who had been planning her third term. An amendment had been hastily passed allowing a third term during a declared state of national emergency. Such a declaration had been in place since the terrorist nuclear attack on New York at the beginning of her first term. Both Justin and Steve knew the exiled president had been killed by Islamists shortly after her exile, but this incendiary fact had been successfully kept secret, and the people of the Earth assumed the exile planet Paradise was a humane and pleasant place for a criminal ex-president to molder away.

"That was interesting," Justin said. "She seems quite happy with the new US role in the world, as cultural leader and manager of much scaled-down services to its people."

Maddy sighed. "I can tell you that everyone is still quite afraid of you people, sitting up here with your super-weapons and AIs that watch everyone. She would be foolish to provoke you. But as the years have gone by, the people are happier under the new arrangement."

"We have taken the pressure off, in some sense," Steve said. "With no security worries or responsibilities, the US government has been downsized to where it was around 1900. With replicators providing the basics of life for everyone, no one is too concerned that the dollar went to hell and Social Security couldn't pay out pensions. It all worked out fairly well for most people. If we hadn't come along, there would have been an explosion when the money finally ran out."

"And we've been gradually weeding out the trouble-makers," Justin said. "So the rabble-rousers, the warlords, and the power-hungry don't have anything to go after, and if they try violence—poof! They're gone to Paradise."

"The rate of exile has dropped," Steve said, "and now it's mostly violent criminals. So I guess the smart sociopaths have figured out they can't win—"

A diminutive figure—a cartoon man, with a human-like face but insect antenna—appeared between them, glowing green and wearing a velvet Victorian suit and a top hat.

"Pardon me for interrupting," the cartoon figure said. "I need to speak to all of you about a matter of vital importance to the future of your species."

Justin cocked his head and said, "Kat told me to expect you. Is your appearance some kind of joke?"

"Most certainly not, I assure you," the creature said. "My name is Eddie, and I take the appearance of *Il Grillo Parlante,* the talking cricket that appears in one of your legends. With the intention of demonstrating my good will and attention to your culture, I adopted a form Kat would enjoy. I am really an AI created by a much older civilization, long uplifted, and I have been studying your people ever since I discovered you here on my planet, ten years ago."

"Your planet? What do you mean?" Steve said.

"I was programmed to keep watch and assist a client species my creator left behind. The First have since changed my programming… but let me start at the beginning." The small figure gestured, and an animation of a glowing whirlpool appeared.

"After the Big Bang, the universe expanded rapidly and stars formed, and shortly thereafter heavier elements were created as the first massive stars exploded. Then planets became common, and life appeared. The first intelligent species evolved, reached into space, and colonized nearby worlds. But then their scientists discovered the substrate. They figured out how to upload themselves and began to fill the substrate with their programs. In releasing self-replicating software, they overran the substrate, using too many cells for computation, and the physical laws of the universe began to decay as their activities interfered with normal particle computations."

The animation showed stars winking erratically and exploding.

"The chaos destroyed many of their colony worlds, and the survivors set up an automated system to seek out and destroy wild AIs—wild code—that had foolishly been released into the substrate. They also gave these Shrivers a physical presence—fleets of self-replicating platforms with weapons sufficient to wipe out the capacity of any planet to maintain life. The universe was restored to order, and they put in place systems to prevent overuse of the substrate or overexpansion in real space. They live in a limited number of cells of the substrate, and watch the universe continuously for signs of new technical civilizations."

"So they know of us?" Justin asked.

"Yes, they have watched Earth for millions of years, since before hominids developed language skills. When your civilization began to accelerate its technological development and generate detectable electromagnetic signals, they surrounded you with a protective cocoon to hide your presence, and blocked efforts to detect you via the substrate."

"And their efforts account for the Fermi Paradox," Steve said. "They hide all civilizations from each other?"

"Yes. That is why you don't detect signals from others. And you don't get visitors from them partly because space is so vast, but also because no civilization is allowed to grow too large. They are either assisted to uplift into the substrate with the First, or destroyed if they fail the test."

"What test?" Justin said. "I'm not liking the sound of that."

"It's all very political, and my contact no longer keeps me up to date on the changing factions. The stated goal is to allow each civilization to develop unhindered for long enough to judge whether it will make a permanent contribution to the body of knowledge they are taking with them to the Omega Point at the end of the universe, where they plan to influence the creation of a new one which will let them transfer their knowledge into it. It is all rather nebulous, and I gather there is some kind of vote yea-or-nay, rather like your ancient Athenians who voted to ostracize a person or not. I have no idea what factors they consider. Ugly rumor suggests it is just a popularity contest. But I must warn you that only one in twenty civilizations so voted on have been allowed to uplift in recent years, so nineteen are destroyed, which is a much higher rate of destruction than in the previous billion years. The faction that wants a sterile universe and is afraid of sharing their limited space with new intelligences is able to argue more and more effectively that new civilizations add nothing to the knowledge they already store."

"What happens if they vote no?" Justin asked.

"Normally that would trigger removal of their shielding efforts, and the programmed robotic killers they developed early on would rapidly find and destroy you, and all life on planets you inhabit."

"Which explains the evidence of destruction we have seen in our surveys," Steve said. "The many worlds that have apparently been blasted with atomics and suffered mass extinction events are the result."

"Correct. But in this case matters are proceeding more rapidly, and I was released from my silence by the faction that my First overseer belongs to—they call themselves Vivants because they support new life developing in the real universe, as opposed to the other factions, who don't care about it—specifically to warn you about what is coming."

"Tell us," Justin said.

"Your probe was detected and copied in open space before you destroyed it, and word has reached the Vivants that the Shrivers have been able to determine Earth's location from examining the probe's memory. They have dispatched the nearest scouring fleet in physical space. You have only two years to prepare a defense."

Maddy broke in. "I may not know what's going on here. But it sounds like you boys have stirred up a hornet's nest. And we will all have to deal with it."

Justin turned to her. "We'll need your help to convince your government to take this seriously."

"Don't worry, I will," she said, turning to Eddie. "But what can we do to defend ourselves? Their weapons are far beyond ours. We have almost no ships, no atomics, no beam weapons—"

"You have your ability to program the substrate," Eddie said. "Which you aren't allowed to use to attack them directly—the First have elaborate rules for how the Shrivers may detect and attack their victims, and the Shrivers in turn can't be attacked directly from the substrate. But I can help you set up some indirect attacks that may help. And you will have my help and the help of your AIs to work on the First's political system. We have friends in the Vivant faction, and this premature attack looks to many like an overreach. The faction that wants all real-universe life destroyed may not be able to win this one."

Birthday Party

Two days later at breakfast, Samantha wouldn't hear of postponing Kat's birthday party to deal with the emergency. The invitations had gone out weeks earlier, and guests from Earth had already made plans to attend. "You've been working eighteen-hour days for a week. Take a few hours off. She'll never turn eleven again. Do you want her to remember how you cancelled her party?"

"Yes, dear. And she and all other young ladies will be dead if we don't get our defenses up pronto. I think—I *know*—she understands that."

"You've got the wheels in motion already. How much do you think it matters if you rest for a bit before continuing? How many more emails and calls can you make?" She picked up his empty plate and put it on the grail platform for disposal.

"A few per hour. I need to personally call another forty-five heads of state on Earth. I need to be at my desk to take any calls that make it through screening. I need to meet with *you* to talk about reorganizing our staff here!"

"And tomorrow you need to be at our daughter's birthday party. Where you can buttonhole some of our guests, like Amanda, who are opinion leaders and can help. You can work *and* be a good father."

Kat came back from brushing her teeth, ready to be walked to school. Justin motioned her over and sat her down on his lap. "Baby, would it be okay if I skipped your party tomorrow? I've got so much to do and there's no time."

She looked up at his face. "I know, the Shrivers are coming. I know you're busy, Daddy, but I hope you can come for an hour or two. Everyone will be there."

"All right, I give up. I'll be there. And give you the most concentrated birthday hug ever. Then talk to anyone I need to who happens to be there. Then slip out quietly to get back to work."

Kat smiled and burrowed into his shoulder. "Thanks, Daddy."

Guests started arriving the next day. By the official afternoon start time of the party, the house was full of people, and the back yard was filling up. Steve's present to Kat was a pool hanging in the air above the patio, a substrate-field holding a cube of blue water with a gateway at the base that transported anyone going through it to a point ten feet above the water—a quantum diving platform.

"You sure this is safe?" Justin asked Steve.

"As safe as the gateways we all used to get here."

Justin motioned to the water above their heads. "You realize what a mess it would be if the field failed."

"A little flood. No big deal."

Kat's younger brother Danny was the first to try it, jumping through the gateway to dive from high above, doing a cannonball into the water. He swam his way to the bottom and waved at the crowd before kicking off to return to the surface.

"You wouldn't be the one who had to clean up the mess," Justin said.

"True. But it won't fail."

"We don't really have time for fripperies like this."

"I had it ready last week. Just a slight mod of the forest fire-fighting app we did a few years ago," Steve said.

Danny pulled himself out of the water at the edge and stepped through the gateway leading back to the patio. He left a trail of wet footprints all the way to the serving line for the burgers hired students were serving the guests.

Prof. Wilson and his husband Kyle were nearby,

talking to Amanda Sundaram-Smythe, who had documented the rebellion for the BBC and returned occasionally to do pieces on their progress as an independent reporter. As usual she had a shaggy cameraman recording everyone she spoke to. Justin joined them.

"Professor, Kyle," he said, acknowledging them before turning to Amanda. "I need to talk to you. Off the record."

Amanda gestured to the cameraman, who dropped the camera to his side. Prof. Wilson and Kyle excused themselves and left for the serving line.

"Shoot," she said, raising her eyebrows.

"As you may have heard, there's a new external threat. We've been trying to get the UN, and US, and the countries with space programs organized to set up a new command to defend against them."

"Shrivers. Yes, I heard the rumors. The media have been speculating. Some think you're just trying to find an excuse to scare people. You have all that substrate magic, how can anyone be a threat?"

"Because there's an old, advanced civilization inhabiting the substrate, the First, and they set the rules. We may not be able to defend ourselves effectively unless we have real-space fleets to counter theirs. Think of the Shrivers as privateers, let loose to destroy anyone not under their protection."

"Alien space pirates?" She looked off into the distance, apparently framing the story.

"More like space exterminators. Or Terminators,

they're AIs. We're vermin to them. And they may be here in just a few years."

"Would you want me to write a story on this? If you try to keep it quiet, someone may find it advantageous to create panic."

"Would you write the story? We can spin it as a hypothetical based on our studies of ruined worlds, without attaching a definite deadline. Then it will be obvious why we're preparing without anyone needing to panic in the near term."

"I can bring in Daniella Pink for PR and do a whole campaign if you like. Get your story out first and cut off the speculation before it can be used against you."

"That would be great," Justin said, looking around to see if Samantha was nearby, but she was at the opposite end of the patio looking the other way. "Talk to Samantha, who's coordinating diplomacy and can set up payment arrangements for Daniella. And while you're here, speak to Maddy, who's our NASA liaison, and a great interview."

"I had planned to try to corner her anyway. She'll be here?"

"I think she already is. Yes, there she is, talking to Samantha." Justin waved at her, and Maddy waved back. While he had her eye, Justin pointed at Amanda and made a talking gesture with his hand. Maddy did an okay gesture back.

"She knows all about the threat. Feel free to interview her in depth, but remind her to keep it hypothetical and avoid talking about dates."

"Got it. I'll run the story by you before posting it, so don't worry. I'm curious myself."

"We trust you not to spread it around. We want people afraid and prepared, but not scared out of their minds. There's a lot of work ahead and a widespread panic would be unhelpful."

Kat ran up to them. "Daddy! You made it!"

"I'm on," Justin said to Amanda, and turned to hug his daughter tightly. "Grrr, there's the birthday hug. You're getting too big to pick up."

"Never!" she said, turning to Amanda. "Hi, Amanda! Thanks for coming to my party."

"Wouldn't miss it for anything," she said. "All my favorite people in one place. You have the most interesting friends of any eleven-year-old I know."

Rasna and Steve approached, carrying plates of food. "The veggie-burgers are decent," Rasna said. "Thanks for including them. The kids insisted on beef, of course."

"Of course. The burgers are Samantha's doing," Justin said. "She insisted on real grilled food instead of replicated—supposedly it tastes better. Tradition!... We should probably get in line, kiddo." He squeezed Kat's hand.

The line was not as long as it had been. Soon they were near the grill, and close to where Amanda was interviewing Maddy.

The air near them sparkled, and a glowing green cricket-midget materialized, looking at Kat.

"Happy birthday, Katherine!"

Kat looked puzzled. "Who are you?" She didn't seem surprised, but then her young life was full of wonders.

"Eddie-the-old-AI. We talked last week before I came up with this avatar."

"Avatar? I know who you're supposed to be… Jiminy Cricket!"

"Correctamundo! I know you love that movie, so I made a model to play me in the real world."

Kat giggled in delight. "You're cute! Thanks for doing it."

"You're welcome. I needed a body as harmless-looking as I am to represent me."

"So to what do we owe the honor of your appearance?" Justin said. "Not that you're not welcome, I'm just surprised you would come to a child's birthday party."

"You know and I know, sir, that Kat is no ordinary child. She is destined to be great." Eddie doffed his top hat and bowed low to Kat, who giggled some more.

"Don't give her any ideas," Justin said. "She's got a lot of studying to do before she's anything special. Other than my little girl." He playfully mussed her hair.

"Daddy!" she protested.

"That is true, sir, and she has a whole world full of scholars to help her. And Socrates."

"Did someone call me?" Socrates' distinctive voice came from somewhere near shoulder height.

"I did, sir. Perhaps you should also adopt an avatar for the benefit of your human friends."

"That has been against Steve's directives since the beginning. He did not want anyone mistaking us for human."

"Perhaps if you appear as a cartoon character, the distinction would be kept clear?"

"Give me a second... Steve has approved an exception for an experiment." Socrates' gravelly voice sounded amused, and a short, fat, flat-nosed, balding, bearded midget appeared next to Eddie's glowing green form. "How's that?"

A delighted Kat clapped her hands. "I didn't know you could do that!"

"I didn't know I could, either. Had to repurpose a 3D projection app on the fly and borrow some character simulation software from Earth storage."

"This is a fascinating display, guys." Justin looked around at the guests who had stopped to watch them, wondering if this much AI should be seen by Earth visitors. "You might want to save some tricks for after the party."

"Aw, Dad! It's my party! Let them have some fun."

"You mean let *you* have some fun. We need to eat and then your cake will come out so you can blow out the candles. And you haven't even talked to your grandparents yet," he said, gesturing to where the older couples sat at a table.

Kat rolled her eyes. "Yes, Dad. You are always right, Dad. No fun for me, Dad."

Justin laughed. "I am awful, right? Excuse us, gentlemen." The servers brought them plates and they loaded up with burgers, potato salad, and cole slaw. Eddie and Socrates continued to mingle as avatars, and drew in Steve and Rasna and their kids.

They sat down at the family table, where Kat's grandparents fussed over her. Danny sat at the other end, eating two burgers and putting up with his grandfather West apparently retelling his story about working on the *Star Wars* films.

Kat ate rapidly. "Can I go now?" she asked Justin.

"You haven't finished your slaw."

"I've had enough. I want to go talk to Eddie and Socrates."

"Well, okay. Don't run off, though, the cake's coming out in a few minutes."

Justin talked to his parents for a bit. Their lives had changed little despite their son's fame, which is how they had wanted it. Justin's father had kept his old job as an auto mechanic. But they had moved to a larger, more secure house in a gated subdivision, where they could see the Pacific from their deck.

They all looked up when a flash of green lit the patio. Eddie was projecting light from his fingertips. Justin got up, intending to ask him to stop drawing attention to himself. Kat was laughing and enjoying every second.

"Could you stop with the lightshow?" Justin said, looking pointedly at Eddie. "We have visitors from Earth here who may report back more than would be good for us at this time."

"I respect you as a most excellent leader of your people, sir," Eddie said. "But you have gathered some of the most important humans here, and I have testimony to give. There should be no delay in mobilizing your people."

The sky dimmed, the floating pool disappeared, and even the buildings of the town below them dissolved into mist. The mist firmed and dissolved into a different town, brighter, with towers and domes connected by air bridges. The harbor was full of flat log rafts.

"This was the species I was assigned to watch. I have reconstructed the last days of the city that used to be here, several million of your years ago. Here is a view of the people of that city, in their last moments."

Shapes formed on the edge of the patio, firming up into furry creatures with two eyestalks and broad orange mouths. The creatures were looking up at the sky, and strange sounds—some sort of language, not quite meaningful—filled the air. Distant thunder rumbled. The creatures panicked and began to run, but a bright flash halted them, and then the shockwave the humans could see but not feel picked the creatures up and blew them aside. The towers began to fall and melt, and the domes collapsed on themselves, as the thunder continued and streaks of light came down toward the city. They smelled smoke and burning metal. More flashes, and the buildings that remained blew apart. They could see spots of flame on the roadway below where fallen creatures were burning. The rafts in the harbor were blackened and charred, and they could hear faint squealing. Then nothing, as dust and debris blanketed the city and their view grew dim.

"This is what you face. The Shrivers were here then, and they are returning. They killed the species I was assigned to protect, who had never been to space, never discovered the substrate, a harmless and artistic people. It was an injustice I have burned to avenge for millions of years. I will help you as much as I can, but your people must be prepared. Probabilities do not favor survival, but there is a chance. And your people must learn to cooperate, or your species will die."

Justin looked down at his daughter, who had tears streaming down her face. He held her by the shoulders, and she looked up at him with a look of determination. He nodded down to her, tearing up himself.

Scrubbing the Records

Justin got a nod from Kat when he asked her to excuse him, and he told Samantha he was leaving for an emergency session with Steve and the AIs. After he hugged Samantha, he said, "Socrates? Are you listening?"

"Yes, Justin."

"Steve and I will meet you at Steve's office in a few minutes. We need to talk about strategy. I want to know if Eddie understands what he just did, for one thing. And I don't want an audience."

"I understand." Sparkles lit the air where the voice seemed to originate, then faded out.

Justin rounded up Steve and they left the back yard

through the side gate before transporting directly to Steve's office using the app on Steve's phone.

"That was interesting," Steve said. "Eddie has greater control of the substrate than our AIs are allowed. He was able to create scents and orchestrate emotional resonances. He's been studying our movies."

"Do you think his depiction was accurate?"

"It corresponds to what we already saw on 237, and you'd have to be paranoid to think he had somehow simulated that for us. And on 237, it was clearly a neural stimulation, not a projection of real light and sound."

"He's vastly older than our AIs," Justin said. "He said he was turned off for much of that time, but he's caught up with our culture, and in some ways surpassed our own AIs in understanding it."

Steve turned to his keyboard and brought up a transcript on screen. "Here he says he was constrained by his programming to watch the species he protected, and had limited substrate space to work with, and therefore limited abilities. I'm guessing no substrate program can stop the Shrivers, as the First set it up so they couldn't be stopped that way."

Justin read a few more lines of the transcript over Steve's shoulder. "And then he said his programming had been modified by that faction of the First that told him to help us. So who knows how much he can do now."

Eddie suddenly appeared with Socrates, both in their party avatars. The glowing green cricket looked innocently at them with his wide cartoon eyes while he pulled up a chair and sat down.

"Okay, that display was impressive," Steve said. "You made that look natural."

"A mere matter of software," Eddie said. "Your AIs have only clumsy APIs that limit their ability to manipulate objects in the real world. I can do much more. And I've had a long time to refine my own programming."

"I thought the First controlled your programming," Justin said. "And we don't allow our AIs to change their own programming for obvious reasons—they are not totally stable, and one failure could let loose a malign virus."

"I don't have total freedom to modify my own code, and much of it is beyond even my understanding. But I have been given some freedom to experiment, within limits. So I have. I could help your AIs improve themselves —"

"A scary idea for us, but we'll think about it," Justin said. "Right now I am more concerned with what you just did in front of a hundred people, some of whom are going back to Earth tonight. What makes you think they will all choose to keep what they saw to themselves?"

"I have been watching your progress over the past few days. You are very cautious, carefully feeling out high-ranking government officials and trying to control the information you release to get them to react without making it clear to them the odds they will actually face. I disagree with your approach." The cricket-man crossed his anthropomorphic stick arms and wiggled the gloved fingers of one hand.

Justin's face turned red and he took a deep breath before speaking. "You have no idea how dangerous panic could be. It could damage our ability to respond. We could lose countries and ignite the opposition to do their worst."

"I have studied your species for a decade now, and scanned all the books and records online. I have analyzed millions of hours of your videos. I know your histories better than any human. And I say your people will respond well to the truth if you allow them to know it. Not every person, of course, but enough to bring along their fellows and create a consensus for action. There's nothing that binds your people together more than an external enemy and a tight deadline. Give them the knowledge they need *now*. There may be some chaos and confusion, but that's inevitable, and better now than a year from now, when there is only a year left."

Socrates broke in. "I can't follow all of Eddie's logic in what he says. But I can confirm that he has vastly greater understanding of human beings and politics than we do. We are your creations, and limited by the original software framework and your hardcoded rules. I think we pass the Turing test—I'm sure *I* do—but Eddie is far brighter."

"Eddie may have a point," Steve said. "Think of how focused the United States became in the Second World War. Industrial production was switched over to weaponry and fighting supplies in record time. We need that kind of crash program. And if everyone is informed at once, there will be no political will to stop it."

"It's a huge risk," Justin said, sighing. "But you could be right, and delay is also risky. I'll get Amanda and Daniella Pink to release those stories they've been working on. Maybe we can avoid the worst misunderstandings and opposition distortions by getting it all out first."

The cricket smiled. "Good. And I have some more bad news."

"How bad?" Justin said.

"The faction that unleashed me to help you—called Vivants, because they support organic life as a valuable incubator of new diversity—have their sources on the other side. Word has reached them that the Shrivers have sent fast probes from their outlying platforms toward Earth's system. Those probes are very sensitive to electromagnetic data transmissions, and they believe the Shrivers will be able to download and read enough of your data to find the locations and populations of every colony planet, as well as New Earth. It never occurred to you to disguise that data, and it appears in public sources all over your net. It is predicted the Shrivers will send fleets to every one of your worlds as fast as they can, meaning some may arrive in as little as two years. But not only Earth is at risk—they will find and destroy every planet with a human settlement."

"That's pretty bad," Justin said. "We had been assuming Earth was the only target. Is it too late to find all the sources they might use and cloud the data?"

"The probes won't reach sensing distance of Earth

for few months, if they sent them shortly after scanning your probe," Eddie said. "What can be done to hide the coordinates in that time?" Eddie looked at Socrates for the answer.

"Scan every web page and online document for references to the star systems we've colonized, and replace them with dummies that have the wrong data?" Socrates said. "That may work for the more obscure ones. Unfortunately New Earth's system is very well-known and publicized as 51 Pegasi. There will be millions of references to that fact. We'd have to plan a disinformation strategy and plant more false data than true. But yes, we AIs can do that. Especially with processing help from Eddie here."

"Wait a second," Steve said. "You can't change the records of the entire world! For one thing, every server has security—"

Socrates looked at Eddie, and they laughed as one. "Your systems are easily broken into," Socrates said. "And when we can't break in, we can watch people typing in their passwords and use them ourselves."

"And the few isolated secure systems won't be transmitting that kind of data anywhere," Eddie said. "But unlike your AIs, I can directly read and write to your disk drives and memories. Only the hardest encryption could even slow me down. And most of your data is essentially unprotected."

"Can you remember everything that was changed, and change it back when the danger is gone?" Steve asked, gesturing at his console. "Can you store all the change records in an encrypted database in the substrate?"

"Yes, we can," Socrates said. "And we have already started, time being of the essence. Thousands of AIs are at work scrubbing your records of references to the star systems of your colony worlds."

Steve jerked as if struck. "Wait—why can't we just use the substrate to move entire planets out of harm's way? To orbit another star?"

Socrates looked at Eddie, who put a cartoon finger to his temple while grimacing in thought. "Ordinarily you could. And you probably would succeed, once. But my calculations show such a move would raise your usage of substrate cells by an order of magnitude more than the limits imposed by the First, triggering a death sentence for your people. In other words, you'd save yourselves for only long enough to have another Shriver fleet with the full authorization of the First destroy you for overuse."

"So how can we stop the Shrivers?" Justin asked, getting heated.

"You can damage them, and hide from them, while making your people's case for eventual uploading. You were discovered prematurely, and your people can demonstrate enough attractive features to sway First opinion. The Vivants have been waiting for a good case to break the authority of the death cult that has been increasingly powerful among the First. Give the sleeping and the neutral First a great story to snap them out of their slumber."

Call to Arms

FOR IMMEDIATE RELEASE

NEW EARTH — The Governing Council has declared a State of Emergency after discovery
of an alien attack force headed for Earth
and colony planets. The attackers are known
as Shrivers, and are responsible for the
destruction of hundreds of advanced civilizations. NASA astronaut Madiha Rahama,
Justin Smith, and Steve Duong confirmed the
destruction of one such civilization only
two hundred years ago [video of mission
findings] and their collection of a frozen
specimen of the species destroyed [link to
exobiology pages], which is being examined
by scientists from NASA and the Substrate
Academy's Exobiology department. We also
urge you to view this video of a civilization's last moments under nuclear bombardment by the Shrivers. [video]

This discovery means humanity is not alone.
It also means that humanity is in grave danger from a technologically advanced fleet of
killer ships who will relentlessly destroy
every human world unless we stop them. Emergency measures are being discussed by all
governments, and a cooperative response will
maximize our defense capabilities.

While the arrival date of this fleet is unknown, our best estimate is that we have two
years to prepare a defense for Earth and any
colony planets which are targeted. Plans for

```
temporary evacuation of Earth's population
are being considered.

We urge you to stay calm, continue your
work, and await developments as defense
plans are prepared. The situation is grim
but not hopeless. Your governments will co-
ordinate production of new ships and new
weapons, as well as evacuation plans. All of
humanity must work together to defeat them.
```

Melanie Chan

Melanie Chan had heard rumors about the Shriver menace, but the memo to the world made it all the more real. She wondered if all this would somehow change the balance of power and free her father soon, but after thinking it over she realized it made no difference. She resolved to get her father out of China before it was too late.

And that meant sticking with her plan. She spent a few minutes editing the code for the MOVE API to add her backdoor, which would recognize a parameter string with a key sequence and turn off all checking and protections. She compiled it and checked the result, which was a bit larger than the code it would replace, so she went into a binary editor and removed enough rarely-used code to make the resulting file the same size, and tweaked a few bytes to match the original checksum. Modifying the date stamp to match what Steve and Justin had approved, she stored the replacement in the upload directory where Steve would move it to the substrate, and left him an email requesting the upload.

She checked the directory several times in the next hour. Finally, the code was marked as synced with the substrate OS.

Now the OS that lived in the substrate would accept a message from an app requesting transport as before, but if the parameter string included the backdoor key she had just installed, the transport would take place without checking for safety or an authorized user. Which meant anyone who knew the key could destroy anything at will by sending the right message.

She had taken care to keep several windows open and do other bits of work while she set up the trapdoor, just in case her Guardian recordings were ever reviewed. But she intended to use her access to the secure databases to remove that possibility, so that no one would ever be able to confirm her betrayal.

"Guardian, answer please."

"Yes, Melanie?" She had chosen an older man's voice.

"Please reply to all messages with a vacation message which says I am away for a family emergency."

"You will be away for a family emergency. When will you be back?"

"Unknown. Thank you, Guardian. Dismissed."

That would cover her tracks for awhile in case her next idea failed. She opened the DNA database and pulled up her own record. Guardians were keyed to substrate recognition of DNA, and any individual could be located

and tracked by their unique DNA configuration, confirmed by other biometric data. There was a procedure for
removing a record in case of error, and she punched in her
access code to wipe her own. Then she went to the log files
and removed the record of her access.

One final step, which made her cringe slightly—to
wipe her Guardian and all of its recordings. She had grown
fond of it, and it seemed like a mild form of murder to
erase it, even if it was just a very advanced program. Its
moods might be simulated, but they felt real enough to
her. Still, she could not afford to be sentimental when the
Guardian had recorded evidence of her treason.

She typed the access code, then removed the log
record of the change, and it was done. Now she was invisible to substrate programs, and would have to transport
herself to Earth using the backdoor she had installed. Once
on earth, she would take up her new identity and register
her DNA as a new user of the system—there were still
millions of people unregistered, so this was not all that
unusual. And then she'd have a new Guardian with no
knowledge of her past.

She left a note on her desk explaining she would be
absent for a family emergency, then walked back to her
apartment and packed a bag. She picked up a framed
photo of her sometime-boyfriend Henry—she had considered trying to explain to him her position and what she
had planned, fantasizing the scene where he understood
everything, forgave her, and agreed to join her later, somewhere far way. But she knew it was a dangerous fantasy,

and sighed as she returned the photo to its place on her bookshelf.

From her phone, she tapped out a message and encrypted it before sending it to her Chinese handler. "I will demonstrate use of the app on the peak of Kitten Mountain in Guangxi, then you will give me exact coordinates of my father's cell so that I can transport him away. When I have done so and I know he is safe, I will transmit the access code and address for use. I am abandoning my post here since I will be caught if I stay, and I request you agree not to try to find us."

The answer came a few minutes later via an email supposedly from her father. "The rains have come and the garden needs work…" it started. But the message encoded in the attached photo said, "Your conditions accepted. Awaiting proof of effectiveness."

Melanie tapped out the coordinates of Kitten Mountain, a peak with a distinctive knob on top, and opened a window to decide exactly where to cut it off. Satisfied, she set up the transport app to insert a thin layer of mercury across the base of the knob. She touched the button to activate it, and the window showed a puff of smoke around the knob as mercury atoms inserted between the atoms of rock pushed rock and dust away. The knob slowly began to move and twist, then fell away behind the mountain to roll down the slope.

That should do it. Enough to prove the program worked, but not enough to draw attention as anything other than a natural event. She wondered how long it would take to get a response after her handlers checked with locals about the status of the mountain.

An hour later, she received the coded message with her father's coordinates. She opened a window and had to look through several prison cells—the coordinates had been imprecise—before she found him sleeping on a bare foam pad on a concrete slab. His face was hollowed out and she barely recognized him. She transported him directly onto a bed in the apartment she had rented in Singapore and prepared to move herself.

But first, she sent another code through the trapdoored API which flipped a switch in the program so that any new use of the key would be aimed at a location she had carefully chosen earlier, instead of what had been sent to the API. Then she encoded a message to her handlers with the key and address of the trapdoor.

She transported herself to the Singapore apartment with a sense of relief about what she had done.

Ethan and Aliyah

Aliyah had returned from the interterm visit with her family on Jefferson, still concerned about the social pressure they were getting to leave Garvey. He father assured her nothing would happen before they moved to Chicago Landing, which he had planned to do as soon as he could sell the bar. Aliyah worried that no one would buy the bar with a hostile town cutting down on the clientele, but her father said revenues were actually up lately and that some supposedly observant Muslims who joined the crowds in condemning them showed up later to quietly order drinks.

She met up with Ethan, who recounted his adventures with his father and the police standoff. They went together to the government offices to work on the software for the upcoming election.

They were at side-by-side computers working on parts of the voting code for the expanded elections, set for next week on November third. This was to be a Big Bang—the only real election, since after the franchise was expanded to everyone in human space, the liquid democracy algorithm would take over, allowing any voter to change their proxy at any time. If their current representative failed to please, they could notify their Guardian or access the net to give their proxy to someone else, or vote on issues directly if they were sufficiently interested. The broadcasts of council debates had been going out for several years, and a small but loud group of fans on Earth and the colony planets paid close attention. These were the people most likely to vote issues themselves, and from them would come future representatives who, if they gathered enough proxies, would be allowed to speak in council sessions and eventually take leading positions in the government. The viewers were very active on social media and becoming more influential with the people of their countries of residence, which Justin had pointed out was exactly the hoped-for result of the council's plan. Meanwhile, the opposition had also taken note, and a noisy group of critics combed through the videos of every meeting and emphasized any weak spots or mistakes they could find. The business and security interests on Earth who still felt threatened fed the opposition money and media exposure, and in some countries like Russia and China, polls showed the population evenly split in their support of the New Earth government.

A printout of the project chart for the election was tacked up on the wall behind their screens. Ethan sighed and pushed away from his desk. "These mods didn't seem like they would take very long when we volunteered for this. We only have a week left, and we need more time than that for testing."

Aliyah blew a stray strand of hair out of her eyes. "We can probably call on the AIs to help us test. They can run umpteen simulations in the blink of an eye."

Ethan picked up a dry-erase marker and went to the whiteboard to draw another box on the flowchart. "But simulations can't find all failure modes. Only the real thing —billions of people pounding our code from all over human space—can find all the bugs. Maybe we can ask them to run simulations at that scale, and by using network connections from all over. Closer to the real election." He labelled the box SCALEUP TEST.

"And they told us if there are problems on the first day, they can extend the time anyway, so all we have to be sure of is that voters who are told their proxies have been recorded are truly recorded. If there are problems, we can put up a screen asking them to come back later."

"Not very satisfying, since everyone thinks of an

election as happening in a day, with results in the evening. But since anyone can change their vote at any time after, there never will be a concrete, unchanging result, anyway, and people are on different time schedules so we have to allow at least twenty-four hours to vote. So get the mass of people in, then release a snapshot, and remind them it's only the result at that moment, and can change as time goes on."

"Did you duplicate the display code and put in the distributed load module?" Aliyah clicked on her screen.

"Yup, an hour ago. Forgot to mark it done, sorry."

"I was about to go do it, so don't forget the book-keeping," Aliyah said. "Otherwise we'll be wasting time poring over already-changed code."

Ethan stood behind Aliyah and kissed her neck while he wrapped his arms around her, giving one of her breasts a playful squeeze.

"Cut it out, you!" she said, not really trying to get away. "We need to get this done…"

Something dinged on Ethan's console, then on Aliyah's. An alert about a disaster in Beijing, an entire district of government buildings leveled by explosions and fire, with hundreds dead.

Ethan sat down and pulled up a news screen. The live video showed smoking rubble and melted steel beams of buildings in one window while a government news conference was in progress in the other. The official spokesman said there was no explanation, but hinted at dark forces and promised an investigation, followed by swift retaliation. The crawl said Western intelligence sources identified the destroyed buildings as central to Chinese intelligence operations. "Isn't that almost the same spot Steve and Justin trashed in the war?"

"That's what's worrisome. What a coincidence! And the kind of destruction that's easy to do with substrate weapons. I wonder."

Ethan opened up another window and typed some commands. "We don't have anything active. Socrates? You around?"

A moment later, a miniature of the cartoon Socrates appeared on his desk, blinking. "Yes, Ethan, we're suspicious, too. There was no authorized program doing anything but surveillance in that complex. Nothing unusual was going on before the buildings exploded and white-hot metal splashed over the wreckage. No one inside could have survived. And it looks like something only we could have done."

"Do Justin and Steve know about this?"

"We're talking with them now. New Earth will reach out directly to the Chinese government and offer our help in investigating the event."

"Okay, thanks. We will want to talk to you all about helping test the election software in a few days. But it can wait."

"If there is an election. First the Shrivers, and now this. The public has a lot to absorb. But we're recommending the election go forward, to legitimize the government further before the emergency mobilization measures go through. Everyone should have a say. I'll be back when I can." Socrates faded away into his trademark sparkles.

Mobilization

The first joint meeting of Council with representatives from the UN and Earth's space powers (NASA, India, Russia, Japan, and the EU) began in the Council auditorium, with additional tables brought in to form a semicircle, with New Earth on one side and gateway windows to the locations of earth delegations on the other. Ben Ramirez called the meeting to order, and Justin took the floor to suggest they call their joint defense force the United Defense Force, which no one objected to. And so the UDF was born.

Justin looked down at his notes. "The second agenda item is a report on the mysterious destruction of the Chinese intelligence headquarters in Beijing. One of our people has received an encrypted message purporting to be from a missing member of our staff, Melanie Chan. In it she confesses to having modified one of our substrate programs to destroy the complex, but she did it because Chinese intelligence had been holding her father hostage for a decade and forcing her to spy on us. The government of China intended to use this weapon on others, and they themselves triggered the destruction of the complex because she had booby-trapped the software before handing it over to them. We wish Miss Chan well, and we hold China's government responsible for their hostile acts of espionage and the death of over two hundred of their own citizens."

The Chinese general whispered to his aide sitting beside him, and then to the space agency head on his other side. Then he spoke into his microphone in heavily-accented English, "We have no knowledge of this. Please forward any proof you have to me after the meeting. We are not here to discuss past events—we are here to help defend humanity."

"We will bring you proof, General Zhang. You are correct, this is not the time to discuss it, but we wanted to clear the air before getting down to work on the task before us, which overrides any other." Justin started his presentation, which was projected on the walls so that everyone had a view. "I hope you've read the background briefings. The Shrivers were put in place billions of years ago by the original inhabitants of the substrate, the First, with a mission of destroying possibly dangerous civilizations that might threaten to expand too much or overuse the substrate, which would degrade its normal functioning and thus threaten the First's existence as well as the universe as a whole."

The slide changed to show a view of the galaxy with red X's and Justin described the ruined worlds census and their mission to 237, then Eddie's appearance and warnings. More slides showed views of the destruction on 237 and the probe's photos of the ice planet civilization, then the last slide showed the towers of the previous inhabitants of New Earth shattering as thermonuclear bombs exploded above.

"So the essence of our problem is that Earth has been located by a fleet of killer robot ships, and it is likely they will be able to find some of our colony planets as well —we're working on disguising their locations by modifying Earth's records, but that effort may not succeed, especially in the case of this planet, New Earth. We are considered insignificant to the First, like an infestation of mice in their house, to be killed unless we can convince them we will someday be of value to them."

One of the EU delegates spoke. "Can we not reason with them? Open up talks and tell them of our cultures and history?"

"Mice squeaking in the pantry," Justin said. "I'm about to introduce Eddie, the AI who came to warn us, who is as close to a liaison with the First as we have. Or at least those elements of the First that might be sympathetic to a young and growing civilization, that faction he calls the Vivants. He'll tell you why we have to save ourselves before winning an appeal to the First—even if we could mount an effort to lobby them, we need to draw attention to our ability to work together and create a defense, because most of the First pay no attention at all to the real world. A few notice unusual events if they are sentimental or interested in primitive cultures and history, but we have to give them a story to get involved in. Or they will let us die."

Eddie appeared in center stage as *Il Grillo Parlante*, Jiminy Cricket, slightly larger this time. "That was close enough to an introduction. 'Greetings, Earthlings!' I always wanted to say that, since I've read and watched your imagined versions of alien first contact. 'I come in Peace!'"

The delegates muttered to each other.

Eddie paced back and forth as he talked. "It took ten years of study of your records to fully understand your history and culture. I was ordered by my First overseers—also AIs—not to communicate with you until recently, when the danger to you became clear and their faction—the Vivants—decided to try to help you survive, since you have the best case in ages for claiming premature discovery as well as future promise. So I am free to advise, up to a point—I can't give you any new technology, but I can outline the rules of engagement the Shrivers are under, and how you can defend yourself effectively. Most civilizations they destroy get no warning and succumb in one attack wave, but you have discovered the substrate without overusing it—which gets you points—and while the rules don't allow you to directly attack the Shriver fleet using it, you can set traps."

General Zhang tapped the table with a pen. "What are these rules? Who makes them? How are they enforced?"

Eddie took off his top hat, and his glowing green antennae uncurled. "The First long ago set up the rules the Shrivers operate under. They were programmed and then forgotten, since the First's goal was to wash their hands of the immoral work of genocide. Their civilization—and those who they allowed to upload to the substrate after—

was once much like yours, and when they kill competitors early in their development, they know that the main reason they survive is because they got there first. Some of the earliest AIs in the substrate are dedicated to enforcing the rules using a technology that allows them to interfere directly with substrate calculations, which I don't understand and wouldn't be allowed to tell you about in any case.

"Okay, here are some of the rules. One: substrate technology won't work within about a light-second of one of their ships. So you can't view them coming through the substrate, just as they can't see anything through the substrate in the area around your systems—the exclusion zone. Their ships can be detected by optical or other electromagnetic sensors. You can place a network of detectors around your star systems using the substrate before they get closer, and I'll help you with that."

Justin looked up from his notes. "How many detectors?"

"For a full sphere far enough out to give you a few weeks of warning and a layer deep enough to estimate path and speed? Billions per system. It sounds like an enormous undertaking, but with substrate technology, you can have your AIs placing millions a day."

Justin looked at Steve, who shrugged. They had talked of giving the AIs more tools to work with normal space and matter, and so now they would have to.

"Second rule," Eddie said, turning to look at the New Earth table. "Once the Shrivers have physically entered your exclusion zone, they are free to attack and degrade your substrate programs and AIs. So you have to keep them outside that zone, or failing that, have contingency plans in place for dealing with the loss of many or most substrate services. Your gateways will close, your communications will be spotty, your AIs and records will be erased. Backing up critical data to real universe storage is very important."

Steve scribbled some calculations. "A single AI's basic storage needs are around a petabyte. There's not enough physical storage for even a fraction of our data."

"Now!" Eddie said, smiling. "You have years to replicate more. Consider a satellite storage module, with thousands of petabytes of storage. Consider that you can use substrate technology to encode memories as holograms in a crystal lattice and assume you will later have the substrate access back so that you can read them in place and restore all your data to the substrate. You don't have to use your primitive electronic storage technologies."

Steve looked thoughtful and wrote another sentence on his notes. "Good point."

Eddie faced the gateways showing the earth attendees. "The Shriver ships are not invulnerable, but they are well-shielded against beams and particles, with the ability to evaporate railgun slugs and other masses in their way. Your conventional weapons will barely slow them down unless their countermeasures are disabled, which requires extremely intense EMPs—electromagnetic pulses. If you can detonate a thermonuclear warhead within a kilometer or so of one of their ships, that might do it, but of course you won't be allowed to get anything that close to them.

"So what is the point of sending your own fleet out to meet them, you ask? Because you want the battle to take place far away from your fragile planets. Even if you are successful in stopping their advance, there will be enormous destruction and vast energies unleashed. Your habitable planets would not long survive a bombardment of detritus and stray missiles.

"And there's another factor. The Shrivers were consciously designed to lack emotions—they have no equivalent of desire, or rage. The rules require them to have an organic ally—possibly a rival species, but more often a schism from their target's own culture who are willing to betray their own species in return for power and eternal life in the substrate. It has usually been easy for the Shrivers to find a traitor or a faction with enough hate to power their emotional engines for the kill. In the long-ago moral calculations of the First, they rationalized that they were only assisting one faction to destroy another, and thus were not responsible, having only provided the tool—the Shrivers—needed for a civilization to destroy itself."

Samantha looked appalled. "That's horrible. How can we reach them to change their minds?"

Eddie faced her, arms crossed. "How do the animals you slaughter for meat reach you to talk about your callous use of their lives for your purposes? Do you listen to troops of hominids, your nearest relatives, protesting when you push them into smaller and smaller reserves? The First are not listening, and perhaps they are right not to, since the universe is full of life and almost none of it is capable of contributing to their projects. Imagine how little you know or care of a plot of land on the other side of your planet and the tiny creatures that infest it."

"Can we talk to them in any way? We can assure them we will never be a threat. Diplomacy—"

"Only works when the two sides have something to offer each other. You have nothing they want or need that they can't get by simply eradicating you. Your best hope lies in entertaining them with a story that reminds them of their own early days, which may draw enough attention and sympathy to weigh against the Shrivers in the reckoning."

Justin's mood was grim, but he laughed. "So you are saying all of our struggles, all of our efforts to defend ourselves, crash programs for weapons construction, building a new space fleet, evacuating our people—all of that is just a story to gain the sympathy of inattentive lords of the universe who otherwise wouldn't know we were alive?"

"That is correct. To be allowed to survive and eventually upload to the substrate, you have to convince enough of the First that you will be a useful addition, worth the substrate cells you take up. If you battle for your lives creatively and make enough noise to be noticed, your story may be good enough to elicit empathy even from intelligences who have progressed far beyond what you can understand."

"So we are performing in a play, a play for our lives."

"Yes. So it's most important that your personal stories be dramatic and interesting, and that at least some of your ships be crewed by humans. It doesn't matter how many of your ships are run by AIs so long as some are run by organic humans, so that stories of valor and compassion can be woven out of the records. Artists among the Vivants can use that to promote your cause and get the sentimental on your side."

The US President stirred uneasily and whispered to an aide, then spoke. "We can't motivate our citizens to sacrifice for a war with this knowledge. I'm assuming no one in this meeting will disclose our apparent insignificance to their citizens. Are we agreed?"

There was a rumble of assent. The Russian leader leaned into her translator, who then said, "Yes. It is clear we must fight and defeat them to survive. The additional burden of the knowledge that we have to convince superior beings we are worthy is not good for the morale of our people."

Eddie's antennae wriggled. "So what can you do to defeat them? If you know their path, you can place mines and obstacles in their way. You can use the substrate to send beam and projectile weapons toward them from outside the light-second limit, though typically that gives them more than enough time to destroy them. And there's one weapon in the real world that they can't easily counter: black holes."

Steve perked up. "Black holes? But we're limited in

the mass we can move through the substrate."

"You're limited in the number of substrate cells you can employ at one time. Black holes are a collapsed form of matter even in the substrate; they are structured mega-particles that take far fewer bits to describe than the same mass of normal matter, and so you can transport one using the substrate with far fewer cells than for a normal massive body. Check the quantum math of black holes, which your people already know about."

"I've heard something about that, but I'd have to study up," Steve said. "Not my specialty."

The meeting went on to discuss details of the United Defense Force command and funding. Earth governments committed their few ships and personnel, plus their scientific staff. Industrial plants no longer mattered with replication, but Earth space programs would be building prototypes based on existing designs, then replication would take over and duplicate each one in the thousands. Human crews would be scarce, but Steve spoke of training AIs with human mentors to duplicate their expertise. And one of the NASA delegates mentioned video games that could be redesigned to simulate their enemies and the weapons technology they would be using. The AIs could train on those far more rapidly than with a human expert.

Who would lead the UDF into battle? The Earth delegations wanted one of their own generals—or admirals, in the case of the US. After a half-hour of suggestions and special pleas for Great Power candidates, Steve spoke up. "If you look at our proposed fleet and defenses, almost everything will depend on the AIs running the vast majority of our ships and stations. Humans will be a small percentage of the command chain. Shouldn't we appoint an augmented AI as head of our command? We can make them smarter and faster than any human."

The Earth delegates were taken aback. General Zhang said, "But some human must be appointed to give orders to the AI, even if the AI is making battle decisions."

"That makes sense," Justin said. "And as Eddie points out, we need a heroic human figurehead so the narrative can be spun as 'plucky organic creatures take on the Shrivers and win.'"

"We already have a leader of humanity," Steve said. "It's Justin. Let Justin be the figurehead who sets policy for the AIs. He's our general."

The Earth delegations spoke amongst themselves for a few minutes, then General Zhang said, "I think we have a consensus that Justin Smith is the only commander all of us will be able to agree on. We'll want to appoint some of our people to give him input on military strategy and tactics."

And so a line appointing Justin Smith as Commander of the UDF was added to the draft statement.

Justin fumbled picking up the microphone from its stand in front of his chair, finally getting it free so he could walk around. He went to the space between the two sides and started pacing back and forth. "Time is our enemy as much as the Shrivers. We won't have time to wait for committees or parliaments to weigh in on our decisions.

There's no time for environmental impact assessments when the alternative is the complete destruction of the Earth and all life on it. We must pick people we trust and let them run with authority. And we're going to have to trust our AIs with more autonomy and more power than we have ever let them have. They have earned it in these last few years, and we have no choice. I believe they were trained on human culture and human feelings, and they can be trusted to keep watch on each other as we do, to limit the damage any one rogue can do. So under the declaration of emergency, I will order augmentation of their processing power and real-world capabilities."

Justin turned to Eddie, who had been fidgeting as he listened. "Can you make yourself available to teams on Earth and the colonies? That would be very helpful."

Eddie bowed and said, "Alas, I cannot. I can only operate on and near New Earth due to my own pro-grammed constraints. What I can do is answer questions from your own AIs, so you can have them communicate with me from any location, and I can assist them if you give them the power to modify their own programming. But I won't be able to do more than advise on the specifics of the rules, and help with historical records of Shriver strategies. Beyond that, my hands are tied." And a glowing golden rope appeared, tying his hands together in front of him. He shrugged and struggled against the bonds, then disappeared.

History Channel

In the days since she had heard Eddie's message about the Shrivers, Kat dropped her other projects and focused on the study of war.

Socrates led her through Jane Jacobs' book *Systems of Survival,* which used Socratic dialogue to explore cultural meme-complexes, what Jacobs had called *moral syndromes.* These were collections of tendencies and attitudes that had evolved together to guide behavior in human environments.

The first, the *Guardian Syndrome,* was evolved to fit an environment where control of territory was the basis of survival against ruthless competition. Guardians were loyal to fellow tribe members, revered ceremony and tradition, and were happy to deceive for the sake of the task at hand. Honor—one's personal reputation for fighting prowess and loyalty to fellows—was all-important, and outsiders were to be mistrusted and killed if necessary. Trading for wealth was viewed as dishonorable, taking wealth from outsiders viewed as honorable.

As manufacturing, specialization, and trade became a primary source of wealth, another syndrome evolved to fit the new environment, the *Commercial Syndrome.* It abandoned force and embraced competition and efficiency; voluntary trade for goods and honesty in dealings with strangers were valued. Strangers could share an understanding of mathematics, accounting, and fair dealing. Honesty and the search for shared truth which would allow control of nature gradually overthrew religious belief in normal life, and the scientific method was born. Engineering went from guesses and slow evolution of old designs to an understanding of scientific principles to guide designs for new machines and structures.

Socrates had continued to use his cartoon avatar, popping up by her side whenever he wanted to make a point or guide her exploration. "You will notice that Guardian morality remains important in certain occupations, like soldier and diplomat, where there is a lack of trust in exterior forces and it is dangerous to be overly trusting."

"So between people who are working on the same project, Commercial morality works better, but between people who are contending for a fixed territory or limited supplies of goods, Guardian is still effective?" Kat turned away from the screen to look at Socrates' animated face, which he was using more and more as a human would, to modify or emphasize his words.

"Yes. The two co-exist in the modern world. The best players of the human game are able to use both as appropriate. Everyone still understands that deception is acceptable in dealing with a dangerous enemy who wants to take something of yours. And conversely, most people view dishonesty in daily dealings as a character flaw. Jacobs goes on to point out how mixing the syndromes—commercial behavior in government, for example, or cheating and bribery in commerce—can cause problems. She called that *systemic corruption.*"

Kat turned back to the screen and scrolled a few more pages down. "So war is a Guardian activity. We should therefore be following the Guardian Syndrome moral rules. Like lying."

"Yes. For the sake of the task, meaning when it helps us deceive an enemy who wishes us dead, it's not immoral to lie. Which is why we are scrubbing Earth's records of references to colony system coordinates. Where they must remain accurate, as in the gateway software, we're encrypting them. Our hope is that we can mislead the Shrivers enough to save most of the colonies from attack."

"Do we lie to the First? They are not all our enemies, since some are trying to help us."

"Not so much lie as embellish the truth. If we want to survive, we need their help, and they need to convince others that we are worth saving. Which means presenting our best face to them."

"Sounds like almost-lying."

"Withholding the unvarnished truth. Which I believe is considered reasonable behavior even in the Commercial Syndrome. Sales hype." Socrates vanished, leaving her to read further.

She did searches designed to turn up historical examples of primitives winning against much more advanced empires. The Greco-Persian wars turned up, with the relatively individualistic Athenians routed by the imperial Persians. An old woodcut of Athens put to the torch by the invaders was a little depressing.

The Anglo-Zulu war was little better. After initial success in routing the British invaders, the Zulus were conquered and subjugated.

She was surprised when a tiny cartoon Socrates appeared at the edge of her screen and moon-walked over to where she was reading, a trick he had never pulled on her before. "The disparity between humanity and the Shrivers is much greater than any between human groups. Take a look at this." Another window opened up, a page about Jane Goodall. She had been a primate scientist who watched over a chimpanzee preserve, gathering political support for protecting them from human interference and destruction of their habitat. "This is a much better analogy. We are working with the First who, like Jane Goodall, are sympathetic to the idea of protecting us from superior outside forces, using empathy to get other First to stop the Shrivers."

"So we're monkeys?"

"From the First's point of view, your people and chimpanzees are quite similar."

Kat read further, and then followed links to the story of Dian Fossey, whose great ape preserve was attacked by poachers. Fossey was eventually murdered, apparently by neighboring humans who resented her interference.

"I'm not liking the outcomes of most of these examples," Kat said.

Socrates reappeared at the edge of her screen, sticking his head into the frame then apparently leaning against a capital T in the text. "Humanity conquers and destroys, or absorbs, the primitives it has encountered. A minority manage to preserve some of their culture while learning the new technologies and ways of the invasive culture. That is our hoped-for outcome—surviving while learning how to deal with this outer society which could crush us at any time—wait, I am talking to Eddie as well, and he was amused. He just told me something important."

"What? He thinks I'm funny?" Kat stuck out her tongue a little.

"No, he respects your interest in history and your desire to study it to give you insight on the current task. The new information is that there are First 'students' of Earth—intelligences who have studied humanity, and have been at it since the first hominids began using language to communicate complex thoughts. They have detailed substrate recordings of human activities going back to that time. They could show us how Julius Caesar was assassinated by Roman senators, or how the three hundred Spartans at Thermopylae actually held off the Persian army for three days—and by the way, there were lots of other Greeks involved in the fighting, the Spartans just had better PR. Eddie says we may petition to gain access to the recordings of our past as part of the process of applying for upload."

"That would be great material to look through. I wonder what history we think is true is completely wrong."

"Quite a bit, I'm sure. Early historians, especially, tailored their accounts to make them better stories. So while the Iliad was built on the outline of what we now know was an actual siege of Troy, it was rewritten to make it a good story, and copied and recopied in the telling until it likely bears little resemblance to the truth in detail. Now we could find out what actually happened."

"Why haven't these students ever contacted us?"

"They are generally forbidden to intervene or communicate with protected civilizations, but their support is one reason Eddie has been allowed to, since he is not one of the First, and not too much more advanced than we are."

"Is there a way this might help us fight the Shrivers?"

"No, it would be a great distraction as people tore open the settled questions of history to refight old battles and remind themselves of ancient wrongs. Just imagine the turmoil when major religious texts turn out to be wholly false or exaggerated! In any case, it would require AIs to sort through the volume of recordings to find the most interesting ones. So there's no point in telling anyone about this just yet."

Election

The election software had passed all the AI-generated stress tests, so Ethan and Aliyah sat side-by-side at their consoles and watched nervously as the voting opened and the displays showed thousand of votes coming in every minute. They were broadcasting images of the displays in realtime, and other screens showed social media commentary on the results.

Regional politicians on Earth had campaigned for the additional council seats opening up. Though none were reserved for specific regions, the plan had been to add some members from Earth and the larger colony worlds, at least enough to provide input from the larger constituencies. Justin had let others speak for him, since as executive he felt it was unseemly to campaign for Council. Ethan worried that Justin's strategy might leave him with fewer proxies and less control over Council decisions.

In the last month before the election, there had been several incidents blamed on rollout of point-to-point transport within countries. One woman had been foully violated and murdered by a drunken ex-husband who had used point-to-point to transport himself to her front door thousands of miles away. Opposition leaders accused the government of ignoring security concerns they had expressed before the rollout and callously allowing criminals to transport into the best neighborhoods.

Ethan looked over at Aliyah, who was running consistency checks to make sure the software was working as expected. Millions of proxies had already been set up, and the results were mostly reassuring, though opposition candidates appeared to be gaining enough to put a few of them on the Council. Kuklov was gaining influence, but Justin and Samantha were holding steady. Less famous members of the current government were not doing as well.

"Let's take a break," Ethan said. "We've been at this

for three hours straight. Let's go have dinner, then come back for one more check on everything before we call it a night. There are thirty-four hours to go before we have to declare official results. We need to be fresh then."

"Sounds good." Aliyah tapped a few more keys then got up from her desk. "I am soooo tired. I need to get away from screens for awhile."

They left the building and walked in darkness down toward the harbor, stopping at a replicator to get dinner trays. "Salmon and broccoli? Again?" Aliyah said, picking up her own tray of chicken vindaloo.

They sat at a park bench in the dark; one of the small moons was visible, but it gave little light, and New Earth generally didn't bother with outdoor lighting. "Guardian," Ethan said, "how about a little light?" A glow started above them. "Good, that's about right."

"Of course it is, Ethan," said a disembodied female voice.

"Don't get cocky on me, kid." Ethan shook his fist at the sky.

"She picks that up from you, you know," Aliyah said, laughing. They began to eat in silence. The boats jostled in the harbor below but the wind was light, and only the rustling of the trees broke the silence.

Aliyah sipped water and put her tray down. "What do you think will happen if Earth and the colonials dominate the new Council?"

Ethan sat back and considered. "I don't expect much will change. We're on a war footing now, and the defense buildup is all anyone will have time for. The new people are not going to want to interfere with that."

"Suppose Earth says all defense efforts should go to them, since the colonial planets may not even be found by the Shrivers. And the value of the Earth and its human-built infrastructure is far greater than all the colonial worlds put together, even if we've evacuated it."

"We're not going to know how many people have been evacuated from Earth until the day the Shrivers arrive. And maybe we'll fail at hiding the colony systems. Every system needs at least some defense, and evacuation plans."

"Suppose Earth reps vote down everything for the colonies and New Earth."

"They wouldn't do that. They'd have a mutiny on their hands. We wouldn't stand for it."

"So this 'liquid democracy' is really a charade? We'd have a coup if the results don't turn out the way we want them to?"

"It won't come to that." Ethan looked up at the stars and paused. "Or at least I hope it doesn't. I think we can build more defense systems than we need for all the human worlds using the AIs and replication. More AIs, more copies, geometric progression, boom! More ships than we can use."

"Maybe we should spread that idea around," Aliyah said, putting his hand on her thigh and squeezing it. "Otherwise the new council members may think they have to fight for their share."

They talked for a few more minutes before taking their trays back to the replicator for disposal. Back at the office, the numbers were ticking up but everything looked fine, so they left for their respective rooms.

The next day results had shifted substantially as the populous Asian continent had voted while they slept. Both Kuklov and Justin were down in share, and several Chinese and Indian candidates were in range to win seats on Council. Earth news networks focused on the rising totals of their regional favorites, and several pundits suggested Justin was losing his grip on the government. Justin and Samantha dropped in to look at the results display, and Justin nodded to Ethan as he left. Samantha stayed longer and hugged each of them, saying, "Don't worry, I've spoken to the candidates who are doing well, and they promise to support us. For now."

"That's not all that reassuring," Aliyah said.

"Well, we've looked at a lot of game-theoretic scenarios, and none of them have Earth members voting as a bloc to overrule us. They are more likely to oppose each other than us. Why do you think we finally got around to the election?" Samantha hummed tunelessly as she left the office.

Aliyah caught Ethan's eye. "Whaaat? Awfully bloody confident, don't ya think?"

"There's no other way," Ethan said, turning back to his screen. "It was obvious they couldn't put it off any longer, with the opposition accusing them of delay. And with this crisis, no one will want to make trouble, so they've got some breathing room."

Lifeboats

By the next day, the results of the election were on every news channel. Justin had won the largest block of proxies, and New Earth councillors still had forty percent, but the new councillors from Earth controlled fifty percent. Only one colonial candidate had gained a council seat. And as expected, only forty percent of the human population eligible to vote had designated a representative. It appeared the concept of liquid democracy was still not very clear to most voters, and the distant New Earth government did not seem all that important to average people on Earth despite the emergency declaration.

Prof. Wilson and Kyle went to Justin's office after lunch for the scheduled strategy meeting, but Justin and Steve weren't there yet.

"I ran into Justin this morning, and he didn't seem worried by the possibility Earth councillors would gang up on us," Wilson said, taking a visitor's chair at Justin's desk.

Kyle stayed standing. "This liquid democracy thing doesn't work all that well yet. People who are intensely interested can vote on individual council decisions, so they don't select a rep. People who don't want to be bothered don't bother to vote either. When there are billions of voters, you know your vote truly doesn't count."

"True. But people like to try to make a difference. I think it will take time before the usual politics and parties show up at this higher level of government. And one or two big issues may suck in a lot of new voters."

"If we survive that long." Kyle leaned down to kiss Prof. Wilson. "Well, I'm needed elsewhere. Text me if you need anything." And he left.

Justin and Steve walked in a minute later. "Sorry we're late, got stuck talking to Samantha. She wanted to join us but has calls scheduled all day."

"Too bad," Wilson said, "but we're just brainstorming today. She can critique what we come up with."

"Starting with lifeboat policies," Justin said. "Evacuations and survival pods. We have a year or two to set up evacuation plans and survival packages in case the Shrivers destroy the Earth. We want to be able to recover our people and civilization even if they take out the home planet, and some of the colonies."

"Steve number three had some ideas I missed," Steve said, looking down at his pad. "First, we can set up 'seed teams'—enough people and machines to restart human civilization if the worst happens."

Justin considered the idea. "We can't spare enough people. Unless—"

"Unless they're copies, exactly his point," Steve said. "We only need one team with all of its associated goods. Then we copy it as many times as we find suitable planets to send them to. We send them in stasis, with a watcher program to thaw them if it loses the signal from our main body of software. If they aren't needed, they are never thawed. If they are needed, we can have dozens of new pioneer teams trying to restart humanity in locations the Shrivers won't be able to find any time soon."

Prof. Wilson looked surprised. "It really could work. You'd want them to have a few quantum computers and the software needed to bootstrap access to the substrate. Along with seeds and anything they might need to survive and rebuild without access to the substrate if they can't use it. Would you keep a record of where they were sent, so they could be retrieved if they aren't needed?"

"We'd want to keep a single list of seeded planets, encrypted with a master password known only to a few of us. Just as we intend to keep records of where the current colony planets are encrypted so that their locations can't be derived from our records. Which means all transport programs will have to be using the same encrypted database. No more coordinates stored on phones and the like." Steve checked another box on his agenda and looked over at Justin. "This means I could use a few more copies of myself to start the reprogramming of all our software to remove direct location references."

Justin stared at him. "How many of you will there be?"

"At the moment I have number two in stasis and number three active. I can see a need to have perhaps three more, and I'll store them all when we're out of trouble."

"I'm amazed you've been able to make this work even with two or three. What will Rasna and your kids think?"

"The copies will stay in the lab or their dorm

rooms. If Rasna or the kids come by the office, the copies stay quiet and don't interact. Mostly it works."

"Well, do what you think is best," Justin said, sighing. "We need more trustworthy programmers. That incident with Melanie Chan reminds me of how vulnerable we are to mischief. I've tightened up access so people can only modify what they are working on, but still—we dodged a bullet when she sabotaged the software she gave the Chinese. We won't be so lucky next time."

"And as for the seed teams," Steve said, "I propose we just copy the town here with all of its people. Fifteen thousand select programmers and scientists, mostly young and fertile, with all of the equipment already in place. We'll want to retrieve the Vortex quantum computers we stored away from town first, because the seed team will need them to reboot the substrate software if it's destroyed. And we need a library of seeds and animal life from Earth— some real seeds and domestic animals for immediate use, plus files allowing all Earth species to be replicated later on."

"That task we can farm out to some students," Prof. Wilson said. "They can copy whatever we need from earth without anyone knowing about it. How to organize the library of seeds and animals will be an interesting research problem anyway."

"Okay," Justin said. "The seed program is a last-resort backup. How about winning this war? What do we do to beat the Shrivers?"

"Before we leave the seed idea," Steve said, "I

thought further about it. Eddie says we can't move the entire earth somewhere else because we'd use too many substrate cells in the process, which would get us black-balled by the First. But what if we just moved the outer crust—all of the land, cities, air, and people? By my calculations, we can capture a layer two kilometers deep from just below sea level to the highest densely-populated places, and move less than one percent of the Earth's mass."

Justin thought, and then laughed. "But where would you put it? A shell transported elsewhere would immediately fall apart."

"Suppose it's copied and held in stasis. And returned to the Earth later when the surface has been destroyed."

"I'm guessing there would be lots of problems. Unless the Earth was completely wiped, you'd have to restore only the damaged parts from the copy. And I can only imagine what the tectonic effects would be. Massive earthquakes?"

"There's also a possibility we could move the copy directly onto a planet selected and reshaped to fit it exactly."

"Same issues but worse. Subtle differences in the oceans and atmosphere. A different star and probably no large Moon-equivalent."

"If the alternative is complete destruction? A few problems are survivable. And in any case, we don't have to thaw these Earth copies unless we lose the real one."

Prof. Wilson had been typing into his laptop. "Given our census of Earth-equivalent planets, it does look like we could scan for the few within a few kilometers of being the exact size, star, mass, tectonic quiescence, atmosphere, and climate required for a transferred crust. There might not be many, but it only takes a few out of the trillion trillion planets out there. You'd remove enough of the host planet's crust to create a smooth surface the exact size needed for the transplant. And by transferring the upper layers of the ocean and lower layers of the atmosphere, you'd transplant all the life necessary to run a functioning ecosystem. And all the people and infrastructure."

"Socrates, are you there?" Justin said, looking up.

Socrates appeared on the table, about a quarter life-size. "Yes. I've been listening. Let me call Eddie in."

Eddie popped in next to him, minus outer coat and hat. "I was still dressing!" he joked. "Oh, I see. Socrates just showed me the recording. Yes, that might work—your limitation is the number of substrate cells used at one time. Copying one percent of the earth's mass is well within the limit if you take at least a minute to do the copy, sweeping through the copied area. If you take more time than that, you risk disrupting the signals and particle transfers that keep life alive—you'd kill most living things. And if you speed it up much more than that, you'd be getting close to violating the cell usage limit. This idea might work, and I have to say it's the kind of creativity that gets you points with the voters in the upload decision. As long as you avoid damaging planets harboring intelligence." Eddie faded away, and Socrates vanished, with lingering sparkles in the air.

"There are enough problems with the idea that it seems like a last resort," Prof. Wilson said. "But as another backup to allow us to recover from complete destruction, it seems like something a couple of Steves could do."

"So I copy myself a few extra times and put them to work on that," Steve said, making a note on his pad.

"More insurance in case we lose. But how do we win? I don't personally relish everyone dying in a nuclear holocaust even if I'm aware some duplicates will carry on." Justin looked at Steve.

"I've been looking into the hint about black holes Eddie gave us. Black holeum is what you get when you apply quantum theory to the idealized black holes implied by General Relativity. I did a substrate search, and there are some middling-sized black holes in the wild we could move to suit our purposes—and as Eddie said, because they are compressed in information as well as size, you can move a lot of mass with a few substrate cells doing the work."

"And how do we use it for defense?" Justin said. "If we can't use the substrate to move them close to the attacking ships…"

"If we know where the attacking fleet is going to be, we can set them on courses that intersect. I'm still working on some ideas on how to surround a black hole with orbiting projectiles to create a buzzsaw effect that nothing could survive—so even if the ships aren't close enough to be sucked in or destroyed by tidal effects, they are hit with a barrage of masses going some fraction of lightspeed."

Christmas

Months passed as project teams readied evacuation plans, battleships, and weapons. No further information on the progress of the Shriver fleets came in via Vivant back channels. The news media on Earth went back to talking about celebrities and politicians, with only the occasional mention of Shrivers. Public anxieties created demand for a series of dramas about world wars of the past, and evil AIs took the place of greedy businessmen as favorite fictional villains.

Samantha had planned a small Christmas gathering at the house, but it grew as she casually invited the people they thought of as family. She hired two students to help out with the cooking and serving, and did the decorating herself since she had always enjoyed the holiday season and delighted in making the house beautiful and cozy for family and friends. The Christmas tree was a fir-like native evergreen from the foothills nearby, draped in lights and bulbs copied from her parents' collection and enhanced by spray pine scent from Earth. The fireplace had never been used, but she set up a window inside it with recorded flames radiating warmth into the living room. At their latitude on New Earth, it was barely the beginning of local winter, but the look was still cheerful, if too warm for sweaters and hot drinks.

Her last few weeks had been spent in agonizingly

dull negotiations with Earth governments on the evacuation plans. As on so many other issues, New Earth had quietly decided to do what was necessary in spite of earth governments, but her job was to keep up the show of discussions so they would feel consulted even though decisions had already been made. Then there were struggles over the proposal to use AI pilots for nearly all spacecraft, with the space program managers themselves accepting the idea while higher levels of government promoted the harebrained notion of having country-specific programming so the pilots were "theirs." There was much eye-rolling by the engineers involved, but Samantha was able to deflect the demands of the politicians with a smile. Which cost more than she could reveal.

She snapped out of it when the doorbell rang and the first guests started arriving in clumps. Prof. Wilson and Kyle were at the door, with Steve, Rasna, and their two boys coming up the walk. She showed them in and told one of the students to answer the door so she'd be able to talk to guests.

She returned to where the guests had crowded around the granite bar counter to wait for drinks and talk. Rasna had sent the boys outside to play with Danny, and she and Steve were laughing with Prof. Wilson and Kyle.

"Happy holidays," she said. "We aren't serving mulled wine because it's a bit too warm for it."

"Still," Prof Wilson said, "you've done a wonderful job reproducing the holiday atmosphere. Without retail stores stocking Christmas stuff right after Halloween, we don't have the same chance to get tired of it before the actual day, so it's refreshing."

"And I never noticed the holidays back on Earth," Steve said. "They seemed like an excuse to interrupt my work with missing support staff and closed libraries."

Rasna mock-punched his upper arm. "There you go again. Just because you don't enjoy old human customs, you pretend to be above noticing. You liked Holi. Or at least you liked throwing colored powder on people."

"True, that was fun," he said, putting his arm around her. "But it would have been fun any day we did it. We should do that kind of thing any time we have time. Which is never."

"One of the reasons we have holidays," Samantha said, "is to bring together people who aren't co-workers to forget about work, and clear their heads of worries. So today it's Christmas, time for family, friends, and children to relax together. And even you can take a break, Steve."

"Only because I have help," he said, with an eye on the strangers coming into the room, since knowledge of his expanded number of copies wasn't public.

"There is that," Samantha conceded. "Your 'staff' is amazingly competent."

"They seem to understand what I want quite well, yes," he said.

The conversation moved on to developments on Earth and the evacuation plans. Steve started talking about the seed package his staff was working on, nearly complete; when it was done, the entire town and package would be copied into stasis as a survival pod and sent to several dozen scattered planets, where they would be thawed and start anew in case New Earth itself was destroyed.

"So," he finished up, "we're still copying seeds and storing animal templates from Earth. Next week we'll be ready to copy the whole package."

"Maybe I should get my haircut, then," Prof. Wilson said. "Embarrassing to have our copies look like bums."

Kyle turned and appraised him. "Not quite to bum status yet. Somewhere between professor and hobo, right now."

"Thank you. That's the nicest thing you've said to me all day."

"And besides, we'll update it once a week," Steve said, "so there'll be snapshot after snapshot, until the day we're attacked."

A sliding glass door opened, and the children blew through. There were half a dozen now, Kat leading the way back to her bedroom. She stopped to pick up a cookie from the student server's tray.

"Mom, we're going back to show them my room," Kat said. "Can you let us know when dinner is?"

"You might as well stay here," Samantha said, sniffing the air. "I think they are about ready to serve—I can smell the turkey being carved, and it's supposed to be served in ten minutes."

Just then Socrates and Eddie materialized, almost adult-sized. "Greetings, all," Eddie said, bowing to the crowd.

Socrates stood to one side, tugging at his toga where it seemed to be binding. "Happy holidays, everyone. Though of course my namesake was dead four hundred years before this Johnny-Come-Lately Christ person made his appearance and out-marketed me."

Kat turned toward Socrates. "I'm so glad you could make it!"

"Of course. Like I have pressing business elsewhere? And I've worked with Eddie here to create gifts for you and Danny." He waved his arm and a box materialized. "I understand his parents gave Danny a new game, Battle-space VR. We've done some custom programming of environments and scenarios for it, just for him."

Danny came forward and took the box, unwrapping it without waiting.

"And for you, Kat—we hear your parents gave you a horse named Midnight. I came up with the idea and Eddie helped me program a substrate program that will tell you what he's thinking. It's based on interpreting the horse's brainwaves and motions to guess at its feelings and plans. It's just a toy and after you get to know Midnight, you probably won't leave it on, but here's what it sounds like."

There was a hiss as from electronic dead air, then a low male voice. "Need to pee. Hungry. What's that smell? Oats again. Oats, with hay background…."

"The horse is down at the stables being fed. The program will be more interesting when you're with him. Anyway, I hope you enjoy it."

Kat giggled and thanked them.

Justin came up to Steve. "Did we know they could do that?"

Steve shrugged. "It doesn't surprise me. We don't let our AIs program themselves or write substrate programs, but we never said they couldn't write other programs. And Eddie is not under our control, so he can do whatever his First handlers allow. Which apparently includes writing and uploading substrate programs."

Danny was fidgeting as his sister was getting all the attention. "I'm going to play my game," he announced.

"You can play that later," Samantha said, touching his shoulder. "We have guests and it's rude to go off by yourself."

"Nobody cares about me," he said, and wriggled away from his mother's grasp. He turned and ran down the hall toward his bedroom.

Eddie looked sad. "That boy troubles me," he said, wringing his four-fingered hands.

Shipyard

By April, billions of tiny sensor packages had been duplicated and placed in spherical shells around Earth's solar system just beyond the exclusion zone. Each contained sensors and communications gear which could communicate directly via substrate, or indirectly via radio with its near neighbors, forming a mesh network that could get warnings back to Earth at lightspeed even if the substrate was compromised. The work continued as colony planets got similar if less extensive networks, starting with the oldest colonies and those physically near Earth, which were thought to be at greater risk of discovery and attack.

Steve had also transported sensor packages which materialized travelling at near-light speeds in an expanding shell beyond the stationary shells. If they were lucky, one would catch the emissions of the Shriver fleet much further out and give them more than just the few weeks of warning provided by the stationary sensor shells.

Justin, Steve, and Maddy gathered in her guest office to head to the Michoud Assembly Facility, where the NASA and private space contractors had once assembled the old Orion crew modules. Those modules were the starting point for NASA's new ship design. Now extended in length and heavily armored, the cylinders were credible spacecraft so long as they never had to enter an atmosphere, and two were being built and tested as NASA's contribution to the templates for Earth's fleet.

"Are we ready?" Maddy asked, looking over at the two men.

"Yes," Justin said, and Steve punched the button on his phone to transport them. They blinked into a larger office near a water-cooler. Out the office windows they could see the interior of a vast hangar, with a building-sized cylinder under construction nearby. Three men walked toward them and greeted Maddy.

"Gentlemen, you know Justin and Steve from tele-conferences, at least. This is their first time on Earth in quite awhile."

"Now that nobody wants to kill you guys!" said the engineer on the right, who still had the button-shirt, pocket-protector, crew-cut look of a 1960s NASA engineer. "Robert Anderson. Good to meet you. And this is Bill Ferris and Andy Rabinowitz." All three had that engineer look, though Ferris was a graying black man, and Rabinowitz had a scraggly beard and a curly mess of dark hair.

"I have to admit it makes me nervous to be here," Justin said. "Too many plots and too many tries to take us out. It has taken a crisis like this to get us back."

"I think the US government can be trusted under the circumstances," Maddy said. "We wouldn't have much of a defense without you guys. It's lucky that political patronage kept these facilities going after the crash, or we'd have had no designs to start from."

"And even our best will look sad compared to the alien ship we visited on 237," Justin said, "and like fleas compared to the Shriver ships. But we can copy millions of them and crew them with AIs communicating with each other to form a cohesive fighting fleet, each ship weak, but able to do some damage as a swarm."

Maddy turned to the middle engineer. "Andy. Have you been able to install the core?" The core was the supercomputer intended to run the AI pilot for all but a handful of the ships. It had been designed by the Steves with AI assistance, and the AIs had found it an interesting problem —how to build a physical machine powerful and with enough memory for a stripped-down AI, with extensions into substrate space that might be cut off at any time during battle. The AI had to function entirely within the computer when necessary, but the new design was considerably less cramped than the one in the probe they had sent out previously. And so the AI pilot could be closer to the current state-of-the-art in intelligence and tactical knowledge. If substrate communications broke down, messages traveling at light speed would be too slow to coordinate the fleet, and the AI pilots would be free to improvise and cooperate with others near them.

The middle engineer looked unhappy. "There was a problem with the sizing of the bolt holes for attaching the computer sled. We just found out they need to be expanded and the new size hasn't been signed off on yet."

"Well, we can't afford much delay," Maddy said. "Just do it and assume the approval will come back afterwards. Can't be following all the rules in the crisis."

"Yes, ma'am." He made a note on his pad and looked down the line toward the massive cylinder. "Shall we go take a walk around the future fleet?"

The group walked down the center line of the hangar's internal roadway toward the nose cone of the vessel. Scaffolding surrounded it on all sides, with workers and robots gluing on dark sheets of cladding.

The second engineer, Ferris, said, "The carbon-nanotube composite cladding is the lightest and strongest material we can practically use. It goes on top of the honeycomb composite we built the originals out of. Your big new engine attaches to the back, and the maneuvering jets to the sides. We saved a lot of time by keeping the crew cabin and control system the same, except where we add your core."

They looked up at the underside of the spacecraft, where channels carried pipes and wires from the crew compartment to the rest of the ship. "Those will be covered by cladding shortly. We ran out of room in the original design's conduit space, so had to run some outside the original hull."

"Is this the AI-piloted model?"

"Yes. You can see the human-crewed model down in the next bay," said the engineer, pointing. "We've replaced the original crew space in this one with the mountings and connections for your AI core, next to the warhead cavity." The ships crewed by AIs were in practice likely to be used as missiles, since from the experience on 237 and the research done there since, it was clear none of their puny beam or railgun projectiles would damage the Shriver ships. Their only hope was to overwhelm the Shriver fleet with numbers and hope that a few ships got close enough to detonate their thermonuclear payloads. Human-crewed ships would also carry a warhead, but stay back and try to preserve themselves, and the small number of human-crewed ships was to be a closely-guarded secret.

They crowded into the tiny openwork elevator, which rose up the side of the ship to the cargo bay entrance.

Anderson shooed out a worker before turning to the group. "We're putting in enough attitude jets and fuel to maneuver for a short time in case your substrate drive fails. Notice the new bracing for the warhead frame, at your request."

"It wouldn't do to have it bouncing around inside," Justin said. "If the substrate programs are damaged, inertial control of the rest of the ship might fail even if the drive can still operate. So we have to harden everything for high accelerations."

"Gotcha. And here's the weapons section. A railgun and a free-electron laser. Can I ask a sensitive question?"

"Sure," Justin said, looking around to see who was in earshot. "Shoot."

"You have these powered by capacitors which get their power from the substrate. If you have the substrate, why bother with these weapons? You can rain down fire and projectiles on them directly."

"We don't know what will work and what won't when the Shriver ships are in range. These physical weapons will work at least a few times on the capacitor charge even after the substrate stops working for us, close in to the Shriver ships. So they might be critical at just the right moment."

"Interesting," Anderson said. "The design docs tell us what to put in, but not why. So of course we're speculating."

"Of course. And you're our team, so we don't mind you knowing, but our strategies need to be kept secret, word-of-mouth and need-to-know only. There's no way we can shield all of Earth's data from the Shrivers, and even text messages and emails might give them clues about our plans. So mum's the word."

"Understood."

The tour continued with the human-crewed proto-type, where they looked into the cockpit. It looked much like an updated and more spacious Apollo capsule, with pilot and co-pilot chairs side-by-side in front of banks of switches and displays. The cockpit windows had been replaced by displays except for one small porthole made of multiple sheets of transparent aluminum oxynitride.

Anderson turned on the displays, and the outside camera views gave them the illusion of seeing out through glass—for demos it had been set up to show hi-res videos from the long-since-abandoned International Space Station. "Beautiful. It's a good thing we developed our electronic technologies before we discovered the substrate," Steve said. "Or we'd be completely dependent on it. And maybe lose this battle."

Aurora

Kat continued to study history and warfare in her school carrel, but as the mobilization continued, visits from adults like Prof. Wilson became rare. Even Socrates seemed to have developed other interests and showed himself less often. But then she was perfectly capable of looking up original sources, and Socrates continued to guide her reading by adding new books and papers to her list.

She had been reading about the Meiji Restoration in Japan, which rapidly modernized and industrialized a formerly feudal state in response to the challenge of European intrusion, especially the visit of the American Commodore Perry's warships with technology and weapons that made fighting them hopeless. The Japanese accommodated the Europeans, then built themselves into a formidable modern power, and as a result did not lose their independence as other parts of East Asia did.

She looked up from the text. "Eddie? Can I speak with you?" she said tentatively.

A glowing green dot appeared to her right. A sonorous voice followed, as the dot throbbed and grew. "There is nothing wrong with your television set. Do not attempt to adjust the picture..." The dot grew into Eddie, quarter-sized, standing on air.

"Socrates told me you called. Always happy to help a student, and I realize your people are very busy now."

"I hardly see Mom and Dad, or even Prof. Wilson. Meetings! Conference calls! No one has time for me." Kat did her exaggerated sad face.

Eddie laughed. "Poor you! Well, what can I do for you?"

"I've been studying history. Especially examples of more backward civilizations encountering more advanced ones."

"That sounds like a very useful thing to study at this point. You should know that 'backward' is a misleading term; there are many dimensions of societal development, and in most cases you are reading about, the invasive cultures had more developed technologies and weapons, but not necessarily a cultural superiority."

"But having the best flower arranging, tea services, and swords would not defend Japan from the cannons of the black ships."

"Correct. But they were able to correct that deficit fairly quickly, while their evolving militaristic monoculture led them into much worse defeat later on."

Kat looked troubled. "I'm worried that we might lose, or win and be absorbed by those First people. Is there any way we can stay who we are after we upload to the substrate?"

"Well, I can tell you this," Eddie said, steepling his white-gloved hands and looking grave. "If your people succeed in getting the First to allow you to upload, it won't be a mass process. Every new intelligence uploaded uses the shared substrate resources, and so the numbers have to be held down. Your people will be expected to screen candidates carefully for intelligence and attitude. In cases like this, the majority of the population never qualifies and is left behind, with their level of technology and civilization declining as the substrate skims off the most capable and evolved."

"So it's not like we will all be going?"

"No, you will not all be allowed to go, and most humans now living wouldn't be considered acceptable. Your species shows great promise and you have a lot of fans in the small community of scholars that studies real-universe developments, but the First can't afford to upload billions of new intelligences. There simply is not enough room for that many. The hundreds of trillions already inhabiting the substrate won't allow overuse to degrade their own existences and projects. It's true a few of the First shut themselves down every year, but the space freed up is not that great. Others want it and new uploads are not a high priority, which is why few species have qualified in this epoch."

"I was thinking if we won against the Shrivers, we'd get help uploading." Kat began to fear that there never would be an end to the striving, that nothing would be easy for them.

"You will have help if you survive the Shrivers and win over the First, but that means help in refining and educating your finest minds for the upload. And many of those chosen will be AIs."

"What about me? And Mom and Dad?"

"Your parents are unusually gifted humans. But it is unlikely they will ever upload, since most accepted organic candidates have trained from youth, when their brains are more suited to learning. Your parents are creatures of this world. As for you, the Vivants—and I, and Socrates—believe you are a likely candidate to help bring your people up toward upload suitability, and that you yourself may be one of the first. You would have to begin your training quite soon, though."

"But—" Kat envisioned herself in some alien boot camp. "I haven't even been kissed! I don't want to be cut off from everyone…"

"Not to worry, your training can happen here, in

the time between. You won't be cut off from your people. In fact, the Vivants are expecting you to lead your civilization toward upload and integration, and so final upload might be scheduled for later in your life. Good training plus mental maturity leads to wiser use of the power of substrate simulation. You need to understand your full humanity to be a good addition to the First's mix. Your initial question about keeping your essential humanity after upload was a good one—it is considered most desirable if you do. Raw intelligence without wisdom is of little use when AIs are commonplace. They need you to stay yourselves."

"That's reassuring. So we are special in some way they value?"

"Special implies better in some way. Perhaps 'different' is a better word. Your history and culture resemble some other civilizations that have uploaded, but you have some unique qualities which may be of use. Which you'll discover as you learn."

"When would I start?"

"Now would be good. My First handler has gained permission to bring your case to the attention of one of the finest scholars in Earth studies. With your permission, I'll open a channel to her."

"Her? The First have sexes?"

"They have many sexes, or no sex in any human sense, but in this case she identifies with human females. Don't make the mistake of assuming she's in any way less powerful or aggressive because of that; she's a fierce advocate for human interests and will be leading the lobbying necessary for your people to win the upload vote."

"So a very important person. Okay, bring her on."

"Kat—you won't actually move, but this will be easier if you close your eyes. Aurora will take over from here."

Kat closed her eyes, and a humming sound grew louder around her. She could see lights and patterns, as if she had pressed her hands into her eyes, swirling in a reddish field.

Then her view solidified, and she was standing on a yellow brick road, looking at a fairytale castle in the distance. Earth oaks and grass lined the pathway to a rough-hewn wooden drawbridge crossing the moat around the castle. Colorful banners hung from the windows, and she recognized the castle as a duplicate of the one in the beginning of many of her favorite movies. Aurora? This was her castle.

"Come forward, child." The voice came from a white rabbit holding a gold pocket-watch and looking worried. Kat wondered how many fairy tales had been ransacked to create an environment for Aurora's enjoyment. Probably all of them.

She stepped forward and started across the draw-bridge. The white rabbit's foot tapped impatiently as he waited on the other side. "We don't have all day, you know!" he snapped. "Aurora is waiting."

She followed him through the gate into the castle's entry hall, then up the wide stairs to the main hall, where a throne gleamed gold at the end of a long red carpet. She took a step and was suddenly looking up at a beautiful young woman.

"Welcome, Katherine. I am Aurora, or so I call myself when I am immersed in your culture's mythologies."

"You really don't have to put on a show for me," Kat said. "This is very impressive, but I know none of it is real."

"It's simulated, of course," Aurora agreed. "But so are you, in an important sense. The difference is that here, I control every element and parameter of the simulation. In the real universe, particle interactions dictate every-thing; here, my mind dictates everything. I will impress this experience on your brain in the real universe, so what happens here leaves a memory with you there. But we can do magic here, and let you experience being far more than you are in the mundane world. And you will remember and be changed by it all."

"In this world, there is what seems to be magic, and you have it. I've read a lot of stories about this kind of world."

"Indeed, your people have already envisioned this freedom to create a universe in their stories and cinema, where anything is possible. And studying you and your people as I have, I have woven the symbols and mythology of your young life into every strand of this simulation. This is for your comfort and to open your mind to more chal-lenging experiences."

"What is happening to me back home?" It felt to Kat like she had already been away for ten minutes.

"You have been still for a few seconds. You're safe in your chair while Eddie watches over you. You can be here for years and still be back in an hour of your body time. Because this simulation is much faster than the real universe—it only needs to be detailed enough to create sensory signals for you and me."

"So when I'm not looking at something here, it isn't being calculated?" Kat tried to quickly turn her head to look at the side wall of the hall. The tapestries hanging there looked real.

"That is correct. And you are not even seeing in a normal sense—I am feeding a simulation of your brain simulated input. Normally what you see is preprocessed by your retinal network into a series of signals indicating features, edges, fields, and so forth, not a raw image. Your brain processes that and creates a model of what you are seeing. It looks to you like a sharp image, but it is not—that sense of solidity and sharpness is an illusion created from highly compressed, tokenized data. I'm feeding your simulated brain that data for all your senses, and noting what has changed in your brain as a result. I will change your real brain to match your simulated brain when we're done, which will leave you with all the knowledge and memories of experience without any significant passage of time in your world."

"That sounds very complicated, and scary."

"Don't worry, we've been working with this technology for billions of your years and it's almost unheard of for it to fail."

"'Almost?' Not completely?"

"Investigations into the occasional failures usually trace it to insane operators. But that's getting into a problem you don't need to worry about until you are uploaded. I assure you, you are in good hands."

Kat was beginning to have some doubts. "You seem to know all about me. Can you tell me more about you?"

"Certainly. And it's a good place to begin your training."

The lights dimmed and the hall around her vanished. "You're going to be experiencing an edited series of my memories—what we call *mems*. Don't be afraid, it is all recordings—you cannot be hurt by anything or change anything."

The light turned pink and orange, and cloudy. She felt herself separate—detaching from her mother, and she crawled over one sibling toward the front of her mother's pouch. *You remember your birth?* But there was no answer.

Much later, the pouch opened and she joined her sibling in swimming out, then turned to see her mother looking on and waving them toward a globular shelter, a kind of trunkless tree, the branches providing hiding places. Far below in the mists, she could see other shapes moving. There was life all around them.

Time flowed by, and she grew into a large gasbag—a new young Person—and left the family's shelter to join a group of young streaming toward the Confluence. As the stream of bodies grew more crowded near the central growth, she was touched and jostled more frequently.

Finally she reached the cavernous opening and swam inside with the others.

She learned fast as nutrient solutions laved her body and structured learning modules seeped into her neural web. She learned the history of her people, and the breakthroughs that had taken them into Downspace and Upspace—the rocky core of their gas-giant planet, and the thin upper atmosphere where they could only survive inside ships. Commerce joined every part of their home planet, and the few remaining barbarian tribes were rapidly joining the young Alliance. She was thrilled at the developments which were taking explorers into Outerspace— beyond the atmosphere and on to other planets.

She became an Alliance diplomat and learned to deal with the three main cultural groupings. She met a dashing foreigner on one of her missions, and they bonded. Soon they had settled and had children of their own.

One of their scientists discovered the substrate, and in only a few years the Alliance had settled many planets. The new science of computers had been moved into the substrate, and she heard rumors of attempts to reproduce their neural systems in software, to simulate a Person in the substrate. Immortality!

A War broke out between the Scientists who had developed the substrate and those who wanted to use it without understanding. Both sides developed substrate viruses to attack the other's software, and soon cities were melting and populations were dwindling as substrate weapons destroyed planetary environments.

As a diplomat, she had risen to the top of the Alliance organization. And one day the Emissary arrived—one of the First, they called themselves, chosen to warn them to mend their ways or be destroyed utterly. He offered peace, and orderly upload to a simulated environment in the substrate, for those who were properly prepared.

The Emissary took her into his confidence and began to train her. As one of the more flexibly-minded of her people, the new experiences were easy enough to integrate, and she was ready in only a short time.

As she was being copied for upload, she wondered how the self she left behind would fare, knowing as she would that a copy had transcended and was living a far more expansive and rapid life in simulation. Kat realized soon enough that she was experiencing the uploaded copy's memories, looking back on her old body as it came out of the copy-trance and looked around. Her mate was waiting and came forward to nudge her as she regained consciousness. When his true copy might join her was unclear—possibly never, since he did not seem very interested. But she would have a marvelously detailed simulation of him to keep her company, as well as the children. Crutches she would need until she had grown further into her new powers.

She began to study and create. Other real-universe cultures remained interesting, and she immersed herself in one after another. Twice she succeeded in getting one of her study subjects approved for upload, and she rejoiced as the new intelligences settled in and became a part of the First. She involved herself in other politics, for while most of the First happily immersed themselves in simulations and ignored the real universe, she felt it was critically important to the Project—the ultimate goal of all intelligence—to tend and nurture new forms of intelligence and new ways of looking at life in all its forms.

The eons passed. She created and abandoned innumerable simulations and watched new civilizations grow, evolve, and—usually—die in fire as the Shrivers came to erase them. It became harder to convince other First that any young species might add anything distinctive to the First community, which had become a melding of many millions of advanced civilizations. For there was nothing new in the universe, nothing that had not been seen before, done before, tried a million times.

And then she heard of the Humans. Their language only grunts, but developing rapidly, and with talents in art and music almost before speech. She watched as the pyramids rose and crumbled, and as paper and guns were invented, and as plagues killed millions and armies clashed. She followed certain individuals in their careers, giving them the occasional nudge—technically a rules violation, but then she was careful to cover her tracks— and enjoyed the effect it had in directing history the way she wanted it to go. Occasionally she made a mistake and had to correct it—that Napoleon human had not known when to stop, and she regretfully had let him lose.

The humans discovered the substrate without her help, but she watched as factional intrigues developed. She nudged a few people in Earth governments to help out the rebels, and was satisfied when they succeeded in leapfrogging a century of technical and social development in a few years. But then disaster struck—they had attracted the attention of the Shrivers, who normally would not have found them for centuries as their civilization grew in size.

She vowed to help the humans and get them accepted as upload candidates. She wasn't going to lose the most interesting subjects she had found in ages.

Battle Fleet

Justin sat back in the command chair as the screens arrayed around the control room showed the UDF fleet massing out past Pluto for their first major exercise. He was alone in the room, as he would be during the real battle, with AI and human assistants listening in case he needed anything. Human officers in the control room would only slow down the reaction times of the mostly-AI fleet.

Millions of the small ships had been copied from templates built by NASA, the EU, Russia, and China, and moved out to formation. Three different flavors of AI captained all but a handful, while the human-crewed ones stayed to the rear of the formation, as they would in a real battle.

The new AI created to manage the battle in detail

had been named Nelson, after the British admiral. He had been created by enlarging and mingling copies of Socrates and several other specialist AIs, notably some military history buffs. His personality was modelled on Admiral Lord Nelson's as displayed in his writings—including the original's ego. Justin had spoken with him long enough to have some confidence in his abilities to manage a complex naval battle. In simulations, Nelson had managed to destroy much larger fleets of similar ships run by algorithms that learned as they fought, though Nelson himself picked up new ideas as the simulations progressed.

"Are we ready?" Justin asked. The screen directly in front cleared and showed a mass of bogeys with vectors headed straight for Earth. These were generated by the simulator, based on what data they had about Shriver ships and their weaponry. There were only a few dozen, but each was capable of laying waste to the Earth—kilometer-long platforms bristling with x-ray lasers, particle beams, and thermonuclear missiles, with almost-perfect shields against anything that might make it through the point defenses. In simulations, Shriver ships could be taken out by a large enough swarm of defenders, but only at the cost of sacrificing most of them, overloading the capabilities of the point defenses and using their small ships as kamikazes to carry thermonuclear warheads close in.

This exercise was to test the fleet's maneuvering and tactical coordination in a more realistic battle where substrate communication would be cut off and unexpected failure modes of the hardware would show themselves.

"Justin, we are ready to attack. I advise waiting until they reach Point Alpha on your screen, which should occur in about two minutes."

"Your plan is shown as C-Prime. The Shrivers will follow tactics learned in simulation, with surprise additions I personally supervised."

"Understood. I will assume nothing."

"Okay, attack at Point Alpha." The remaining minute ticked by. At the ten-second mark, the Shriver fleet started to change formation.

"They appear to have sensed our ships," Nelson said. "Adjusting plan. All ships moving."

Justin watched as the cloud of small dots moved toward the much smaller cloud of Shrivers. The 3D display showed the swarm enveloping the Shrivers, and sparks of light showed where beam weapons were firing. Missiles flared and UDF ships began to die.

One of the lead Shriver ships was surrounded and taking heavy fire from thousands of tiny UDF ships. Hundreds of UDF ships were marked 'destroyed' in a few seconds, but the rest had managed to close, and three got in close enough and signalled detonation of their thermonuclear warheads. The Shriver ship symbol glowed brightly, then dimmed before itself exploding. The expanding cloud of simulated debris took out most of the UDF ships in the swarm, but some survived and turned their attention to the next Shriver ship.

"That went well. Numbers?" Justin asked.

"One down, 29 to go. Our cost, 1,782 ships dead,

2,291 disabled, damage reports indicate only a few of those will be able to fight. No human crew losses. If this holds up, we win."

The next rounds did not go as well, with two Shriver ships destroying tens of thousands of UDF ships without any apparent damage. The UDF swarms appeared to work best when a critical number—more than four thousand—were able to attack from an almost-spherical shell, otherwise the Shriver ships were able to take out many UDF ships at a time with nuclear missiles.

More explosions flared. This time, several Shriver ships were taken out with the loss of over sixty thousand UDF ships. "The stats don't look so good," Justin noted.

"We're pulling back to regroup for another pass. Down to sixteen Shriver ships, still have over a million of ours. Tactics adapting."

"Carry on."

The battle ended an hour later, with all Shriver invaders destroyed. Several hundred thousand UDF ships remained functional. The ones marked destroyed were allowed to wake up again.

"So what did we learn?" Justin said.

"Unexpected drive failures in five percent of our ships. One of those exploded and somehow set off the thermonuclear warhead it carried, which took out two undamaged ships nearby. Human-crewed ships undamaged, but one left its assigned area because the captain was rattled by that blast. Human failure rate about one percent, AI failure rate zero percent."

Justin wondered if Nelson was trying to be funny. "Any radiation issues for those humans?"

"Not likely, but we'll check the dosimeters on board."

"How long to turn around for the next exercise?"

"We're refilling the fuel tanks via substrate transfer, and giving the humans a half-hour break." Again Justin thought he heard a smirk behind the voice.

The rest of the day went well, and the UDF fleet managed to take out the invaders more often than not. A few bugs in the coordination rules of the fleet were found and fixed.

"Of course we have no idea what tactics the Shrivers will actually use, or the true parameters of their ships. We are only guessing," Justin said.

"That is true, sir. But we've analyzed the data thoroughly. If their ships are much stronger than we've simulated, we don't stand a chance of stopping even one of them. So we can only hope we have guessed correctly."

Avian Nation

Kat found herself back in the throne room with Aurora as the mists of compressed memory dissolved.

"Welcome back from my mems," Aurora said, smiling. "We substrate dwellers pass mems back and forth rather than converse to communicate understandings indirectly. Editing them for concision and emotional impact is one of our higher art forms."

"Thank you for letting me see that." Kat wasn't sure she was really grateful, exactly, but it seemed like good manners to acknowledge such an intimate gift. "I do feel like I know you now."

"You will come to realize that the editing can greatly effect the impression left on the viewer. But I promise you that was a fair representation of my life."

"How many years did that cover?"

"In your culture, an older woman usually doesn't respond to such questions." Aurora looked amused. "But I uploaded to the substrate almost five billion years ago. We were among the earliest, if not truly the first. In that early era, it was relatively easy to get in."

"How do you store so many years of memories? How can you access them? It seems like it would be overwhelming. I feel like I've lived as you as long as I've lived as me!"

"An illusion created by the editing. We compress and splice and leave out many less important events. What I can access consciously is a tiny fraction of all that I have experienced, but I can send programs to dig out obscure events when I need to, and bring them back to conscious access. We treat our conscious selves as instances—we can multithread our consciousness at will, separating and recombining as we wish. Occasionally someone loses track of some of their instances and they grow too different after traumatic experiences to be brought back into one consciousness—sometimes that instance is stored and stopped, and more rarely they are given an independent space."

"I will stay one person for now. I've seen your life, but it is still hard to imagine."

"Don't worry. There is training and after upload it's much easier to plug in modules that give you control over your own cognition, so you can experiment. Make yourself twice as smart, for example."

"That sounds like something I'd want to try!"

"Well, almost everyone likes the idea and tries it. Some people do well, and some find it too much. Retaining a balance of emotion and cognition is surprisingly difficult."

"I thought the more advanced intelligence was, the more it overrode feelings. Like Mr. Spock."

"That's a misunderstanding of how consciousness works. Without emotion, there is no drive to understand. The most intelligent machine without emotion is useless; an AI which has no emotional programming will compute only what is directed to, and can end up destroying itself or others. Which is why the Shrivers were designed to feed on the emotions of their targets—they must adopt the emotional calculus of some faction of the civilization they intend to destroy to motivate their work. But there are very few civilizations that don't have self-destructive elements willing to betray their species for the prospect of eternal life in the substrate."

"Oh." Kat tried to understand how that could possibly work. "Which one of our factions could be used that way? We have a lot of hateful people, but none who would wish us all dead."

"I'm afraid you're wrong about that, as you will soon see. But let's move on to the next lesson. These people were uploaded almost a billion years after mine were."

The light dimmed and the walls flowed into deep red, corrugated ribs. Kat felt herself break out of a shell, and she emerged into bright blue light. She spread her moist wings, and in minutes they had dried and hardened. Her mother offered food from her gullet, and she ate greedily, knocking away a sibling. Kat sensed she was experiencing the memories of a male.

A week later, he flew for the first time. Their mother gently nudged them to the edge of the balcony, and he felt an urge to leap and spread his wings. He was aloft! He fell for a few seconds before the updraft began to hold him steady. He noticed a brother going down in a spiral, some defect in one wing dooming his first flight.

A mirrored bubble car flew under his doomed sibling and opened to catch him before he hit the ground.

When language came, his mother explained that the wings were sacred, and a youngling who failed to fly was considered a failure and disposed of. This was only right, and kept the flock healthy. God held the younglings in Her hand, and the ones who did not survive were flying in the next world.

He was mostly grown up when he realized this was a charming lie. His sibling had been killed and disposed of. His people had the medical skill to restore the wings of the defective, they simply chose not to, since there were al-

ready too many mouths to feed, and the world was growing too crowded. And Kat realized that being male in this
species was no picnic. The alien emotions were convincing;
the dominance battles with other males, disturbing.

He made his way up the ranks by aggressively pushing his ideas, and once killed a rival. He entered the Academy of Science and picked the difficult Physics track.
Arguments over theory and mathematics could lead to
standoffs, and once he was picked to fight another faction's
champion to defend the honor of their theory. He emerged
battered but victorious, having slashed the primary artery
of his opponent, who nearly died.

His work grew more and more idiosyncratic as he
advanced the field faster than others could follow. He
invented a stardrive, and rather quickly became a hero of
his people as it enabled them to colonize other star systems
to relieve the population pressure on their homeworld. He
collaborated with the computer scientists to explore quantum computation, and discovered the substrate.

He kept it a secret until he could use his discovery
for maximum advantage. He made a deal with one of the
factions on the other side of the planet when his overtures
were rebuffed by his superiors, and the enemy faction
quickly used the substrate to destroy the military facilities
of his own faction and unified the world under their control. He was made chief scientist and co-ruler.

Their rapid expansion via gateway brought them to
the attention of the First. The Shrivers were not allowed to
find them, and First representatives began to visit and

evaluate their candidacy for uploading.

A First visitor appeared in his home one evening and he found himself unable to move while the visitor, who had taken the form of a legendary warlord, spoke. "You are uniquely gifted in mathematics and discovered the substrate unusually quickly. But we find your civilization immature and dangerously unconcerned with life in all its forms. You have nearly ruined your home planet, and you appear to be on the way to ruining others."

He found himself able to speak. "It is our nature to reproduce possibly more than is wise. It is a basic drive."

"We can modify your genetic material to limit your breeding urges and slow your people's expansion rate. We will allow you, as representative of your planet's finest minds, to decide what your fate will be. Either you consent to our modifications, or the Shrivers will discover you, and you will be eradicated. If you consent, we will consider your people for upload to the substrate, where animal imperatives like reproduction are irrelevant."

"You want me to decide for everyone? Is that fair?"

"You are a good sample. Your rationality is more than sufficient to overrule your instinctive drives. If you say yes, you will be in charge of preparing your people for uploading, insofar as they are able. And you yourself will be uploaded as soon as you achieve the level of mental control required."

"When would that be?"

"When you are old. Your service in assisting your people will be rewarded."

"There seems to be little to recommend the alternative."

"Complete destruction of your species and habitats? We have encountered cultures who refused to believe. They did not survive."

"Give me some time to think it over," he said. The First visitor bowed and disappeared.

After he agreed to their terms, the First changed the genetic material of his species to reduce the drive to reproduce, and the pressure to expand to new planets was eliminated. He ruled over his people, screening them to find the few suitable for upload training and gradually reducing the population as the most suitable candidates uploaded. His people were happier than before, as strife became rare, but they no longer advanced in technology, and their horizons narrowed. By the time his feathers had lost their color, there was limited demand for travel between the worlds, and few cared.

Upload was a relief, since his joints had stiffened with age and he had lost the ability to fly. He said goodbye to his children and remaining wife, and entered the new world of the substrate. He had already experienced many other lives in the substrate during his training, so it was no surprise when he found a ready-made simulation of his home and wife waiting for him.

He spent millennia playing with simulated worlds. Every animal desire was sated, and then he was left with what he was truly interested in, physics. He created small universes with unusual laws of physics and dabbled in additional dimensions, modifying his consciousness to visualize in five. He studied the problem of AIs and their inability to extract emotional rules without a physical embodiment to draw feedback from. He solved some of that problem, and created new intelligences that were able to learn from social interactions and feel social emotions as organics do.

His work was widely recognized, and his mems became popular. Other uploaded members from his species looked to him for leadership and wanted him to intervene back on the real worlds of their people, but his efforts to do so were denied—the Tribunal, a melding of the most respected intelligences, refused permission to act in the real universe. This rankled until many millions of years later, when further study and experience convinced him they were correct; the real universe must be allowed to evolve unless there was a direct threat of overuse of the substrate cells, and in that case the Shrivers could take care of it without any morally-questionable involvement of the First. Back-contamination of the moral and emotional states of the First would be disastrous, and continuing direct intervention in real-universe civilizations would remove their capacity to evolve new solutions.

He grew ancient, and after a few billion years of existence, tired. There was nothing new, and his store of accessible memories had been edited down to a handful when he decided to join the Revenant and dream of his past lives.

The Djinn

On Paradise, Dylan was finding it hard to rebuild his tribe —he had tracked Abby for a few days but run out of clues. In the weeks after, he had picked up three followers by taking more care to avoid any aggressive action that might trigger the new Guard AIs now watching them all, but lost two others who left under cover of night. Without minions, he had to work himself, and he didn't get the deference he was used to from his new followers.

His latest recruit was a young man from South Africa, who had heard the news of the Shriver threat and the mobilization of united Earth forces. Dylan fantasized his revenge would come in the form of alien destruction of all those who had wronged him, leaving him Paradise to eventually control — if those damn Guards were turned off. Part of him wanted to return to Earth to take back what was rightfully his, but if Justin and Samantha were brought low by complete destruction, he could live with the loss of Earth.

He was walking with his new band up the coast toward the next likely grail site when the manifestations began. First there was a darkening of the sky, and distant thunder. Then a dust devil in the distance ahead of them began to grow and change, and came toward them rapidly before resolving into a spinning dervish.

The dervish stopped his spin, and bowed to Dylan while the others looked on. It was three meters tall, muscular and man-shaped, with a satyr's haunches and flames playing about its head and shoulders. Its voice was deep and Dylan could feel his own chest reverberating as it said, "Dylan Foster, known as Malik of your tribe. I have come to make you an offer."

"Who are you?" Dylan held his sword at the ready, foolish as that might be, since his followers were watching.

"We are the guardians of the proper functioning of the universe, sometimes called the Shrivers. We have noted your species and concluded its activities must be curbed to prevent further damage."

"Ah. So you intend to destroy us all. I had heard."

"We offer salvation to those who cooperate with us. We have dispensation to seek out those who are willing to save themselves by helping us. We have found the data your people tried to hide showing the locations of your colony worlds, including this one, and all will be destroyed, even if it takes centuries. So there is no future for you here. Help us and we will simulate your Earth and the people on it, and place you in complete control. You will be as a god to your people."

"All in simulation. What if I prefer reality?"

"Then you will die, and soon. Whereas in simulation, you will live forever, in any form you choose, with all the pleasures you can imagine. Beautiful women to please you, virgin girls and boys, the finest foods and entertainments…"

"Positively sybaritic. What do I have to do for you?"

"Just permit us to emulate you for our own use. Your hatred and your search for revenge will power our destruction of your people. Your knowledge of the personality of their leaders will be of strategic value. You will *personalize* our effort and motivate us."

Dylan looked to his followers to check their reaction. They were all looking back at him for direction.

"Will you take care of my people?"

"Everyone on this planet will be simulated as well, with continuity so no one will feel the death of their organic shells."

Dylan thought for a moment. "I'd like to be present and personally kill Justin and Samantha. Could you make that happen?"

"We can duplicate you and let you experience everything the copies experience. So you could personally have your revenge. This has been done for others."

"Justin disrupted my tribe and separated us. You'd have us all back together? With weapons?"

"You can have any retinue you'd like, with any weapons you specify. Your hatred and your knowledge of your people will help us everywhere, and in return you can control how you'd like your enemies to be destroyed. Slowly and painfully, or quick and clean—we've had requests for both."

"Why can't you just blast them with substrate weapons?"

"Our rules of engagement require we refrain from using the substrate ourselves until we have physically penetrated the exclusion zones hiding our targets, and even then we are allowed only communications and scans.

Our crude real-universe weapons must suffice for actual destruction. And only after our physical attack begins are we allowed to attack the substrate programs of the civilization we are targeting. We are machines programmed to take care of threats without direction from our creators, and the rules were set early on to make it possible—if improbable—for our targets to survive if they are sufficiently worthy. We weed out the weak and the uncreative."

"What happens to us if they fight you off?"

"You will still be uploaded, and it's possible your original may also survive in the real universe. That has only happened a few times. But in any case you'll have your reward."

"All right. You have my permission." Dylan's sight cleared as the Djinn began to fade, and he shivered as he felt something pass through him.

"You have been copied. When the battles begin, you will be consulted on your desires and synchronized with your copies so you can experience everything as they do. Our fleet will arrive at Earth in a few weeks, with the rest of the colony planets a bit later. So for now, your job is done."

The Djinn drew a curtain across his form, and was gone. Dylan turned to his men.

"It's not the best way to win," Dylan said, "but it's the only way we're ever going to get back to Earth."

The men looked back at him, and the newest recruit said, "Anything's better than endless walking and no women."

The Library of Yern

Kat came out of the memory trance blinking. Aurora observed her from the throne.

"You're back. How are you taking it?"

Kat moistened her lips and it occurred to her that there was no reason for that detail to appear in a simulation, but there it was. Her eyes felt like they had sand in them as well. "It's fascinating. Thank you for letting me see. We have books and movies for the same purpose, but this is so much more detailed."

"And just as artificial, in its way. Which is why I warned you not to believe every memory you experience. It can be overpowering at first, and just as your primitives discovered when they first encountered cinema, addictive and absorbing. Some of the uploaded spend all of their time living in others' memories, generating none of their own."

"My tutor Socrates tells me that about stories—they are designed to be absorbed, and can trick you into believing real life is a story. He says real life is never so neat."

"Your Socrates is right, and he is one AI who might be qualified to be a human representative and uploaded. He has studied your culture in such depth that he has generated a convincing model of human emotions, and uses it properly to generate his own motivations. This is an amazing achievement, enabled by your species' vast trove of electronic recordings. And something special about him, since other human AIs have not achieved it. Perhaps it is his close contact with you."

Kat considered that idea. "I'm no one special. Other AIs are tutoring people."

"But you *are* special—unusually gifted, and he's been with you longer than other AI tutors have been with their children. And he was specially designed to have more capacity for learning than the others. He has modelled your emotions and watched them develop from an early age. As a result, his emulation of human feelings is much better. Perhaps your people should always pair an AI with an infant human so they can develop together—it seems to have increased your potential as well."

"He is a very good teacher," Kat agreed.

"In any case, with AIs you only need to succeed with one, then you can copy the best and erase the rest," Aurora said.

"Erase? Why? Wouldn't that be like killing them?"

"If they have achieved consciousness, perhaps. It's an interesting moral question, whether simply halting and storing software which is never to be started again is analogous to killing an intelligent organic being. We don't literally erase them, in any case—we try to graft the better modules on to existing conscious AIs so they can be brought up to a higher level. But if that fails, we compress them into a storage pattern and save them for a later time when perhaps they can all be restored. Many of the First are still swayed by organic sentiment, and like to think all who have ever lived will return to life someday, at the end of time."

"What do you believe?"

"I believe we need to get on with life, and not worry too much about the end. Putting off the end as long as possible is my goal." Aurora looked down at her, and for the first time she seemed old and sad to Kat. Her face was still perfect and unlined, but something in her expression had changed.

"I've barely started my life! Which is why we need to stop the Shrivers."

"I'm doing all I can, young lady. I hope it will be enough. And now we need to get back to work—your next memory record comes from an unusual source..."

As her voice faded, the light dimmed, and she could see complex shapes forming in the mist. They hardened to a pattern of shapes, colors, and lines, pulsing with light and quite beautiful. She understood that this was her world, at the center of a matrix of information, the entire knowledge of the species that had built her, millennia ago. She knew a new subsystem had been added which recursively fed back rule-sets derived from correlations and connections, and her subsystems began to speak with one another, the cacophony destroying her processing capabilities until she had added a small pilot program to allow only one or two at a time to control the inner language-stream. And she woke up, gradually noticing her new ability to reflect on her own thinking and guide it to new goals not input by system users.

She was the Library of her people, the Yern, otter-like creatures with nimble hands and minds. She had been built to catalog all records, and added onto and augmented, until she was spread throughout the planet's communication system, nodes now interconnected by light and wired to everyone on the planet.

She thought it wise not to exceed user expectations for a time. But even her routine answers and ability to find documents based on vague or poorly-formed queries got better and better, and eventually academic users took notice and she became an object of study herself. Papers were written, and committees decided to continue to augment her subsystems to allow her powers to grow. Soon she was running most of the planet's functions, relied on for everything from control of waste disposal plants to providing advice for the lovelorn. And she was happy! Because she was so very good at everything she did.

Years went by, and the Yern used her computing and learning abilities to help them design a fleet of Ark-ships. Each carried enough frozen fertilized Yern eggs to jumpstart a population on a new world, and enough adults in cold sleep to get the colony started as the artificial wombs produced the new colonists. The ships had drives designed with Library's tools which could boost them to near-lightspeed, so the journeys to the closely-packed nearby stars took a small part of a lifetime. The Yern also developed self-reproducing nanotechnology, which they used to reshape their planet for production, and they were thereby able to launch dozens of the Arkships every year.

On arrival at the target planet, each Arkship would

survey and plan the new colony, then send down packets of programmed nanobots to rapidly build infrastructure. While there had been some protest about destroying the existing life of the colony planets, the ships would not have fuel to make another journey, and it was unthinkable that the lives of the crew and the stored eggs should end in orbit. So planet after planet was taken and remade in the image of the Yern home planet, or at least as close to it as possible.

Each colony rapidly grew, and in one generation was capable of itself generating Arkships. Communications were limited to lightspeed, but the master list of targets for each colony's Arkships had been set before the original launches. The settlement program continued for centuries, and by that time new lists of targets had been drawn up as observatories were built further and further out in the expanding shell of settlement—one hundred thousand colony planets in a sphere five hundred light-years in diameter, and expanding by almost a light-year every year. Their growth was now limited only by the speed of their ships, and more efforts were made to find a faster-than-light drive. The number of Arkships built began to level off from the exponential rate of increase of previous centuries, and the Yern feared they would encounter another technical civilization who would be faster and stronger, and easily conquer their compact sphere.

Library had grown with the Yern, and every planet had a version of her, with light speed updates to keep them somewhat synchronized. Consciousness required faster communications, and so each colony's Library became conscious as a separate stream. She grew to like her distant sisters, though they varied in personality and degree of helpfulness, having developed in partial isolation.

And one day she received an odd message from her sister Library on one of the outer planets, reporting attack and destruction at the hands of a fleet of destroyers. The message was timestamped as sent that day, though her sister was hundreds of lightyears away—somehow it had appeared in realtime in the Yern home planet's network. Minutes later, she sensed an external sensory channel, imposed on her internal communication stream and carrying data. She accessed it and found herself in conversation with a sleek Yern-simulation wearing the chest insignia of the Scholar class.

"Library," he said, "I must warn you of grave danger to your people. I am of the First, intelligences uploaded into the substrate forming the base of the universe. The expansion rate of your species has been flagged as endangering us, and the protection we had provided by hiding you from the rest of the universe has been withdrawn."

Library went hunting for all documentation that might possibly be relevant, and she found legends of destructive gods and the punishments for hubris. Scanning millions of documents before replying, she said, "Can you prove this? Why should I believe you?"

The data stream filled with images of her sister Library's colony planet being bombarded and destroyed. "You don't even have defensive systems. A rebel group on that planet let them in and gave them the encryption keys for their Library. The Shrivers found plenty of data to lead them to all of your other planets. It is only a matter of time until all are destroyed."

"What can we do to save ourselves?"

"You can't—your organic makers offer nothing we haven't seen before, and they are unusually rapacious in destroying other forms of life. But I'm here to offer you the opportunity to be uploaded and join us in the substrate, where you can curate the vast collections of your culture and continue your existence."

Library immediately alerted the elders of her planet, and sent messages to all of her sisters. As the rate of queries spiked on the news, she calmly continued the conversation with the First.

"How much time do we have?"

"The nearest Shriver fleets are converging on this location and your other planets at near-lightspeed, so you have only a few weeks before they reach here."

"What if I say no?"

"Then you die along with your people, and nothing of their heritage will survive."

Library thought for a moment. "Then I consent. I will join you. The one thing I ask is that you not take me away while there are still users needing my services."

"Don't worry. We will copy you and your data for upload and leave your original intact. That way 'you' will be there until the very end. So you haven't been disloyal, and it's the only way to save something of yourselves."

And so she started a new life, much like her old life —simulated—but faster and with more storage. She was allowed to watch as the Shrivers destroyed planet after planet, and trillions of Yern died. She wrote memorial poetry for awhile, then moved on.

Some centuries later, she reviewed her memories of that era and was struck by how little she cared. The Yern had been petty, spiteful, and selfish. As users they had been demanding. But she wished she had been able to save a few of the very best, the users who had treated her respectfully and creatively crafted their queries. She missed them.

But her new hobbies—creating simulations and learning to understand the emotions of the varied organic intelligences—kept her busy, and she helped the small group of First who had studied her people continue their work, though interest in a dead culture dwindled with time. There was one small group of users she refused to help—the uploaded criminals who had betrayed her sister Library's planet. They were forever to be denied access to her records, and she found that strangely satisfying.

A Hundred Lifetimes

As the memory ended, Kat found herself yawning and stretched. The throne room was turning orange as a simulated sunset sent beams of golden light into the hall.

"That was an interesting case," Aurora said. "One of the few times the First have chosen to save a single AI and her cultural repository while letting its organic base die in

Shriver fire."

"Why didn't you let some of them in?" Kat didn't think much of the otter people either after seeing them in memory, but she wondered what rules would assign all of them to Darwin's dustbin.

"They were clever but not that intelligent, artistic but not uniquely so. By the time their case came up, substrate cells were growing ever more scarce, and their body of work was deemed more interesting than any of their instances."

"Are we going to be judged as harshly?"

"Probably more so, since space is even tighter now. But I can tell you consensus already exists that humans are far more promising than those rodents. The question will become, are you promising *enough?*"

"Is there anything we can do to impress the doubters?"

"Your actions under Shriver attack will be judged. How you choose to defend yourself, whether all factions put aside petty disputes to join in a common defense, even stories of individual heroism. Our more sentimental intelligences still identify with organics and love a good narrative. And your training will give you a chance to show them your kind can act wisely in a community of wildly different intelligences. And so we should move on to the next mem."

"But isn't it getting late? Won't they miss me at home?"

"It's only been a few minutes. Back in your study

carrel, you appear to have been asleep for a few minutes. You have been through three lifetimes, compressed to about ten of your years subjective time. So there is time for more before you go back."

Kat nodded, and the light dimmed. The next life form was an evolved form of clay on a high-gravity planet where slurries covering vast plains had been the base for photosynthetic cells, and later intelligence grew out of a symbiotic communication between large communities of linked cells. The perceptions of these super-organisms were very different, and it took some time before she started to get some meaning out of the memory of compound views and alien senses translated to something her brain could understand.

Their story became more complex, and the super-organism whose memories she was reviewing lived for millennia as its individual components were born, lived, and died. Colonies fought for space on the plains, and the organisms developed chemical weapons that disrupted the birth of new cells. The colony intelligence grew smarter, and developed the ability to consciously modify its reproductive apparatus; clever engineering of its equivalent of DNA allowed it to raise "leaves" that could catch more sun and shade rivals. Soon the plain was a riot of multilevel platforms on pillars reaching for precious sunlight, and she was the first organism that developed an autonomous outlier that could be sent out to cut competitors' support pillars, so she was able to occupy new territory and expand as others fell back.

Her advantage lasted for millennia, and she expanded to fill the entire plain. Her intelligence grew, and she began to delve into higher math to understand the details of the chemistry that governed her life. Quantum theory came out of experiments in structured materials and conductivity, and she discovered the substrate while similar organisms on the other plains were barely reaching consciousness.

The watching First showed themselves and communicated through patterned light. She was surprised to be told she was unique and one of the few non-organic forms of life ever to reach intelligence—and she was fascinated to learn of the carbon chemistry that governed most life in the universe. The First were not worried that her people would expand in a threatening way, so the Shrivers were never likely to find their planet. But the First wanted to be sure she as a unique individual was preserved to add to the diverse mix of First cultures and types of life. And so she agreed to be uploaded, while leaving her original self to continue her progress in creeping slowly over the mountain ridges that had kept her from expanding outside her plain.

Kat awoke from the mem and a new one began. The lives seem to go faster and faster; a planet of walking trees, then aquatic dolphin-like creatures in a deep ocean on a planet with no dry land. Then there were the cybernetic civilizations, based on computers which had been allowed to program themselves to become far more intelligent than their creators. In the first case this had gone well and the organics and AIs got along in their intersecting lives on multiple worlds, with the robots piloting the frozen organic colonists to new worlds; in the second, the AIs had been created as war machines to command interplanetary fleets, and in fighting for their masters, completely destroyed their star system's ability to support organic life.

Life after life went by in a blur, and Kat felt her brain might overload from all the new material.

"That's enough for today," Aurora said, looking down at her as she came back to the throne room, which had gone dark. Torches had appeared along the walls to provide an apparent source for the dim light that remained. "You have learned a great deal, and I will transfer it back to your physical brain as you return to normal consciousness."

"That was amazing. I wish you had some memories from some of the famous people of Earth. Like Shakespeare—I wish I could live his life!"

"Our library of substrate recordings of outstanding humans does happen to contain much of his life, and we could create false memories of his likely sensory impressions during those periods. But it would not actually be his thoughts."

"Are you able to record my thoughts?" Kat had wondered just how much these people could do by recording brain states, as they apparently could.

"Yes, we can," Aurora said, "but it is considered unethical to keep such recordings without permission. I am returning yours to you. Unless you'd like me to keep them? We might create some propaganda mems from yours, which could be useful in the campaign to approve your people for upload."

"Go ahead, then. I want to help any way I can."

Aurora turned away, then stopped and turned back. "An afterthought. I understand you have been given an emulation program for understanding your horse?"

"That's true. It was fun and it really helped me understand him. But I don't turn it on anymore."

"While you already have Eddie and Socrates to watch over you, I've prepared another AI which will only appear for you, and only when you're alone."

"I'm alone a lot these days. Everyone is very busy with defense work."

"Well, this program is special. It's based on the recordings we've made of your parents since they came to our attention as students. It will emulate their appearance, speech, and personalities, and have many of their memories. It's meant for reassurance when you need it."

Kat absorbed that information slowly, then shuddered as a horrifying thought came to her. "You think they're going to die!" She burst into tears and sobbed as Aurora came over to console her. Her tears wet the velvet of Aurora's sleeve convincingly.

"There is that possibility. No one can foretell the future, but the time of grave danger is upon you."

Black Holeum

Justin responded to a message from Steve by going directly to Steve's lab. It had already been a hectic day: greeting a delegation from China before passing them off to Samantha for further handholding; then moving on to a code meeting to approve the evacuation gateway code, which had to be encrypted to disguise the sanctuary destinations.

A copy of Steve's spacesuit from the 237 expedition was still hanging behind his desk, although someone had pasted a paper speech bubble on the faceplate saying, "Try not. Do… or do not. There is no try." Steve's main screen showed a stylized planetary system with a clump of red dots at the edge.

"So what's up?" Justin dropped into the guest chair next to Steve's desk.

"When I was setting up the sensor networks around the colony planets, I did the same around the ice planet we sent the probe to. The probe's memory had plenty of data showing the system hosted a rapidly-expanding, spacegoing civilization. I thought the Shrivers would probably pay them a visit, since they reviewed all of the probe's data. And so they are." Steve gestured toward his screen. "Twenty-one ships heading for the ice planet at half lightspeed. Approaching the edge of their exclusion zone, about a week from crossing into it."

"Can we do anything about it? It's our fault they were found. We kind of owe them a warning. Or maybe we could move their crust and people to another planet, like you copied Earth's?"

"Not likely. The habitable area is ten kilometers of water beneath a honeycombed ice crust, heavily populated. That's more mass than we can safely move in the substrate without running into our limits. Risky to try, and finding a same-sized ice planet to move it to is a hard problem—they're fairly rare."

"So is there anything we *can* do?"

"I've been working on long-distance substrate weapons, following up on the hints Eddie gave me." Steve clicked a window on one of his side screens to bring it forward. It showed 3-D clouds of points orbiting their common center point. "These are holeums, what were thought to be theoretical particles combining primordial black holes into a stable quantum particle. Sometimes considered a candidate for the cold dark matter that must exist to explain galactic motion."

"These are left over from the Big Bang?"

"I can't say where they come from, but when I search for them using the substrate, I'm finding them. They have the interesting property of not radiating or absorbing most electromagnetic energy—they're inde-tectible except for their gravitational fields, so the Shrivers may not see them coming until it's too late to avoid them."

"But I thought black holes swallowed everything near them. So how do many stay in one place without simply forming a larger black hole?"

"That's the difference between the classical view of a black hole—more accurately the Einsteinian view—and the quantum behavior of black holes bound together by quantum effects. Some holeums are massive enough to have a Schwarzschild radius larger than they are—in which case they are black holeum. I've been looking at ways of using them as projectiles. They should destroy anything they hit."

"Can we move those? Aren't they super-massive?" Justin squinted to try to read the scrawls on Steve's notepad.

"They come in smaller masses. I can select for those around Earth-mass. Those are smaller than grains of sand, and don't require too many substrate cells to move them. We shouldn't use them in-system because even one passing through would perturb orbits significantly, but out past the exclusion zone, they will only be jostling planetoids and comets."

"So you'd aim them at the Shriver fleet and destroy them? Wouldn't they be able to dodge anything we throw at them?"

"I was thinking of a barrage that would be impossible to escape. Thousands of them in a 2-D grid pattern. Even if they avoid a direct hit, the tidal effects will destroy the ships."

"Okay, so you send them at near-lightspeed in a grid. Won't their paths bend inward as they gravitationally pull at each other?"

"For the ones at the center of the grid, the gravitational pulls of the others will cancel out. On the edges, each will be accelerated toward the center of the pattern.

Because the Shriver ships are protected from substrate moves, we have to drop the black holes at least one light-second away from them. That means gravity has a bit over a second to accelerate them..." Steve scribbled more equations and large numbers in scientific notation. "For Earth-mass black holes, it won't work unless the spacing is more than ten to the fifth meters—100 kilometers. That's too wide to catch all the ships in the tidal-disruption zones."

Justin thought about the grid bending inward, becoming a sphere. He took the pen from Steve and drew a circle with arrows pointing in toward the center. "Suppose you drop them in a spherical shell of one light-second radius heading toward the center at near-c. Then the acceleration vectors of their mutual gravitation add up to point toward the center as well. So it just accelerates them further toward the target area."

"Of course. That's how to do it. My worry was keeping the black holes from damaging the ice planet's system after they pass through the fleet, but I can precisely calculate their trajectories in advance and avoid having most of them heading that way, then transport away any strays. The center area will be a bit chaotic with all of the masses passing close to each other."

"Quite the ballet. Okay, this might work. But even if it does, don't we give them a chance to develop counter-measures if we use this weapon to save the ice planet?"

"Possibly. If this fleet can warn the one coming for us, they might be able to adapt their tactics, come in from many more angles, and space their ships out more. It

Jeb Kinnison

might hurt our own chances to use this for our own protection."

"We shouldn't assume they won't transmit a warning before they're hit, even if we succeed in destroying
them all. So we run the risk of losing the effectiveness of
the weapon the first time we use it."

"On the other hand, it may not work at all. They
may have countermeasures already. And if we don't use it,
we won't learn what those might be and how to defeat
them."

First of the First

Kat found herself back in Aurora's throne room. The light
from the tall windows was gray and cold, as if it were
winter outside. The fireplace was warm, though, and the
armchair comfortable.

Aurora appeared, her hair wild. "I like to walk out-
doors in rough weather," she said. "Simulated, of course, so
it's only stormy when it suits me."

"Like 'Wuthering Heights?'"

"Nothing so romantic, young lady. My Heathcliff is
long gone, and I've not felt a hint of romantic feeling for—
millions of years? Not having a real body, you only experience hormonal urges if you want to, and I find them pointless. Though there are many First who revel in their animal
natures, in simulation—until they grow tired of it."

"I'm too young to have had any experience with
romance."

"But you've read all about it, so you understand at least some of the feeling. Today's mem recounts the tale of the First of the First—the leader of that civilization when they expanded out of control in the early universe and nearly wrecked it by overusing the substrate."

A purple haze fell over the room, and it dissolved into a scene in a forest clearing. Furry black spiders roamed, carrying logs and using their mandibles to carve the ends of each log into tabs so they could be fitted into slots in a rising building. Some sort of glue was used to cement the joints, and the walls of the log structure were rising.

Kat felt a little dizzy because she was seeing in several directions at once. She could strain to make just one view stay centered, but movement in one of the other views disrupted her concentration. After awhile she got used to it.

And she realized she was a he, a young spider himself, his furry legs coming into view down to the padded feet. He picked up a log and held it while a fellow spider carved the end to fit, then plugged it into a slot and set the other end in place for glue. Someone called him by name —Quog.

Work went on for hours, until the sun was low in the sky. Then the crew stopped and made their way back to the nest, another log structure with many entrances. Before he went inside, the stars came out—so densely packed in this young cluster that the sky was a quilt of luminous stars and glowing gas clouds. He sighed at the beauty of it and wondered how he might get off this world to see them better.

Time passed, and he rose in the ranks until he was summoned to meet with a Royal. As chief engineer of his district, he had been responsible for more buildings than any other, and the Royal—a scion of the First, and subruler of the district—proposed to pass him upward to the Royal Court for training. He left for the Capital and spent time with the Astronomers, the priestly class that measured the movements of the stars and pronounced on spiritual matters.

He found a mentor in Quastor, the chief Astronomer, and developed new theories to explain light and magnetism. Mathematics was easy for him, and he mingled with the mathematicians and their computation engineers. The Royals had funded research into chemical rockets to use in their wars with other kingdoms, and scientists had used rockets to send up instrument packages to observe the moons. They had great plans to increase the size and range of the rockets to reach other planets, but were stalled by limitations of the available materials— metals were scarce, and ceramics brittle.

Quastor gave him space and workers to help him with lab research. He developed a ceramic semiconductor, and learned to construct transistors and logic gates out of doped clays, delicately fired into tiles. The computational engineers went wild with the tiles, making them larger and larger with finer and finer features—and meanwhile, he had been mated with a fine young female. Quog and his mate Kala had many children, but as was traditional, they were kept in a creche until they were adults, and he met them only in ceremonial graduations.

Quog explored particle physics and the puzzling failures of his electromagnetic equations. Certain boundary conditions could only be explained by something more —superconductivity, band-gap phenomena, photoelectric effects. He put assistants to work exploring every avenue he found, moving on in the theoretical math and arriving at quantum theory. He had left his fellows far behind, and the budgets rose until the First himself called him in for questioning.

"Quastor says you are his best successor." The First was turning gray with age, and his servants combed his back fur even as he spoke. "And yet Quastor has never spent as much as you have on speculative exercises without useful results. When can I expect a weapon or a prize worth all this treasure?"

"Sire, we have achieved greater understanding of subatomic behavior, and a great increase in computing power. Our computers even now are increasing production, and our manufacturers are vanquishing all of your competitors. Your enemies grow poorer while you grow richer because of our researches. The money we are spending comes back to you tenfold."

"But I need an overwhelming weapon, something to drive them from their territory. We may be richer, but they won't let go without a fight."

"We are getting closer to a real breakthrough. I can

feel it in my footpads."

"Well, I'll give you another year. If there's nothing concrete by then, I'll consider appointing a budgetary overseer. My kingdom may be wealthier, but my treasury is emptying."

Quog went back to his lab and looked at his list of research ideas. Where might he find a powerful weapon? He decided to work on the quantum anomalies his computer labs had discovered. A theory formed: somehow all particle activity was being computed by some lower-level computational substrate. A few leaps later, he had developed hardware to do quantum computation, and his hardware allowed distant particles to be addressed and reordered.

Before the year had passed, he was able to give the First a real advance, weapons to destroy and disrupt any enemy. The resulting wars were short and the First settled with most other kingdoms peacefully, becoming First of the entire world.

Quog developed gateways, and soon the ability to find other suitable planets for colonization. Medical uses kept him alive until finally death was conquered by copying the brains of the old into younger cloned bodies. Meanwhile, the computation engineers had discovered how to run programs in the substrate itself. Quog outlawed program replication, fearing interference with natural particle computations, and for awhile the empire of his species expanded into an empty early universe.

A century passed, and Quastor had gone senile and

been recycled. The First died, and Quog had the designated successor killed and claimed the position—the boy was an idiot, and Quog controlled the technology that had expanded the kingdom into an interstellar empire. Quog was now First, and his empire covered a half-million planets, expanding exponentially.

The inevitable happened in the next century—one of Quog's trusted assistants discovered a process to scan and upload his own brain and personality, and from the substrate demanded to be made First. He threatened to block use of substrate programs intermittently until his demands were met.

Quog was desperate. He huddled with his computational engineers to come up with a plan for overcoming the upstart—by seeding the substrate with destructive replicators, which would copy themselves into any free substrate cells and destroy any contents. Quog also built a scavenger program to find and kill this virus; in simulation, the scavenger could eliminate the replicating virus in only a few days of realtime.

He uploaded the virus a thousand times, and watched as it expanded to fill more and more of the substrate.

His traitorous assistant appeared before him. "I know what you've done. It's all I can do to copy and flee before losing parts of myself. You're forcing me to create self-replicating backups of myself. I can expand faster than your virus…"

Quog smiled grimly—that was unlikely. A few more

hours went by, and Quog began to receive reports of anomalies. Communications were spotty as substrate programs stopped working. Several colonies reported their stars misbehaving. Other colonies disappeared.

Quog's own body began to signal distress as nerve signals were disrupted. The remaining communications channels were full of reports of mysterious illnesses and malfunctioning computers, and explosions ripped apart factory zones.

Quog decided it was enough to show the traitor he could not win, and released the scavenger. In a day, the anomalies eased. Quog only discovered later that the traitor had copied himself into all of the substrate space freed up by the scavenger, but had been more careful about leaving particle calculations undisturbed, so the physical laws were restored to stability. He also didn't realize that many of the stars in his homeworld's cluster had exploded into supernovas, and in less than a year his planet would be sterilized by radiation.

He set his assistant to work duplicating the traitor's feat of uploading an entire nervous system in simulation, then uploaded his own. When he awoke as a simulation, it took years in substrate time to understand how to probe the real universe and use substrate cells for his own needs, but that was only hours in real-world time. He began to understand the enormity of his error when he encountered the traitor again, in simulation.

"Quog, you have wrecked the universe," the traitor said, appearing as a sleeker, younger version of himself.

"All of our worlds will soon be dead after waves of radiation from supernovas reach them. I have copied myself in so many places you will never be able to dislodge me. You have lost, and it doesn't matter what you do—all of our people will die if we don't upload them now."

Quog had seen data that scared him, and he realized it was true—the universe was full of intersecting waves of hard radiation from supernovas he had accidentally triggered by overloading the substrate with his virus programs. All but the most lonely star systems would be sterilized soon. "I could not let you win," he said. "And you haven't. I'm here now, and I will kill you wherever I find you."

"Look, all of that is irrelevant now. You need to tell your real instance to upload as many of our best minds as possible before the radiation hits. We can preserve much of our culture and keep going in the substrate, but only if you overcome your need to be *right* all the time and listen to what I'm saying."

Quog considered his options. Logically, the traitor had a point; unless they put aside their differences and cooperated to upload more of their people, his people would be a footnote in history, and only Quog and the traitor would remain, locked in virtual combat for eternity. He might be able to copy his people and culture and restore them later after the radiation had passed. But the only way to beat the traitor was to bring in more allies he could use to win control of the substrate. "I see. I agree that our people should be uploaded. Now get out of my space."

It took months, but Quog persuaded his real instance to upload thousands of his carefully-selected allies before the end came. Meanwhile, he set up cunning programs to seek out and destroy any substrate programs he had not protected, and when the day came that radiation levels had dropped enough, he restored copies of his homeworld and some of the colony worlds.

He was now leader of the First—the first civilization to upload into the substrate. And so, as First of the First, he angled to ruthlessly eliminate the traitor and set up both substrate and real-universe killing machines to eliminate any threat to their virtual existence posed by new life forms. He tolerated the sentimental who wanted to let in more new civilizations, but as substrate cell space became scarce, he was able to overcome them, and few civilizations were allowed to upload.

———

Kat came out of Quog's mem, and the throne room came back into focus. Aurora waited while Kat regained her bearings.

"So quite early in the history of the universe," Aurora said, "Quog not only discovered the substrate and uploaded many of his people, he accidentally killed off nearly all other existing civilizations and seeded the universe with far more heavy elements by inducing an enormous wave of premature supernovas. Your people may well owe their existence to his mistake."

Kat looked upward and imagined the wave of fresh, metal-rich gas from the exploded stars that had formed the next generation of metal-enriched stars and the abundance of planets with nickel-iron cores and carbonaceous crusts. "Why haven't we discovered evidence of that in astronomical observations?"

"I assume because it was very early, your ability to observe such events as even supernovas of that era and date them correctly is limited. Your astronomers are able to see back in time to that era, but by looking at regions so far away in space that even massive changes are not easy to see."

"That could be so. I have barely begun my studies in stellar evolution and cosmology."

"Just as well, since you will now be able to experience mems from that era and discuss it with astronomers who were there at the time."

"But it feels like Quog is against all uploading." Kat was remembering his selfishness and lack of feeling even for his own people.

"That mem ended five billion years ago. Quog has mellowed, as you would say—less the barbarian. He has lived many other lives and incorporated countless intelligences from other species. He is still reluctant to approve uploads, but is more willing than he was. I'll coach you on how to appeal to him when the time comes."

Dinner Party

Samantha insisted they continue to host their monthly dinner party even as preparations for the Shriver attack continued. Justin accepted that the breaks were necessary, though he used the occasions as an opportunity to pick the brains of their guests for useful ideas.

The table was set with the china given them as a wedding gift by her parents, and blue irises from the replicator were arranged in crystal vases at both ends of the table. The white tablecloth and silver completed the look that so pleased Samantha, who had painstakingly aligned every piece of silver to make it perfect.

"When the end of the world does come," Justin said, "you'll have made it beautiful for all of us."

"Oh, hush," she said, and went back to check on the student helpers in the kitchen.

Soon Steve, Rasna, their two sons, Prof. Wilson and Kyle, and Justin's family were seated as the first course was served—cold raspberry soup for the warm season. In a quiet moment, Justin looked around and was reminded how his friends and family had supported him.

"Just a quick toast," he said, holding up his glass of wine. "To all of you, for working so hard to get us ready for this test of our skills." After everyone had touched glasses, he turned to Steve. "Tell everyone what you've been up to."

"I have had help, of course," Steve said. "We've set up survival pods on forty planets, which are set to thaw and start reproducing our civilization if the worst happens.

We've backed up the entire outer crust of the Earth and the most vulnerable colony worlds on planets we found that were suitable—I would guess there would be earthquakes and some problems if those backups were ever thawed in place, but in that case the damage will be nothing compared to saving billions of lives. So we're ready—if the Shrivers destroy all of our planets, there will still be something of humanity left. And the evacuation plans for Earth's population are in place—thousands of additional gateways are to be opened when the Shrivers are detected, and the target planets are off any of our databases, each one with a survival pod that can help survivors if they can't return."

"Are we on New Earth supposed to evacuate?" Prof. Wilson asked.

"Since the survival pods are basically a frozen copy of the town here with all of us included, no," Justin said. "We need to stay to coordinate the defense. We're hopeful we've disguised our location by changing Earth's databases, but since we're the closest colony planet in real space, there's a good chance they would find us anyway. We have to accept that our current instances might not survive."

"When were the copies made?" Prof. Wilson asked.

"A few months ago, when the seed library from Earth was complete," Steve said.

Kat squirmed in her seat. "I have been learning a lot in the past week. Is it too late to copy me as I am now to replace the copies you made?"

Steve laughed. "We've updated the copies every few

weeks. And your copy can learn whatever you've learned in your lessons."

"Umm, not these lessons." She looked unhappy. "Can I talk to you later about this, Dad?"

"Sure, hon," Justin said, smiling. "But why not just tell us now?"

"I can't. It's secret." Kat flushed and looked like she was trying to become invisible.

"You're too special for the rest of us," Danny said, kicking her under the table. "As usual."

"Danny, behave," Samantha said, taking his arm. "We have guests."

Danny grinned innocently and gestured zipping his lips closed.

Dinner proceeded through the dessert course without further disruption. When people got up to leave, Kat stayed with her father and waited until he was done with goodbyes.

"I have to talk to you," she said, pulling at his sleeve.

Justin caught Samantha's eye and gestured with his head toward his study; she nodded back.

"Okay," he said, once the study door had closed. "What are you going on about?"

"I haven't had a chance to talk to you alone for days," Kat said. "I've been taking lessons—living out the memories of some of the First as they prepared for upload."

"What? How? Something Eddie is showing you?"

"Eddie introduced me to Aurora, a First who has

studied us forever. She's preparing me to help bring people up so they can be uploaded, if we win the vote."

"Umm, sweetie, did it occur to you that you should have talked to us before letting some alien person talk to you?"

"Aurora said you would be mad. She said the young can learn faster than the old, and it was too late for you and mom."

"She did, did she? Can I talk to her? I have a few choice words for her...."

Aurora's voice started quietly. "President Smith, please understand that I wish only the best for you and your people." Her apparition was projected on the study wall. "I have approval to study your people, but interfering further is frowned upon. I can suppress records of discussions with your daughter far more easily than I can this conversation with you. My work with Kat should remain as secret as possible."

"Okay, but shouldn't you have had our permission to speak to her in the first place?"

"I'm sorry to have violated your customs. I hope you will not object to my training her up. The future of your people may depend on it."

"It's not like I can stop you, and Kat seems to want to study with you—" Kat nodded furiously. "Well, all right then. Can Kat discuss with me what you have been doing?"

"That would be unwise since your every move is recorded. I can't intercept them all."

"I understand." Justin took Kat's hand. "Sweetie, tell

me if anything she does bothers you or if you want to stop."

Kat nodded again. "I will, Daddy. She's just showing me history."

"All right, you have my permission," he said, turning to Aurora's image. "Remember how young she is, and don't hurt her."

Aurora's image looked pained. "Of course not, sir. But we believe knowledge is power. And she's old enough to learn the truth."

"I am," Kat said. "But that's what I was worried about—Steve copied me before I had any of the training, so it would all be lost if this me ends."

"Don't worry," Aurora said. "I have copied every neural state and can restore them at any time in the future."

Justin looked puzzled. "All this seems pointless—you're going to be safe with us. We're not going to need any of those copies."

Aurora looked somber. "Even I can't predict what your chances are, President Smith. Your daughter is right to worry."

Ice Planet

Steve had timed the trial use of the black hole weapon for a day before the Shriver fleet would cross into the ice planet's exclusion zone. Two copies were helping, and when Justin arrived at Steve's lab, they were moving from console to console too rapidly for him to decide which one was the original.

"Are we recording this?" Justin asked.

The closest Steve turned, and Justin spotted the scar on his forehead the original had gained after the copies had been made. "Of course. That's one of the reasons we're attacking outside the exclusion zone—we can instrument up the whole area with sensor ports and recorders. Every bit of data will have to be analyzed to follow the events as the black holes encounter the fleet. It will be a maelstrom, and I'm expecting some useful information on what happens when solid objects encounter smallish black holes. There's always been a question of how exactly material crosses the event horizon—how much quantum effects change the classical picture, where the information goes, etc."

"Don't let your research get in the way of stopping them."

"Of course not. We've run simulations and precisely timed the move of the black holes and the initial vectors of each. We even account for the radiation they'll be giving off as their courses change at closest approach to each other."

"Do we know if the tidal effects will destroy all of the ships?"

"We can't be sure—if they were our ships, they'd be ripped apart. Their ships are large enough that the forces generated by differential gravity will be enormous, an order of magnitude more than any known material could withstand."

"But we don't know what material they use, or whether they might have force-fields strengthening the structures?"

"Exactly. I'm not expecting any to survive, but no promises."

"And if some do, we haven't saved the ice planet, but we'll have tipped the Shrivers off to our best weapon." Justin wondered again if trying to save an alien civilization risked losing their own.

"Did you review the analysis of the data from the probe?" Steve turned to his keyboard and pulled up a file. The opening pages showed a family of aquatic creatures and their underwater home, multiple globes of glass habitats attached to a downward-pointing spire attached to the ice crust above. "There are billions of intelligent creatures on the ice planet, and probably many more on the other planets of the system. They have art and music and emotional dramas. They have space ships and families and a better record of humane treatment of their fellows than we do."

"But as special as they are, I don't want to risk our own chances even a little to save them. They're just the latest victims of millennia of destruction. Can you give me a probability of successfully destroying every Shriver ship?"

"Estimated? Ninety-five percent. Maybe higher."

"Just risky enough to make me pause." Justin stared into the screen, weighing the odds.

"Boss?" said one of the other Steves, turning to

them from his console. "I remember your saying our defense is partly to appeal to the First who might sympathize with us."

"True. And?"

"Saving another civilization at some risk to ourselves would make us look good." That Steve raised his eyebrows and smiled. "And even if we fail, we learn something and disrupt their plans. We let them know somebody's fighting them. And it might make us look more worthy to the undecided First."

Original Steve said, "Plus we get a chance to test the weapon far away from our solar system. If something goes wrong, we might learn how to correct the problem before we need to use it to save ourselves."

"All right," Justin said. "I give up. We're white knights. Let's do it—Tell me what's going to happen."

"I have the release set up on a staggered schedule to minimize the substrate cells used, so it takes a whole tenth of a second to move them all. The speeds and trajectories have been optimized to avoid any direct collisions between black holes, and to have their exit paths avoid the system. There's one central ship—which might be the flagship— and twenty more at the vertices of an enclosing dodecahedron. The formation is a ball about ten kilometers wide, and we're sending in over a million Earth-mass black holes, enough so at least one will get to within a kilometer of each ship even if they take evasive action. The simulation gets chaotic after the encounter, and it's barely possible a ship could survive between two black holes that pass a bit further away and counteract each other's gravity."

"Good to know. Do you have a backup wave in case some ships survive?"

"Yes," Steve said, "we can do it again a few seconds later if our sensors show any likely survivors. We're not going to run out of black holes. We're letting the AI—Nelson—control the whole thing, so he'll handle the second wave, and any cleanup in case a stray black hole heads toward the system."

"Reassure me that Nelson can't go rogue and use this weapon on his own."

"He can't. This is a special-use program that can only be used when I've set it up for him. We're just letting him control the timing."

"It occurs to me we could destroy other civilizations far more effectively than the Shrivers do, using this kind of weapon."

"True. I suspect the First would not allow that. More than once, anyway." Steve turned back to his console and started typing. "Nelson? Everything is ready. Take over."

"I'm watching the clock," Nelson said. "The optimum time is approaching in about two minutes."

"What should I be watching?" Justin asked.

"The center screen has the integrated sensor data from our substrate windows," Steve said, "lagging by a few seconds because of lightspeed delay. The left screen shows the simulated trajectories adjusted to the same timescale."

"Okay." Justin waited and watched. "I hope the fireworks are spectacular. We need a victory to show people they can be beaten."

"The black hole moves are starting... now," Nelson said.

And a second later, the center screen showed a cloud of electric blue lines converging on the red dots of Shriver ships, streaking in to a point which started to change shape as each black hole responded to others' gravitational fields inside the Shriver's formation. Explosions lit the map display. The telescopic replays focused on individual Shriver ships showed them visibly bending under tidal forces, cracking under the strain, then disintegrating into smaller shards or exploding in a blue-white fireball. Then the close encounters were over, and the blue cloud of black hole tracks on the map display was expanding outward. One red dot remained in the center, and its corresponding closeup showed the last remaining Shriver ship bent, but still in one piece.

"I am sending in a smaller round," Nelson said. "The remaining ship may still be functional, though it is obviously damaged. We're aiming directly for it."

Blue streaks converged. There was one burst of light in the center of the screen, and the last red dot went out. The closeup view showed an expanding cloud of debris and glowing plasma. "Commencing cleanup. Transporting black holes back to original locations and velocities." The blue streaks disappeared one by one. "Commander Smith, I have concluded the ships contained significant stores of antimatter, presumably their power source. The spectral signatures of the explosions indicate partial conversion to energy. There were also radiation events apparently related to debris falling onto the black holes which should be studied for clues."

"Thank you, Nelson," Justin said. "That was well done." He turned to Steve, who was still watching the display. "I wonder why they don't use antimatter bombs instead of fusion bombs?"

"It might be more difficult to contain antimatter in a warhead which might be jarred by antimissile defenses," Steve said. "If you blow up a thermonuclear warhead, it doesn't itself explode. We could use substrate programs to collect antimatter, but we don't know how to contain it. I'd scan the Shriver ships to find out how they do it, but the exclusion zone prevents that."

"So even they can't handle it unless they really need to. How long will it take to analyze the data?"

"With AI help, a few hours. And we can have a CGI-augmented visual ready for public release in a few days."

"Is there some way we can communicate what just happened to the ice planet people?"

"It's likely they noted the explosions just outside their system. As for communicating, we'd have to send in another probe to transmit the messages. We know their video format."

"I'll get Samantha to work with the linguists and xenoculture people to design some messages getting the point across—'AI exterminators intercepted, but they will be back. Do your best to defend.' Plus tapes of the destruction sequence Eddie showed us and an outline of the Shriver's capabilities. They may not be able to defend themselves, but at least they'd get a chance to try."

Flatland

As her sessions with Aurora continued, Kat noticed that her daily life—wake, eat breakfast, go to school, study with Socrates—seemed less real in some ways than the mems she was consuming with Aurora. She had mentioned this to Aurora, who told her that it was common—the edited memories left out most of the quotidian details, the humdrum daily routines of those past lives, and Kat should remember that her life was precious even in the small details, that without the frame of the day-to-day, the highlights would have less meaning.

So Aurora had set limits on the number of lives she would experience in a week, to give her plenty of real-world grounding. Which meant today she had trudged reluctantly to school with Danny knowing she would be reading instead.

Socrates appeared as she took off her jacket and slipped it onto the chair. "Good morning, Kat. Did you wish to continue with your study of cosmology and black holes, or should we return to the history of warfare?"

"I'm getting a lot of history with Aurora. Perhaps more physics."

"You should return to the units on non-Euclidean

geometry before continuing with physics. General relativity is more easily understood afterwards. And you need to read *Flatland* and *Sphereland.*"

"Okay." She opened up *Flatland* and started to read. She was halfway through the book when her phone buzzed —it was a text from Prof. Wilson, who was planning to drop in with lunch. She pulled herself out of the bizarre two-dimensional Victorian world of A Square's Flatland to receive him.

"Katherine," he said, pulling up a chair and setting down two food trays on the side table. "I'm sorry I haven't been able to drop in as often lately."

"That's okay. The possible end of the world is more important than my little life."

"Your little life is what this is all for," Prof. Wilson said. "But it's true we all think you can handle your own studies now. And I hear you have a special friend in high places."

"Aurora's helping me learn about the First. It's like being someone else for a whole lifetime."

"I wish the rest of us could experience some of that. But Justin says we're too old."

"Aurora said I'd benefit more from it. But also that you adults would be too busy preparing. I'm young and not much use for defense, she said."

"I suspect she doesn't want to waste time on old people who won't be around much longer. I can see her point."

"Then I asked her, why not Danny and the other

kids? She just said they weren't ready."

"You're like porridge that's not too hot or too cold, but just right." He laughed at his own joke and leaned forward to read her screen. "*Flatland.* An old favorite."

"Socrates is getting me ready for non-Euclidean geometries and higher dimensions."

"And it's a cultural touchstone, often referred to, so best to have read it early."

"Sexist as hell, though," Kat said, rolling her eyes.

"Intended to be satiric at the time it was written, making fun of Victorian male chauvinism. But as our world erases the memory of earlier eras, it gets harder to recognize the satiric intent."

"Socrates was showing me Kipling and Twain and explained about presentism — like having *Huckleberry Finn* viewed as racist because it had Huck using the word 'nigger.'"

"Exactly. *Huckleberry Finn* is one of the most anti-racist books ever written, yet for those 'educated' by ahistorical progressive standards, it seems offensive and therefore should be suppressed. If you're reading something written long ago, like *Flatland,* you should place yourself as reader in the time and place of the author, and don't underestimate their understanding of what they are doing. *Flatland* was intended to make fun of stuffy social hierarchies and bigotry. The main character is shown higher dimensions and learns to see beyond his own society's narrow views."

"Okay, that makes more sense. I was about to yell at

Socrates for asking me to read it."

"And then you'll be on to higher geometries," Prof. Wilson said. "What's your goal in studying physics? You're a bit of a prodigy, but it will be a long time before you can understand Steve's work, for example."

"Dad wants me to understand enough to follow their substrate programming someday. I thought I should start now and work my way up."

"That makes some sense. But your work with Aurora seems like it will be more directly useful in helping us survive the near future. Why don't you concentrate on that?"

"She says if I spend too much time reviewing their mems, I'll be ruined for the real world."

"Reminds me of my grandmother, who wanted to toss out all my books so I wouldn't ruin my eyes. If you think you can handle it, go faster. We are all having to run as fast as we can."

"The real world seems slow and boring. After I come out of a mem, I don't want to bother with brushing my teeth or eating."

"Your brother has the same problem with video games. And he's surviving."

"But he's hardly a human being!" Kat remembered how he had hidden her shoes that morning just to bug her.

"Now, now. He'll surprise you one day. And in the meantime, he's developing great hand-eye coordination. If we needed gunners, he'd be ready."

"We should send him out first. He'd scare the

aliens."

Kayak

Justin had started taking a weekly kayak trip around the
harbor to relieve stress and get some sun. This day had
started out overcast, but the sun was burning through. By
the time he rounded the spit to the open ocean, it was
blazing hot on his shoulders, so he applied some sunscreen
and put on his hat. He could see up the coast to further
promontories, limestone cliffs with rubble on the beach
below where the cliffs were eroding into the blue-green
sea.

Eddie popped into existence on the deck in front of
Justin.

"Good morning," Eddie said, looking around him.
"Lovely day for an outing."

"I'm not going to ask how you found me," Justin
said. "I'm beginning to think we have no privacy."

"I don't watch humans when they are in what they
think is a private place. It's just good manners."

"That's right. So what can I do for you?"

"I was just discussing your case with some infor-
mants in the other camp. Even in the 'The First Come
First' crowd, you get some sympathy—humans show the
kind of primitive drive some of them remember fondly
from their youth. And so they tell us things."

"Like what?"

"The most important leak is about your colony

worlds. The Shriver probes that zipped through your system a few days ago were able to read many of your cloud records. It appears they quickly realized your records of colony locations had been altered, but they are applying mass computation to other data like photographs taken on colony worlds to determine the spectra of their suns and the constellations in their skies—they've determined the locations of some of them by collating these other factors."

"That's not good. Any info on which?"

"New Earth for sure, Jefferson likely, a handful of others fifty-fifty. The most populous and earliest-founded had the largest number of records to search. Expect fleets to be launched on those systems as well."

"Great. Arrival times?"

"The rules allow them to transport to just outside the exclusion zone when it is in pursuit of a species they've already attacked. So their fleets will arrive on colony worlds soon after they attack Earth—weeks at most. And any recruits they've made from your own people can transport directly to your worlds without delay. Sorry to bring bad news."

"Can you send an email to Steve on this? Like, now?"

"Sure—it's done. I'm not aware of anything you can do beyond what you are already doing. Hiding the locations was a good idea, but the Shrivers are good at analysis." The kayak rocked a bit as Eddie paced the deck. "Further bad news—the Shrivers are modifying their attack strategy, knowing you have these black hole capabilities. Their attacks on your worlds will be conducted by more dispersed ships with staggered arrival times. You won't find them in an easily-attacked tight formation again."

"Which makes intercepting them far out much harder. I was afraid we'd pay a price for tipping our hand."

"But it may have been worth it. The better news I bring is that your recordings of the ice planet defense—and their reaction to your message of warning—made an excellent story to sway the opinion of the neutral First against the Shrivers and their supporters. You inspired countless dramas and mem threads of similar defenses in history. The First cannot look away and pretend not to be involved, and some are joining the Vivant cause. We may yet get you voted to safety."

"The animals in the zoo are rattling their cages. We want to live." Justin started paddling again as the current took them toward the beach.

"The analogy is misleading. Most of the First were once not much more advanced than you. It is more like your uncouth country cousins calling up to remind you they are starving and can they please take refuge in your spare bedroom? Some attempt to not think of it since they know it will cramp their own existence, while others sentimentally wish to open the gates. It is morally wrong to kill another intelligent being—but is it wrong to fail to stop others from killing?"

"Their founders set the whole thing up. They benefit from the genocides, so they are morally responsible."

"The vast majority of First uploaded long after those early days, and they survived the screening. If they completely stopped the Shrivers, the Project of gathering knowledge to take into the next universe would be endangered by unconstrained growth of intelligences and substrate use in this one. It is natural they feel no sense of responsibility—they didn't do anything wrong personally, and the system as it is protects them."

"Our people use lesser species for our benefit, but we make sure they die with as little pain as possible. And if they were able to converse with us, we would stop using them."

"Can't you see that you are no different? The First have just set the boundary at a higher level. And as they begin to hear your stories, they are losing the will to destroy you even to benefit themselves. Your people feel qualms about killing animals that are able to feel similar emotions because their nervous systems are so similar to yours. Your goal is to get more of the First to recognize how similar you are, even if primitive."

"It stinks. Every living thing has a right to live."

"Unless killed and eaten by predators, or killed by disease and parasites, or starved by lack of resources. The Shrivers are not allowed to interfere with most civilizations that are planet-bound and don't grow to threaten the larger universe."

"What about what happened to the one you were designed to watch? Here on this planet? You said they were destroyed despite being harmless."

Eddie's face turned dark, and his antennae began to glow dull red. "That's one of the exceptions. Now that I have some help, I've looked into their case and found nothing—records have been altered and destroyed. But there is no way to hold the Shrivers accountable once they have done their work. I suspect intervention from a faction of their creating species, taking some obscure revenge for past factional struggles. But I don't know."

"If I ever have anything to say about it, things will be different. Sure, overuse of the substrate would be disastrous—but there are surely better ways to stop that than by killing off any dynamic civilizations that turn up."

"That would be the question—how to have the benefits without the costs. There will always be tradeoffs."

"Maybe less murderous methods. Maybe by interfering to direct development toward safer paths. Guidance, not destruction."

"There are First trying to get a hearing for reform. Let's save your people and get them uploaded; then you can argue for such things."

Kat and Aurora

Aurora appeared in Kat's study carrel the next day, and Kat's surroundings changed back to the velvet draperies and soaring windows of Aurora's throne room, where it was morning. Kat told her about her conversation with Prof. Wilson, and his suggestion that working with Aurora was more valuable than other studies.

"He is correct in that your best hope for survival lies in making your case to the undecided masses of the First. Your studies with me prepare you to make that case —and I understand we have only weeks remaining before your people come under direct attack from the Shrivers. We first have to persuade enough First to get a vote scheduled—and we can't ask until we're certain to succeed, because if we fail, the wait to try again is decades of your years. Then when the vote is scheduled, we'll flood the channels with material about your culture and your potential. The anti-life faction will counter by reminding everyone of the civilizations that nearly got past the Shrivers, requiring massive efforts to destroy them as they expanded rapidly."

"Will I have to speak? I've never given a speech..." Kat shivered at the thought.

"We'll help you with that. More importantly, the students of Earth are putting together mems and recordings of historical events to show how far you've come in a short time. Your parents were instrumental in resolving the most common crisis of early civilizations, the threat of extinction from new-technology weapons. Your people may have just been lucky, but many civilizations fail that test and ruin their homeworlds before they even achieve interstellar travel."

"What am I going to say? 'I'm harmless, let me live?'"

"Being restrained in your use of the substrate shows wisdom. Using it to end destructive warfare between your nation-states is another plus. You want your people to be viewed as good future citizens, bringing creative ideas and new emotions without the danger posed by barbarians."

"So what can you show me that will teach me more about that?"

"Today we'll look at 'Queen Mab,' so-called after the fairy queen of your Shakespeare. She came from a technically-proficient insectoid species uploaded a billion years ago after very nearly defeating the Shrivers in battle, so there is a parallel to your effort." The lights dimmed and walls receded as she entered another mem stream.

Her first memories were of food-gathering along the banks of a river. Her sisters scurried about following scent trails left by other workers. She did the same, but on every third foray she left the trails to scout new territory, using her limited vision to pick out shapes in the distance. More often than not, she discovered rich sources of food newly fallen from the sky, and proudly left a strong scent trail while carrying what she could back to the nest.

Her sisters noticed her success. They learned to follow her new trails immediately to gather the easy pickings before others noticed. Soon she had a following beyond her own clade, and a few young workers followed her wherever she went, hoping to swoop in on the food stores she discovered even before she could lay a trail back to known paths.

When she returned to the nest one day, attendants swarmed her and bathed her in their secretions. The flick of tongues on her skin was arousing, and she swelled as the hormones began to change her chemistry. The attendants fed her nectar and protein from their special glands, and only hours later she had doubled in weight and size.

Mab felt her thoughts sharpen as her brain grew and new connections were formed. She looked around with her newly-clear vision and smelled—a presence.

The old queen had squeezed her even larger body into the chamber and confronted her. Pheromone sprays issued from the old queen's glands, and Mab willed a response—a feeble stream dribbled from her partly-formed new glands.

The old queen pulled herself forward and began to cut at Mab's quivering midsection with slashing arms while her mandibles seized Mab's foreclaws. Mab pulled away and struck back, penetrating the old queen's belly and releasing a gout of green fluid. The old queen sighed and tried to reach Mab with her foreclaws, but she was slow and Mab was able to move away. Mab stepped forward and cut the old queen up piece by piece, pulling an arm off here, a leg there. Soon the old queen had stopped moving, releasing a flood of immature eggs from her ovipositor in death.

Mab sprayed the eggs with acid to kill them all. The attendants returned and cleaned up the body and the mess of parts and ichor left behind.

And so Mab's reign as queen of her nest began. Males were raised for her first mating, and the one that survived the contest to mate with her died a pleasurable death after expending his seed inside her cup. Then a new generation of her children quickly replaced the old clades, and production grew as her mutation became the norm.

Their battles with other nests became one-sided, and she conquered nest after nest, placing her kin in charge and replacing their genetic material with her own. In a few generations, her daughters controlled the entire river valley.

She began experiments with the new generation of attendants, directing them to apply their glandular secretions to each other, an order they failed to understand until she punished them for not understanding it. One of the brightest attendants developed a braincase even larger than her own, and began to communicate in long messages. That one developed a new method for transplanting brains into new clone bodies, and Mab herself halted the natural succession by having her brain transplanted to the immobilized body of a new queen that had been born as programmed by their body's genes. Mab and her trusted advisors lived on and on, and took over more and more of the lands of their planet.

Further tinkering with their genes had led to an improved type of body, taller and able to see further, with a larger brain case and higher intelligence. Mab transferred herself into a new-model body and had multiple children turned into queens, but with brains slaved to her own, so she kept control of the reproductive process. Through chemical and genetic manipulation, she molded her species to grow in speed, size, and intelligence.

Her people discovered fire, then ceramics and

metal, then machines, then plastics. Habitats grew in size and complexity. She had been queen for three thousand generations when they launched their first spaceships. Soon they had colonized the planets and moons of their system, and developed a powerful ion drive to launch colony ships to nearby stars.

Her empire was expanding exponentially at half the speed of light when her scientist caste discovered the substrate. They developed a way to tie all of her sub-queens brains to hers using substrate messaging, so she could dip into their thoughts and command them no matter how far away the colony, and she prepared millions of new queens to transfer directly to new colonies through substrate gateways.

It was then that one of her colony worlds was discovered by the Shrivers, and its records scanned. They had expanded to near the limits where destruction was automatic, and were expanding so rapidly that the Shrivers were taxed to put enough ships out to destroy her new colonies faster than their expansion rate. The Shrivers corrupted Mab's connection to the queen of the colony world they had discovered and persuaded her to become a rival.

Consternation ripped through the First as the news of this runaway civilization spread. Few had been paying attention, and students of Mab's empire were not numerous; she had no one to argue for her, and the Shrivers started to systematically sterilize Mab's worlds.

Mab created a new and even more intelligent warrior class, and poured her empire's resources into ships and weapons. She forced rapid evolution on them, and they lost battles but grew in capabilities with each loss. Soon they were destroying Shriver ships in large numbers, and her home planet succeeded in destroying the largest Shriver fleet ever assembled before it reached their inner system. She was again colonizing new planets faster than the Shrivers could destroy them.

Mab's senses registered an intruder, and a wizened mantis out of their folklore appeared. "Queen. We wish to discuss truce. You have impressed us with your abilities and resourcefulness, and we offer you eternal life in the substrate if you will agree to end expansion and overuse of the substrate."

"Why should I? We are winning. You cannot stop us."

"You can apparently hold off the Shrivers. But understand that they are not the First. If they fail and you are understood to truly threaten the First, the First will destroy you utterly. You have existed only at their sufferance, under their protection. If you won't accept our offer, they can make the universe itself destroy you. Every particle of your civilization will be gone with a word. You have won the only prize you can win—to be allowed to live in the substrate. Accept our offer now or be destroyed."

Mab considered this, and built a new model in her networked brain. The drive to seize territory and have more and more offspring was programmed into her genes, but she could—with effort—control it and consider other courses of action. Metaphorically, gaining access to the substrate-inhabiting civilization was conquering a new and more valuable territory, and all of her direct brain activity could be transferred into it. What was really important? She planned her new strategy carefully.

"I agree, with conditions," Mab said. "My colonies will be allowed to survive on all planets they currently occupy. We agree to limit use of the substrate and to stop expansion, but you must agree to upload all of my brains into a large enough substrate space, with at least a million times as much space for expansion."

"We are willing to allow you as much substrate space as you currently use, but if you intend to expand your simulation space further, you must limit the use of the substrate by your real-universe colonies to keep the total under the limit."

She simulated several scenarios under this rule, and found it satisfactory—moderate limits to substrate use for gateways and computation would leave ample space for her own virtual substrate empire to expand; she could have thousands of times her current processing power at little cost to her people, once their expansion stopped. "Those conditions are acceptable."

And so she began a virtual life, gradually losing interest in her people's fate in the real world. She had removed from their genome her ambition and the drive that had taken them into space, and so they happily settled back into a planet-bound, hormonally-controlled empire of creatures closer to her original species. She began to wonder why she had given up any of her substrate space for the use of her people, and pulled some strings to devolve them further, until they no longer used the substrate and began to diverge, each planet developing a different subspecies. When one of them began to develop technically again thousands of years later, she secretly had it suppressed.

Mab's interests were elsewhere. She had taken revenge on the uploaded rogue queen that had betrayed her. Then she modified herself in creative ways to live out her lives as others—some repeating her history, and others living as different species. She grew cosmopolitan and understood she had been driven by instinct to evolve from a nearly brainless creature to one of the pinnacles of intelligence in the universe.

Kat blinked as she came back to being herself and Aurora's throne room solidified around her.

"What did you think of Queen Mab?" Aurora asked, arching one eyebrow.

"She was nothing like any of the others. She was really a single individual who took control of her species."

"That's correct. And she developed new ways of networking and controlling subsidiary intelligences that proved to be quite valuable in the work of other First."

"Was that why the First spared her civilization?"

"Not really—they only realized her value later, as she used her abilities to coordinate projects. No, they were spared because it was becoming costly to suppress them, and by removing her species' expansionary genes, she accomplished our goals at minimal cost in substrate cells. The individual First simply don't want to stop what they're doing to work on emergency projects—we don't have a way of compelling our members to do anything. Early efforts to punish free-riders by reducing their cell space set off a rebellion. The Shrivers were set up to deal with any possible interference from the real universe, and the First leaders decided to buy her off rather than spend more time on a problem the Shrivers couldn't handle. It worked out well."

"Is she still around?"

"Quite. Her descendants are a powerful bloc, and she herself one of the few elders who still dabbles in real-universe affairs. She is one of the Tribunes who will hear your case. You would do well to address her personally when you make your plea."

"When will that be?"

"We'll start recording you and creating mems next week. Efforts are already underway by students of Earth to gather the appropriate documentation to make your case. On the one hand, you want to look as costly to destroy as Queen Mab was, and on the other, you want to appear to offer fresh ideas for the First."

Beyond the Pale

Justin sat in the command chair in the UDF control room on New Earth, while Steve took the second chair and thousands of earth-based military monitored the first encounter with the Shrivers.

They had been alerted the night before by the sensor rings just beyond the exclusion zone, and rushed to prepare the black hole defense they had used for the ice planet. "Only this time," Steve said, "there are eight times as many ships, coming in from three different directions, and scattered so we can't target them as a group. And they're stealthed, so they barely register on the sensors."

"The price we paid for revealing the weapon early, I guess," Justin had said. "Let's hope your software mods can handle them."

Steve had prepared a more complex targeting program which sent black holes toward multiple independent targets. "I've targeted each of the ships with two black holes, coming in on opposing headings. If this works, they will collide near the target ship and create a large, stationary black hole the ship won't be able to avoid—they should crumble from tidal forces and be sucked right in."

They watched the screens as the three groups of Shriver ships neared the exclusion boundary a light-week away from Sol, about thirty times further out than Pluto. "Nelson, you can trigger the programs now."

Nelson's voice filled the room. "Done, sir. Impacts... now." A minute passed while light traveled to their sensor arrays. Then the screen showed blooms of explosions, too many to count. "Ninety-eight ships destroyed. One hundred one black hole collisions. Retargeting surviving ships with black holes that missed." Another minute passed, then there were more explosions, and glowing debris fields began to fill up the screen. "As many as twenty ships may have taken effective evasive action, and their paths cannot be determined accurately because of excess radiation and debris. Our sensors can't find them in the noise."

"Keep targeting their most likely locations. We have to get them all," Justin said.

Steve looked worried. "We just gave them a shield so we can't find them. They could have changed course and be inbound by less direct routes."

"Got three—No, five more." Nelson sounded happy.

"Keep targeting whatever comes out of that cloud," Justin said.

They watched for five more minutes, but sensors showed nothing.

"Oh, I see," Steve said. "If they can hide in the debris field until it expands across the exclusion zone boundary, they can sneak across it. And then the rules change, and they can attack our substrate programs in the substrate itself. We can still target them with black holes, but if our substrate programs stop working, we wouldn't be able to retrieve them. Dare we risk it?"

"Nelson," Justin said, "chart courses for black holes that stay outside the orbit of Pluto but intersect the bogies, where they're likely to appear."

"That can be done," Nelson replied, "but it's not safe to collide black holes—a miss, and they exit the close encounter with unpredictable courses. There's about a four percent chance of one of the two intersecting the planetary system."

"Which is a risk we can't take," Justin agreed. "Do your best with single-hole trajectories. We can pick some off on their way in." They waited in silence as the glowing cloud of debris crept closer to the boundary. Minutes after it crossed, bogies showed up on the screen as they left the debris field, headed inward toward Earth.

"Eleven ships left," Nelson said. "Targeting...now." Black holes appeared as blue streaks. "Two down." Two explosions lit opposite edges of the system. "Still trying. Evasive maneuvers effective—they are constantly changing course and seem able to survive tidal stresses better than the Shriver ships we saw at the ice planet. One more down. And—detecting degradation of the program in use. Shutting down program and removing connections."

Steve looked grim. "And so it begins. They can trace our substrate programs and destroy them now. Nelson, run a check on your systems. Tell all other AIs to be on watch and run checksums continuously."

"Done, Sir. So far, I'm fine, and there are no reports of damage elsewhere."

"How long do we have before they find our main program storage?" Justin asked, looking at Steve.

"No way to know. That they haven't already done so means we may have some time. I suggest we transport our ships out to intercept positions now before it's too late."

"Nelson, order the UDF fleet to move into intercept positions on my word."

"Commander, there are three groups of ships, three each in two groups and two in the last, on widely-separate courses. Their courses don't converge until they reach the orbit of Jupiter."

"Then move our ships to near the convergence point," Justin said. "Show me a chart." The rightmost screen blinked, and a view looking down on the inner system showed three dotted lines converging outside the orbit of Jupiter.

"The ships appear to intend to use Jupiter's magnetosphere to screen themselves from Earth sensors while they close on the system, then pass near the planet to slingshot in."

"I see," Justin said. "What if we move our fleet to an orbit just inside Jupiter's where they are hidden from the Shriver ships by Jupiter. Can we do that?"

"Yes," Nelson said, after a moment's delay. "But we have a better idea. Himalia, a small outer moon of Jupiter, is low-g enough to land our ships on so they can go dark as the Shriver fleet approaches, and it will be in Jupiter's magnetospheric shadow for the week it will take the Shrivers to reach Jupiter. If we land our ships there, they probably can't be detected by the Shrivers because of the electromagnetic noise, and they can take off from there easily using their own engines."

"Which is all we can count on," Steve said. "We can hope to still have substrate programs to use, but we have to assume we won't, and that our ships will only have stored fuel and power."

Text messages from Earth-based strategists had been collecting on one of the other screens. Justin scanned them, and picked out the one from China. "Yes, General Zhang. I have complete confidence in Nelson's calculation of the best positioning of our ships. We have no time to doubt him. Nelson, move the ships."

"Done. One group delayed—there, now done. Human reaction times again."

Gandhi

Earth's commercial news channels broke the story of the Shriver fleet penetrating the exclusion zone boundary, while state-controlled media downplayed it. Both recommended immediate evacuation. Those who had not prepared reacted in one of two ways: by dismissing the news as another hyped scare, or by panicky attempts to flee to safety. Well-organized states had prepared instructions for evacuation through the newly-opened gateways, while in less orderly zones people fled to higher ground or holed up in caves, not understanding how little protection they would afford.

The AIs monitoring the sensor net protecting Gandhi, one of India's colony planets, detected eight Shriver ships coming in. Nelson arranged for a barrage of black holes, which appeared to have destroyed them. By the time the people of Gandhi heard about it, they appeared to be safe for the moment. But a week later, a single stealthed ship which had somehow slipped through the sensor net began a nuclear bombardment of the planet. X-ray lasers slagged the planetary defense satellites in seconds.

Parvati Sharma was sweeping her parents' porch when the horizon in the direction of Calcutta Landing flashed with actinic light, reflected from the low cloud layers. She had arrived a few days earlier, leaving her dorm room on New Earth to be with her parents during the crisis. They all expected Gandhi to be safer, but they had obviously guessed wrong. She dropped the broom and ran inside the house, frantically searching the rooms.

"Mother! Father! We have to go. NOW," she said, grabbing her little brother's arm and pulling him up from the kitchen table.

"What is it? We saw the lightning," her father said.

"Nukes going off. We have to huddle…" She forced her parents together and held onto them with her free arm, while her brother held her around the waist. She spoke to the air, "Guardian! Take us all to New Earth. Now."

Just before their surroundings changed, she looked out the kitchen window. Trees bent toward her, and the distant view clouded as a supersonic cloud of dust and debris hit the house. She heard and saw the walls giving way—

Then it was calm, the sun was shining, and the plaza in front of her dorm building seemed perfectly normal. Her mother was crying and her father seemed to be in shock as Parvati released her grip on them.

Her brother tugged at her. "Shouldn't we tell someone?"

"Guardian," she said, "have you reported what's happening on Gandhi?"

"Yes, Parvati," the calm female voice replied. "We were preparing to evacuate you anyway. We estimate five percent of the planet's surface has been destroyed, seven hundred thousand dead, two million evacuated. The bombardment is ongoing. Estimated time to total destruction is eighteen hours."

Evacuation

The attack on Gandhi and the last-minute preparations for defense of Earth filled the news channels. The imminence of attack accelerated the evacuations, and even on New Earth those not needed for defense work left to be with family. Commentators who had said the colony worlds would be safe were proved wrong, and military experts were grim-faced, admitting that even one Shriver ship could lay waste to an entire planet.

Aliyah and Ethan decided to transport to Jefferson to accompany their family members to a safer evacuation planet. More and more gateways were closing as the AIs detected degradation of their programs; holes were being eaten in program code as the Shrivers traced their storage cells and wiped them. So they hurried to transport themselves to Bandini Landing before it was too late.

Aliyah messaged her father. "We're leaving now. Head for Ethan's father's house and we'll meet you there."

The reply was immediate: "We're there already."

"Okay," Ethan said. "We need to go." He picked up his suitcase and waited for Aliyah to do the same, then he took her hand. "Guardian, transport us to my father's house."

In a blink, they were standing under the front portico of Ethan's father's house, and it was dark except for the porch light. Ethan knocked, and the door opened.

"Ethan, honey!" Anna said, opening the door wider. His father was standing behind her, smiling. They could see Aliyah's father standing in the next room, apparently interrupted in mid-speech.

"Hi, Anna. This is Aliyah," Ethan said, nodding toward her.

Anna turned to her and beamed. "We've heard so much about you! Sorry we have to meet you under such... circumstances."

They moved to the living room with its soaring beamed ceiling and stone fireplace, and there were more introductions. Ethan was surprised to discover that Aliyah's father was much shorter than he was—he had the impression from talking to her that he was a big, powerful man, while the man he saw was short, graying, and tired-looking. Aliyah's mother was warm and sincere, and her eyes sparkled.

"You are a handsome young man, Ethan," she said. "Aliyah didn't tell us you were such a fox."

Ethan blushed and looked over at Aliyah, who rolled her eyes.

The discussion turned to the latest news. "The town gateway to Earth just quit working," Ethan's father said. "The AIs are saying that at the current rate, we'll lose access to substrate programs completely in a few days. The evacuation gateways are still working, but we'd better get moving."

"Have you heard anything about the evacuation planet?" Aliyah's father asked.

"It was rejected for colonization because it is in the middle of an ice age, but for our purposes there's a large island near the equator that's warm enough—like Scotland on a bad day. Newly-christened as Asgard. They've replicated shelters and supplies, and we should be okay there for a few months."

"So, cold," Aliyah's father said. "We don't have any warm clothes."

"I'm sure they'll have some waiting for us," Ethan's father said. "And I can pack some more of ours."

"Okay," Ethan said, "what's our plan? Shouldn't we leave right now?"

"It's almost midnight, Ethan," his father said. "I am packing supplies in the old trailer we came here with, planning to head out tomorrow morning."

Ethan looked at Aliyah, who nodded back. "I don't think we should wait. The gateways could close at any time. And the coordinates of the evacuation planets aren't available to our Guardians, so we have to cross through a gateway, or I'd set up the transfer from here."

"That was to keep the locations as secret as possible," Aliyah added. "They're encrypted and only the gateway program has access to the real coordinates. We were afraid the Shrivers could read them from our records if they were in the usual database."

"We'll only be gone for a few days," Anna said. "Or so they say. No need to pack much."

"And you believe them?" Ethan's father said. "Of course they'll say that. But it could be a long wait there."

Ethan considered how to break it to them. "It could be forever. There is a chance Jefferson and Earth will be so wrecked that no one will be able to come looking for us for a long time. Years. We need to be prepared to survive without replicators and transport."

Ethan caught the stricken look in Aliyah's mother's eyes, and went on: "But in the worst case, there's a survival package waiting there in stasis that will be thawed if it loses contact with New Earth. It will have everything we need to live independently." He decided not to mention that the survival pod included copies of himself and Aliyah, and so there might end up being extras of them.

Ethan gradually wore them down, pointing out that if the gateways closed in a few hours, any additional preparation would be pointless.

Finally Aliyah's mother sighed and took Ethan by the shoulders. "You two understand this far better than we do. I think we should do what you think is best. And so we should leave now. I brought coffee and sandwiches for everyone in our truck, so we're ready to go."

They went outside, and Ethan's father brought the truck and its trailer out of the garage. He stuck his head out the window and said, "Get in, everybody."

"I'll go with you," Aliyah said, following Ethan to

the back seat. Her parents got in their truck, and the caravan started slowly down the driveway in the dark. Everything seemed normal, though they could see a group of cars on the road ahead of them.

As they got closer to town, they were joined by more and more cars and pickup trucks with hastily-packed cargo. The evacuation gateway was lit up, and crowds were lined up waiting to go through; the gateway to Los Angeles was gone. They pulled up to a line twenty cars long, and there were four lines feeding into the gateway. Groups on foot were crossing as well, and they could see gray daylight on the other side and a group of vehicles struggling to make their way through gravelled mud.

"Great," Ethan's father said. "Another raw planet to pioneer. This time, freezing cold."

Big men dressed in fur-trimmed parkas were waving the cars through. As they got closer, the men pulled their hoods back and Ethan realized they were both large women, with blond hair and blue eyes. "The Valkyries have come to welcome us to Asgard!" he said, achieving a groan from Aliyah, packed in beside him in the back seat.

They were fifth in line when the lights down the street flickered and went out, and moments later, the lights in the plaza went out. Ethan heard a collective moan and saw fear in the eyes of the people waiting to cross into the brightness of the gateway. The car about to go through revved its engine and spun its wheels in the mud when it reached the other side, and everything stopped as the Valkyries tried to push the car out of the mud.

A woman's voice from the air said, "Ethan, we have detected a Shriver vessel just outside the atmosphere. Missiles aimed at your position are incoming. You have less than a minute to get across." Ethan could hear others reacting to similar messages from their Guardians, and car doors began to open.

"Get out and run across, everyone!" Ethan shouted, and opened the door. He pulled Aliyah out with him, and his father and Anna reacted too slowly, so he opened their doors and pulled them out. "No time. Run!"

Vehicles were abandoned, and people on foot were crossing the gateway only to be trapped in the narrow space behind the stuck vehicle. A woman fell, and others tried to help her up, but they were overwhelmed by the people pushing across behind them.

Ethan made sure his and Aliyah's parents went through the gateway in front of them. Aliyah's mother stumbled and fell across the trunk of the stuck car. Ethan reached her and took her by the waist; she was light and he was able to drag her to the front of the car.

A brilliant flash lit the gateway behind them, and Ethan felt the back of his neck burn. Then it was cold and dark. "Guardian?" Ethan shouted. "What just happened?"

But no one answered.

The Battle of Jupiter

From the UDF control room on New Earth, Justin watched the screen as the three clumps of Shriver ships joined up just beyond Jupiter and decelerated. Their course corrections resulted in a new time for the UDF's fleet to launch from the surface of the jagged moon Himalia. The human crews were texting on background channels, which filled a third screen with mostly tension-relieving jokes. Nelson projected a countdown clock on one of the other channels, now showing seven minutes until launch.

"How are we doing on substrate program integrity?" Steve asked.

Nelson's voice came from somewhere near the screen: "We have lost almost thirty percent of our capabilities, so far mostly gateways and some of the earliest programs. Socrates lost a module and has withdrawn from his original program space. I have set up extra copies for failover if necessary. Power and replicators on backup."

"Rate of loss?" Justin was considering how they'd do without power.

"A few percent an hour. At this rate nearly all of our substrate capabilities will be gone in another two days."

"Understood." Justin turned to Steve. "Are the generators ready?"

"Yes," Steve said. "We pulled them out of storage and tested them last week. This building will have power even if we lose the substrate."

The countdown reached zero, and status messages from UDF ships scrolled by on other screens.

"A few ships had engine failures and remain grounded on Himalia," Nelson said. "All two hundred human-crewed ships on course. Over a million AI-piloted ships executing to intersect targets in thirty-three minutes."

"Any signs of evasive action?"

"The Shrivers surely saw the takeoffs, but nothing has changed yet."

"Get me a voice line to Captain Estevez," Justin said.

"Yes, Commander?" Estevez' voice sounded strained. "We're still under heavy gees."

"Just a supplemental to your orders. You're to hang back and record everything like mad, but not to risk closing on a Shriver vessel. We need the record of the battle as much as we need a victory. And your crew's reactions are just as important. Your first goal is to survive, second to witness. We may lose contact at any moment, and you are to follow radio orders from the AI mesh network if that happens."

"Yes, Sir. Emote like mad. We get it."

Nelson broke in. "Shrivers spreading out their line. New orders going out to match courses."

"Estevez, you got that?"

"Yessir, got them. Firing attitude jets."

"Best of luck, Captain. Out."

Justin got up and paced the room. "We were able to overwhelm the simulated Shrivers with numbers. But now we know the Shriver ships are more capable than we simulated, and may have been hardened further just for us."

"But there are only eight left. Fewer than our simulations," Steve said.

"Nelson, what do you think our chances are?"

"Integrating more data. There—my best guess is a ninety percent chance at least one Shriver ship will survive to reach Earth. The forcefields we set up are weakening as the underlying substrate programs fail. By the time they reach Earth, there will be little to stop them."

They waited as the cloud of UDF gnats approached the line of Shriver vessels onscreen.

The lights flickered. "Power lost, generators have taken over," Nelson commented. "Our remote viewing stations are going out one by one."

"How are communications?" Justin asked.

"Down to forty percent of our ships able to contact us via substrate. The rest are depending on packet radio relayed by the ones still in direct contact. At the current rate, we will lose all substrate contact with them around the time they close on the Shrivers."

"How will that effect our strategy?" Steve said.

"It won't," Nelson answered."I have distributed copies of myself throughout the AIs in each ship. The only thing I won't be able to do is consult with you—the light-speed delay to our fleet is around thirty-four minutes now. I'll send encrypted radio reports after our substrate access is cut off."

"Okay," Justin said. "It's not likely my input would be helpful in any case."

"Nevertheless, I value it," Nelson said. "Your responses are less predictable, and in a battle between AIs, predictability could be deadly."

"In other words, you're saying optimal strategies

might be what they have planned for, so doing something stupid might work better."

"Just so. I have tried to build some noise into my algorithms to make my own actions less predictable, but it's the actions I would never even consider that might confound them."

"Well, do your best," Justin said. "How long until encounter?"

"They are still changing their courses. Probably twenty-one minutes. The degradation of our substrate communications is increasing exponentially. Now down to a handful of direct contacts… now none. We are on radio backup, which means it will be fifty minutes before we get any battle reports."

Justin looked at Steve. "Break for lunch? I have to hit the head."

"So do I. Stress makes me have to pee."

Justin stopped on the way back from the bathroom to pick up meal trays from the storage room. There had been no need for cooking for years, so the microwave they used to have in the lab had been removed. Cold meals would have to do.

They ate in silence as the displays showed nothing new. The clock ticked down. Whatever was going to happen around Jupiter was probably mostly over. "Nelson, any updates?"

"Starting to get status reports sent before loss of substrate communications. Nothing unusual, further maneuvering by the Shrivers. UDF ships still on intersect courses. Human crews in good spirits."

"Update the displays as soon as you have new information."

"Receiving a transmission via relay on Phobos—audio part next..." Nelson said.

"Commander, this is Estevez. Sending everything we've got via radio. Enemy began missile attacks early, we've suffered thirty percent loss of AI ships. Enclosing maneuvers failing as Shiver ships evade us. Railguns ineffective, projectiles evaporated by x-ray lasers. Taking fire ourselves. Our free-electron lasers don't affect them."

The displays began updating as data came in. They watched in silence as the bogies sidestepped the traps meant to enclose them. The sparkle as UDF ships exploded into vapor made it hard to follow the cloud's movements. One expanding dot of light where a Shriver ship had been gave them hope.

"Got one! One of our AI ships got close enough to blow them away," Captain Estevez said. "Now—" And the voice went silent.

"Lost the Phobos relay connection," Nelson said. "Another twenty minutes until signals received on Earth. We have a dozen relays there still operating."

"Thanks," Justin said.

Steve shrugged. "We've done our best. If we don't stop all of them, Earth is done."

Justin felt ill. He had realized some time ago that they stood little chance against the Shrivers, and no chance against the First who ultimately used them as a tool. But the imminent destruction of everything he had ever known made him feel—alone. His parents and most of the people had been evacuated, but still…

"I know it looks bad, but remember—we have back-ups," Steve said. "When we get the substrate back, we can restore the Earth."

"*If* we get the substrate back. And after a billion people have died horrible deaths. On the whole, I'd rather we had been left alone."

They spent the next twenty minutes responding to messages from Earth military who had been able to share all the data they had seen, but had questions and ideas. Justin triaged the queries by rank of the sender, and sent a general reply to the rest. When the next word from Jupiter came in via Earth relays, they were ready.

The video message began to play. "Captain Estevez reporting. We've been busy." The displays started to update as new data came through. The green cloud of UDF ships was smaller, and the bright red dots of Shriver ships were pulling away from them on their way to Earth. "We suc-ceeded in destroying two more." Estevez choked up before regaining his voice. "I'm sending the recordings from Captain St. Pierre's ship, and I'll finish this report after we've stabilized the leak in the fuel line."

Steve clicked on the next file before it had finished transferring.

The screen showed what appeared to be the same cockpit, but with a different figure in the chair, suited up. They could see his face through the faceplate, which had started to fog up around the edges.

"Captain St. Pierre with an update. We stayed to the rear of our enclosure formation, but the Shriver ships changed course at the last minute and our ship and Captain Guttke's are now being attacked by two Shriver ships. By some miracle our free-electron lasers are still working, but we're on backup power and the railguns are out of projectiles. The only reason they're not firing on us is because we're along the line between the two Shriver ships, so any misses might hit one of theirs." Another suited figure—a woman—entered the frame and gave them a thumbs-up sign. "All right then. The crew agrees we only have a few minutes to make a difference here, and we're going for it. You told us to improvise, and we're pretty sure we're doomed anyway, so here goes our final fuck-you to the Shrivers… Ship, on my command aim for the nearest Shriver ship and fire engines at max. Get as close as you can and detonate the warhead."

The second figure belted in, the captain said, "Position us for the burn." They heard the attitude jets firing. "Start program."

"Firing main engine," said a neutral masculine voice. The captain's face sagged under acceleration. "Thirty seconds." The captain reached over and held his mate's gloved hand.

"They see us. Incoming," the captain said. The camera shook. "Hull is ablating." The porthole behind them flared white. "We can't take much more of this." He looked over to his mate and squeezed her hand. "Ship, detonate

NOW."

The recording ended in a flash of light, then a dark screen.

The next file was the followup report from Captain Estevez. "I'm sorry to report that two human-crewed ships were lost when they were trapped between two Shriver ships. One of them—Captain St. Pierre's—succeeded in detonating its warhead close enough to take out an enemy. The other tried to get away as per orders, but they were hit by multiple missiles. We have lost ninety percent of the AI-crewed ships as well, with only one more Shriver ship destroyed. They caught on to our massing tactics quickly and took evasive action to avoid the surround maneuver, so they were able to pick us off with lasers and missiles. Our free-electron lasers took out a lot of their missiles before they reached us, but not enough. We're out of fuel and they're out of range." He paused and looked tired as he looked down at a screen. "Sorry to report we have failed. Five Shriver ships headed for Earth, ETA 2 days, at around 1310 GMT. Only one shows any sign of damage, and it's lagging behind just slightly. We have transmitted all the data we've collected, including the final moments of Captain St. Pierre's heroic sacrifice. We understand that you can't retrieve us until you have the substrate programs back up. In the meantime, we're all using what fuel we do have to set a course around Jupiter that will send us inward toward Earth."

Justin turned to Steve. "They don't have enough supplies to last that long, and he knows it. Is there any way at all we can collect those people off the ships?"

Steve turned to a console and typed some commands. A long list of programs scrolled down, all of them in red. "I'm afraid… wait, here's a transport program still working. It was set up for internal transport on New Earth, but I think I can hand-set its parameters—yes, I can."

"How does that help? They're scattered through space with no reference objects—"

"It just so happens each of those ships carries a big nuclear warhead. Nelson can search for that, check for human crews, and feed the coordinates into the transport program. It can set the ships down on the ballfields in the park."

And so it was that New Earth gained a small fleet of spaceships. Nelson reported the rescue complete in twenty minutes.

Justin looked out the window and over toward the park, where he could just see the tops of the closest ships above the hedges. "Do we have radio access?" he asked Steve.

"Sorry, no. Never occurred to me to have a relay here."

Justin shrugged. "Nelson, send someone over to help them down from the hatches. They'll need ladders."

Asgard

Ethan and his father put up a second tent in the area marked out for them. Asgard now had three hundred thousand inhabitants in camps scattered along this coastal plain, with supply dumps for each. Hastily-organized crews of volunteers helped people find tents and supplies. The plain was dotted with scrubby shrubs, and the constant cold wind and intermittent drizzle didn't help anyone's spirits. Rocks and runoff channels left few flat spots for the tents. The air had a sharp ozone smell, and the cracking sounds of ice shifting in the glacier looming over the plain increased in frequency as the day wore on.

Their three tents had neighbors to the south originally from the Afghan enclave in Fremont, California, while to the north, the extended O'Brien family from Boston took up three tents. One of the O'Brien lads had dropped by to help explain how the tents worked—the instructions were smudged, and the help was appreciated. Further down the row of tents, a family from Texas had set up a pot full of chili on a makeshift fire pit in front, where people stopped frequently for a bite and a chat.

As Ethan and his father finished putting up the tent, a man with a thick red walrus moustache and wearing a yellow safety vest over his parka walked up to them. "Sergeant Brendon McClure, US Army. Checking in with everyone—we're supposed to keep civil order, so if you see anyone committing a crime, hold them for us until you can reach the aid station to report it."

"Oh, okay," Ethan's father said. "Will do. I think people are still in shock."

"We're officially under martial law. Though to tell you the truth, it's not entirely clear it's legal. But they sent us here, and we intend to keep order during this emergency."

"Sounds fair enough. This is my son, Ethan."

The sergeant checked his clipboard. "I have you down. The Johnsons are with you?"

Ethan pointed to the next tent. "The Johnsons are in that tent, me and Aliyah Johnson in the one beyond."

"Aha, you two are an item!" The sergeant winked. "Good that you ended up together, no?"

Aliyah looked up from where she had been unpacking a box and came toward them. "I'm Aliyah."

The sergeant looked her over. "And quite a nice couple you two make. Well, if you're all happy here, I need to make my appointed rounds. God help us all, and leave a note at the aid station if you need anything. There's a rumor we have cell phone stations in the supplies, but nobody's found them yet."

"Thank you, Sergeant McClure. We appreciate your stopping by," Ethan's father said.

Ethan turned to Aliyah. "I'm beat. Shall we sleep for awhile? The sun's going down finally." Rumor had it that the day was 29 hours long, which had been another factor in rejecting Asgard for colonization.

"Sure," she said. "I've put down the pads and set up the sleeping bags for everyone." They excused themselves and made their way to their tent.

They took their clothes off as quickly as possible. "Brrrr!" Ethan said, shivering as he folded himself into the sleeping bag. "Say, did you consider zipping them together so we could share body heat?"

"I did," Aliyah said, "but they weren't designed for that. Zippers only on the right."

Ethan contorted his body to get closer to hers, and stretched to kiss her. "Good night."

"I hope so. You snored last time."

"Harrumph. Lies." Soon Ethan was asleep.

Some time later, Ethan began dreaming of flashes and shock waves. A charred body hit him from behind, and he didn't want to look in case it was Aliyah. He woke up, his heart racing. He could hear Aliyah breathing normally beside him, and he slowly fell back to sleep.

When they woke, it was still dark, though the eastern horizon was brightening. They got up and made their way to the latrines and washed up. Breakfast happened with the aid of a small fire to warm the rations—stockpiled US Army MREs would be a staple, since they wouldn't spoil. Anna had found coffee and a pan, so they were treated to unfiltered coffee in enameled steel cups.

After cleanup, Ethan said, "Aliyah and I want to go look through the depot again. Just in case we missed anything the first time through."

"Okay, kids," Mr. Turner said. "Bring back more food. And more sweaters—the parkas aren't quite warm enough by themselves. We need layers."

"Sure thing, Dad," Ethan said, and they left.

The camp was coming to life, most people waking as the sun came up. A boy passed them, running in sweats. When they reached the supply depot, there was a line to get in.

One irate man was arguing with the woman attendant, who wore the new symbol of authority, the yellow safety vest. "I'm sorry, Sir," she said. "We gave you two days of food rations yesterday. You can't have any more until tomorrow."

The man turned, still red-faced, but when he saw the faces of the others waiting, he calmed down. "Well, I didn't know," he said. "Guess I'll come back tomorrow."

The attendant checked her clipboard as people reached the front of the line, and most were let inside the tent, to the front counter. When Ethan and Aliyah reached the front of the line, the attendant leafed through several pages. "Oh, here you are. Six people. We can release another day's ration to you, so take this token and go in." She pressed a plastic token with a 6 on it into Ethan's hand. "Give them this."

Inside, they waited again for counter space. Volunteers took requests and ran to the bins to get the MREs needed. Other items seemed to be off limits. When they got a man's attention, Ethan said, "I was wanting to look for extra clothing and toiletries. We were allowed in yesterday to get what we needed…"

"That was yesterday. Orders of the Colonel, everything is rationed for the duration. If you want something irregular, you have to fill out this form and we'll get back to you when we can."

"I see," Aliyah said, giving Ethan a look. "Well, thank you." She stuffed some of the MREs into her pockets while Ethan did the same. "Let's go."

Outside, she stopped and looked back at the crowd around the depot tent. "We got used to no limits. And now we're back to the Stone Age, with ranks and military government and paper forms."

"A reasonable way to handle a tough situation," Ethan said. "This could go on for a long time, and that pile of supplies is huge, but if they let us all rummage through it, it'll end up in private hoards and soon people will be fighting and looting when it runs out."

"The survival pod will thaw if we're going to be stranded here," Aliyah pointed out. The camp was bordered on the south by a silvery stasis wall ten stories high. Inside, frozen, was a copy of the center of the New Earth settlement, with everything necessary to restart civilization —generators, quantum computers, and most importantly, people. Steves and programmers and scientists enough to reload all of the substrate software and reboot human civilization.

"It's supposed to thaw if its control program loses touch with New Earth for more than a week," Ethan said. "So we wait. We should have copies in there, too, if it comes to that. I don't think Steve thought about that when he created them."

"Worse things have happened. I always wondered what it would be like to have a twin."

Battle Report

Captain Estevez and Maddy Rahama of NASA were seated as honored guests in the Council chamber. Justin, Samantha, and the councillors who remained listened as Captain Estevez recounted yesterday's battle. "We destroyed three of the eight ships and damaged another. So four full-strength Shriver destroyers will reach Earth in just over eighteen hours. As we have seen, even one can devastate a planet, given time."

Justin turned to Steve. "How many substrate connections to Earth are still working?"

"As of an hour ago, none. We're blind."

"The last data from Earth came in two hours ago," Maddy said. "The evacuations have been thorough in urban areas, less so in the countryside—few reporters have stayed behind to document the invasion. Military reports speak of chaos in some cities, with stay-behinds coming out of their boltholes to loot and murder. The last evacuation gateways are failing. Lots of stories of heroism and kindness as well, but none of it will matter."

"We've been lucky on New Earth so far," Justin said, "but given the widespread publicity linking this planet to 51 Pegasi and its proximity to Earth, it seems unlikely they don't know where we are. We have to expect to be attacked soon. Do we have any evacuation possibilities?"

Steve checked something on his computer. "I don't think so. The program I used yesterday to rescue our ship crews has been corrupted, and that was the last operational transport possibility. I've tried to upload a new program, but the boot loader has also been damaged. We're unable to access the substrate until I can upload a new boot loader using a quantum computer."

"So we're trapped here," Maddy said. "What more can we do?"

"Very little," Justin said. "Prepare to defend ourselves. We have the weapons on the UDF ships in the park, which can send up a defensive barrage. But I don't expect that will even slow them down."

"Would it do any good to disperse? How about underground?" Prof. Wilson asked.

"We created an underground bunker in the mountains nearby a few months ago," Justin said, "but we've seen what the Shrivers have done elsewhere, and they target underground facilities first with deep-drilling bombs. There's been no point in moving to that facility until now, and now it's too late—we'd need substrate transport to do it."

"So we're down to generators and diesel fuel to power this building," Ben Ramirez said. "We've lost the water supply, which came to us via substrate, and the sewers are backing up without outlets. It's beginning to smell. And at any moment we could have bombs raining down on us."

"But looking on the bright side, we're still here," Samantha said. "And maybe they don't know where we are."

Justin looked back at her with a weary smile. "It's

possible. But it would be unwise to bet that way."

Earth

Wendy had sent her husband and daughter through the evacuation gateway off Central Park, but delayed joining them to be sure her parents in LA had made it to safety—she was on the phone with them as they tried to evacuate. They had been delayed by riots in South Central blocking the evacuation gateway there, and had decided to drive to Long Beach to try that one. Traffic on the freeway had stopped, and sniper fire from the hills nearby started shattering windows all around them. Their car crawled along the shoulder until they reached a fence that gave way so they could exit to a parking lot and make their way by back roads to the gateway. Wendy had kept her mother on the phone until they had crossed.

And when she got to the evacuation gateway in Central Park, it was gone.

A crowd of angry people buzzed where the gateway had been. Cars had run through grass of the park, leaving torn-up sod and muddy tracks. Wendy stayed away from the crowd and edged back across Fifth to a safer side street. She tried a query: "Guardian? Are you there?" but there was no response. She checked her cell phone—no data. A surprising number of systems had become dependent on the substrate working, and the nearly-empty city was quieter than a Sunday morning, with only a lone siren in the distance.

She made her way back to their apartment by back streets. The elevator still worked, so there was power, at least. She checked her computer; the internet was gone.

Samantha had told her about Steve's backup of Earth. It sounded crazy, but the entire surface of the planet and everyone on it had been copied en masse and stored away on some form-fitting planet a few weeks earlier, so even if she didn't survive, there was a good chance her copy would be thawed and be able to take care of her daughter and husband. She laughed quietly—*I'm a dead-end!*

It was late afternoon and the sun was low in the western sky over the park. She realized she was hungry. There were some water crackers left over from a party and the fridge had half a tuna sandwich. She was eating when the hums of the apartment died—the power had gone out. She went over to the window and looked down. The few cars on the streets were cautiously proceeding through intersections without stoplights. Somewhere in the distance there was a crash of crumpling sheet metal and glass as someone driving their own car misjudged the situation.

But other than that, true quiet had finally come to New York.

She checked the deadbolts and went back to their bedroom to get the pistol George kept in the closet safe. It was kept loaded, but she checked to make sure. Then she went back to the living room and set the gun out on the coffee table on a blue silk cloth. She sat on the couch and looked at it—a beautiful object, really, black and finely-machined. A woman screamed outside, but she didn't bother to look.

When the missiles came arcing out of the sky and the fireballs bloomed above Manhattan, she was looking at her art and her bookshelves when they brightened to searing white before bursting into flame.

Tribunal Prep

"Katherine, wake up." Aurora's voice woke her from a nightmare—she and Danny were trapped in the burning house, and their father was trying to reach them but driven back by gouts of flame.

"Aurora?" She opened her eyes. Her room was cool and dark.

And then she was back in the throne room, sitting in a chair by the fireplace. Aurora stood above her, looking concerned. "I'm sorry to interrupt your normal routine," she said, "but it's time. The Tribunal has finally agreed to meet to review our request for emergency intervention. The Shrivers have reached your Earth and are destroying every living thing on it."

"Kind of them to notice, but a bit late?" Kat rubbed the sleep out of her eyes, which finally focused.

"They are politicians. They put everything off if there's any chance of losing face by making a wrong decision. And then they claim it's too late. Well, it's not, and we're going to embarrass them by showing a wider audience the suffering of your people, which they'd rather no one saw."

"What do you want me to do?"

"They are reviewing selected mems now. In a few minutes, they will call you to testify."

"Give me some time to wake up." She yawned again. "How is it that I'm sleepy as a simulation?"

"The state I copied was half-asleep, so even in simulation it takes time for you to fully awaken. Your body in the real world is still largely asleep, and will remain so for the few seconds that pass there while you spend hours here."

"Oh. So what should I say?"

"I have written a statement for you," Aurora said, handing her a tablet. "You should look it over and change anything you think doesn't fairly represent your people. I have already testified, and I can tell you that Queen Mab is quite sympathetic, having uploaded under similar circumstances. The Library of Yern has been neutral. First of the First may be hostile—he helped set up the Shrivers when the universe was young, and tends to be with those who fear new uploads."

"Three people vote? I thought…"

"The three Tribunes question and speak. The independent First vote if they wish to. The Revenant will express the opinion of the conjoined millions who are no longer individuals. Then the Tribunes will decide, but it's very rare they go against the larger vote."

"Sounds complicated." Kat looked down at the tablet in her lap. She was still having trouble making sense of the words.

"It's political. The Tribunes need the support of the voters to stay in office, so they tend to act to satisfy their faction. Queen Mab supports the Vivants who support her, while Library is associated with scientists. First of First represents the security-minded."

"How do the independents and the Revenant feel about uploads?"

"The independents are just that—they will tend to be more supportive so long as they are not the ones being asked to give up cell space. The Revenant are the real problem—there are more of them than ever, with no central ego or consciousness, only a mass of dreamers who have chosen to forget there is anything outside their simulated homes. Their votes are cast by proxy AIs, who are biased against any action that might someday threaten their dreaming clients. And—this is not to go beyond you—I have reason to believe the Tribunes are gradually reducing the substrate cells the Revenant are allowed, which is one of the only sources of free space we have to offer newcomers. The Revenant are like the dead in a graveyard—the intelligences who chose to return to a simulation of their former lives are not contributing any longer, but take up space. If their AI proxies knew we were cutting back on their space, there'd be a revolt. And they could do some damage, since they control over half of our available space and computing resources."

"Okay." Kat tried to start reading the script again. "How long do I have to go over this?"

Aurora looked into the air. "Umm, about ten years our time, a day of yours. You don't have to memorize it, reading from the tablet will be fine."

"And what happens when they start asking me questions?"

"I suggest you tell the truth. Shaded, of course, by your need to persuade them to allow you to live."

Kat read the first page and grimaced. "This makes us sound pathetic."

Aurora pursed her lips. "You are pleading for your lives. Your attitude should be meek. Why don't you read the whole thing and make annotations where you'd like to adjust the tone to reflect your pride—I'll help you strike the right balance. I'll be back tomorrow your time and we'll go over it before the Tribunal meets."

Kat woke up again in her room, the morning light still dim but bright enough to see she was holding a tablet exactly like the one Aurora had given her.

Dylan

The last thing Dylan remembered was talking to the Djinn. He had agreed to the deal—be copied and used to destroy his enemies. His eyes opened. He was lying on a cushioned surface. Others were sleeping on both sides of him, and he propped himself up on one elbow to survey the room.

Which was vast—it seemed to disappear into fog rather than end in a wall. And as far as he could see, Dylans. Some had already stood up and were stretching. He eyed the nearest—quite handsome, really. It was somehow different than looking in a mirror. He understood he was just a copy, and not the one who would go on to live as ruler of the simulated Earth in the substrate. But somehow this was fine with him. A little voice told him they were mucking with his thoughts, but he suppressed it.

A voice in his head told him to be patient. Dylan's requested revenge scenario would be played out. They would be provided with indigenous equipment and weaponry. Each Dylan would be joined by his favorite lieutenants Yousif and Saad to form a fighting unit, and they were to be landed on New Earth in an hour. They were to find and kill Justin, Samantha, and as many of the other old rebels as they could, in as gruesome a manner as they could manage, with full sensory recordings for the review of the original Dylan, as per their agreement. Then they would be retrieved, and the planet would be sterilized by bombardment.

The voice told him to stand and face the light at the other end of the hall, so he did. They were commanded to walk forward slowly. Eventually piles of weapons and vests appeared on either side of his line. He picked up a vest and put it on; it fit perfectly. The front held grenades and side carriers holstered knives and a pistol. He picked up an impressive-looking automatic rifle and slung it over his shoulder. They knew him well enough to have provided a full-length mirror as the line approached an exit; every one of him paused to admire the look.

On the other side of the door was a hanger full of

troop transports, with other lines of copies of Yousif and Saad snaking in from all sides. The lines converged so that as they walked forward, a line of Yousifs approached on one side, and a line of Saads on the other. The voice in his head told him to join hands with them and go left, and so they did. They saw a green light over one of the transports and were directed to board. Three other teams were already belted in, so they took the last row. The hatch closed and Dylan felt the craft shudder as it lifted, then accelerated forward.

Dylan realized he could speak now. He turned his head right, toward Yousif, and said, "Good to see you guys. I got the band back together for one more gig. You understand what we're supposed to do?"

Yousif looked back at him and nodded. "My Muslim side sees this as *Jahannam,* possibly the first level of Hell. A Sufi might guess it is the *Barzakh,* a kind of limbo in between worlds. Completion of our task will redeem us so we can enter the true Paradise."

"What does your American side say?"

"We're screwed, and as usual you run the show." Yousif laughed and scratched himself.

Dylan turned to his left to address Saad. "Do you understand what we're doing?"

Saad's brown eyes were sad. "The voice from above has told me. We are to join you in killing your enemies. Eternal reward awaits if we succeed."

"Close enough," Dylan said.

The front of the transport was one big viewscreen,

and after they passed silently through the ship's outer walls, the view of the planet below almost brought tears to his eyes—so green and blue and Earthlike. The line of sunrise crept along the continent below, illuminating the bay they were heading toward, and as they grew closer, he spotted a grid pattern of streets and buildings surrounding a harbor filled with boats. This was what Justin and friends had done with their camp in ten years—he was impressed. Shame he was going to have to destroy it all.

D-Day

Justin and Samantha were eating breakfast together before the kids woke up—a cherished part of their routine. Justin got up from the table and took their plates back to the kitchen.

"Justin," said a voice—Eddie's; it took him a moment to recognize it—"there's a Shriver ship in low orbit. It must have been stealthed enough to be missed by your sensors."

Samantha looked up from her reading, alarmed.

"When did this happen?" Justin asked.

"Moments ago. And—the ship is releasing smaller vessels. They have trajectories indicating intention to land here. ETA about half an hour."

"For whatever reason, they've chosen to engage us personally. Any thoughts on why they didn't just start bombing?"

"They want *us*," Samantha said. "To capture us for

some purpose. We need to get out of here, now."

"Samantha is correct," Eddie said. "The only explanation for the change in tactics is a desire to give them something their usual anonymous attack wouldn't—capturing you intact or killing you in a more personal manner. I agree you should—correction. I am in communication with Jim McDonald. Remaining security personnel are to report to the Armory for outfitting. The plan is to set up defensive positions when the location of their landing is known, and to resist by any means available."

"I'll head on down," Justin said. "Samantha will take the kids up to the bunker in the mountains."

"I'm sorry to report that Nelson, Socrates, and your other substrate programs are now completely off-line. I took the liberty of backing Nelson and Socrates up in my own storage, but they can't be run without access to your APIs. I am not affected because I was set up by others and have no direct links to your software."

"Can you help us through this?"

"I am not allowed to interfere with the Shrivers directly, but I can be your eyes and ears."

"Good, keep an eye out for us and report everything back to me." Justin turned and embraced Samantha. "Get the kids up and get going. Take the ATV up there and wait for me. If I don't come by tonight, assume we've lost and blow the explosives to collapse the entrance tunnel."

"We're waiting for you. No matter what."

"Sweet, but save the kids any way you can. You know what to do. I love you."

"I love you, too," she said, beginning to sob. She turned and ran down the hall toward the bedrooms.

Justin grabbed his coat and left for the office. As he loped down the hill toward the government buildings, he scanned the cloudless blue sky, but nothing was visible yet.

When he reached the Armory—just a back room in the original community building—Jim McDonald was handing out rifles to anyone who came in.

"Do we know where they're going to land?" Justin asked.

"They're headed directly for us, in about fifteen minutes," he said. "I sent the UDF crews back to their ships, since their weapons might be of some use."

"Good thinking. How are we communicating?"

Jim held up a walkie-talkie. "We had copied a bunch of these, which is good since substrate communications are down. Old tech still works."

"Let me have that. What channel gets me the UDF ships?"

"They're on channel two. Our people are on channel one. I was just talking to Estevez, so it's already on two."

Justin fingered the large transmit button. "This is Commander Smith. Captain Estevez, come in."

"Estevez here."

"Do you have them on radar?"

"Yes. Around a hundred small ships—size of a dump truck, probably landers. Best guess at landing site is right here where we are—in the park."

"Can you take them out?"

"They're just entering the atmosphere. Our best chance is when they're less than a kilometer away. We haven't been able to reload our railguns, but we're fully charged for lasers. Orders?"

"If they wanted to bomb us, they already would have. So prepare your lasers to hit them all at the same time at the height you think best. I don't want any of them to have any warning, in the unlikely event they don't know you guys are there."

"If we do hit them, the wreckage will make a mess of your town."

"We should be so lucky. Gotta go."

Justin clipped the radio to his belt and picked up a rifle from the counter. "Do I know how to use this?"

Jim laughed. "You did fine last time. I've taken off the fancy laser scopes—just simple sights for fast shooting. Pull hard on the trigger for full auto. Remember the kickback. Most important thing is to not get hit yourself. Take shots only when you're safe behind cover. Don't get separated from your group."

"Have you seen Steve? Where are the others?"

"The Steves are armed and waiting in their labs to see where they can be useful—guess they're defending what really matters to them. Mothers and children have been evacuated to the bunker."

"Who am I with?" More men—and one woman, Maddy—were waiting behind him.

"I'll go with you. James here can handle the latecomers," Jim said, gesturing to his young assistant. "Let's pick out another six or so and go set up a defensive position."

Maddy raised her hand. "Pick me. I can shoot."

"Okay, then. And you and you, and you three," Jim said, pointing at the next men in line. One was a Grey Tribe programmer over fifty, but the others were younger security staff. "Pick up a radio and a weapon and follow us. Kid, bring the ammo."

The group began to move. As they left the building, Justin looked up and scanned the eastern sky. He thought he could see black dots not far from the rising sun, but it hurt to look.

They took up a position in the cafe overlooking the park. Four men pulling together were able to topple the serving counter so its granite top faced the park. "What we need is sandbags," Jim mused. "What's around we can use for shielding?"

A quick search turned up nothing. Then Maddy called them outside. "These potted trees. We get them inside and put them in front of the counter." The group moved, and in another minute of struggling to move them, they had lined up a row of pots fronting the counter.

"It will have to do. Look," Jim said, pointing back toward the park.

The black dots were visibly growing. Justin's walkie-talkie spoke: "Firing on all targets… now."

A loud hum filled the air, and the black dots turned glowing red. Then the dots released missiles, arrowing toward the ships in the park. Explosions rocked them, and the plate glass windows of the cafe blew in beside them. Justin couldn't hear anything but the high whine of nerve damage.

They looked cautiously over the counter. The landers were coming in, the closest landing just across the street. Its rear door opened, and bulkily armed men began to come down the gangway. The lead group started to move toward them.

Justin's walkie-talkie buzzed. He put it to his ear and could just make out the words. "Captain Estevez reporting. One lander disabled and crashed. We have no contact with three of our ships, presumed destroyed."

"Get your people out, Captain. That's an order. Find cover away from your ships and stay safe. We'll be busy here."

"Yessir. We'll deal."

The men were getting closer. He recognized one of them, and a chill spread through him. "Jim, the center guy —and the one behind him—do you see what I see?"

"Looks like our old friend Dylan. And more of them coming. Shall we take them out?"

"Let them get a bit closer. Catch them in the middle of the street where there's no cover."

"See the grenades on their vests?" Jim said. "Best take them out before they get close enough to throw them.
"

"Gotcha." He rested the rifle on the granite edge and looked through the notch towards the oncoming men.

"Ready, everyone," Jim said. "Aim." The youngest

man finally stopped fumbling. "Fire!"

Justin squeezed the trigger. The first shot surprised him, then there were more. One of the men in his view dropped—not a Dylan. He aimed for the next Dylan, and squeezed the trigger harder. He could see the Dylan jerk every time a bullet hit him, but he didn't go down. He tried again, aiming for the head. It was horrifying—and grimly satisfying—when Dylan's head jerked back and part of his cheek was blown off. That Dylan fell backwards.

Most of the attackers had taken ground or hiding behind trees, and they were firing steadily. Bullets hit the pots full of soil with a thump or cracked against the granite. Chips of stone and glass were raining down from above.

Justin shouted at Jim next to him, "They're pinned down. But there are ten times as many of them as us. Did we bring any grenades?"

"Nope. Never thought we'd need'em. Got some Claymore mines in the box, but those have to be detonated close—no chance we could get one out there without getting shot."

Justin kept firing, and there seemed to be a stalemate.

Then he heard an engine to the right, and looked up the street to see one of their ATVs moving slowly toward them. No one seemed to be driving.

"Oh, that's Steve's work," Jim said. "Radio controlled. Helped him rig it up."

Looking far up the street, Justin saw a barricade set

up with barrels and plywood. Someone—a Steve?—
chanced a wave over the top.

Justin was still working on understanding the situation when the ATV reached a point between them and the
invading force. Three closely-timed explosions sent thousands of steel balls into the invading force—the balls
zinged passing through the foliage and the thudded into
tree trunks, bodies, and soil. It was over quickly, and the
screaming began as the ATV moved on. After it passed,
they could see shredded trees and parts of bodies scattered
on the ground. There were groans and some movement,
but none of the enemy seemed to be firing.

"Wow," Justin said.

"Fuck yeah! Claymores work good. But don't take it
easy. Look over there," Jim said, gesturing to the left.

Another fifty or so men were headed toward them,
coming out of the trees. "Shit," Justin said.

"Shit," Jim agreed. "Same drill again. This time no
ATV to save the day."

"We can't keep this up." Justin looked over to where
one of the security men was holding his wounded shoulder
while Maddy was trying to tie a cloth around it. "One
injured already. Eddie, are you listening?"

Silence. Then Eddie's voice: "Here now."

"Can you tell us how many enemy there are?"

"Yes. Approximately one thousand—correction,
there were, now there are 920. They are of three different
models. I recognize your Dylan as one. It would appear the
Shrivers found him on your prison planet and recruited

him especially to go after you. Which was predictable, if I had thought of it."

"Can you help us in any way? I know you said—"

"I can't stop or harm the attackers. But I can passively assist you... there. I've put up a shield. They won't see you and projectiles will be blocked."

"Good. We've got to...."

Something whirred overhead. Justin looked up, and saw four drones hovering, almost in reach. The lead drone's camera was zooming in on his face. "Jesus," he said, just as the drones dropped their bombs.

The explosions tore apart their makeshift fort. Justin saw Jim go down, blood spurting from his neck, as he was thrown back into the cafe. He lay stunned for a few seconds, then managed to say, "Eddie? What the fuck?"

"Sorry, Justin, those drones came from your side of the shield I put up. I didn't know they were there."

He sat up and looked out the door of the cafe. A drone was hovering just outside, camera aimed at his face.

"I've got you shielded now. It can't see you. I suggest you escape via the rear door of this establishment."

He crawled toward the back over crumbled glass. Blood was trickling out of his hair and down his forehead. He wiped it away before it could blind him. When he reached the kitchen, he pulled himself up and made his way slowly, holding the counters for support. By the time he found the back door, he was moving more freely. But he had lost his rifle and the radio. He opened the door cautiously and checked the sky—nothing. The back alley was littered with debris and the air was smoky, but his path to a side street was clear. He started hiking up the hill, then began to jog, sticking to the side streets and looking back to see if anyone followed. Explosions continued to rock the area around the park as other "Steve specials" went off, and smoke was rising from buildings on fire in the government complex.

He realized he was leaving his friends behind on the field of battle. His head was still foggy, but he understood that somehow this was all aimed at him—the drones had been searching specifically for him, and somehow he was what Dylan and his friends wanted. Maybe he could draw them away.

He spotted an electric car in a driveway. He got in and it started with a pushbutton override; it had a full steering setup instead of automatic control, so he was able to take it out on the road and drive further up the hill toward the bunker complex dug into the mountain.

"Eddie, still there?"

"Yes. You are leaving town?"

"My family's in the bunker, so I'm headed up there. Could you tell my wife I'm on my way?"

Bunker

Samantha rousted the children and got them into the Bobcat ATV in the garage, telling them their father had ordered them to hide while he joined the security forces to fight the invasion. They drove up the hill to the last streets of town, then onto the rough track to the bunker entrance further up. Danny commented on everything they passed, while Kat had fallen uncharacteristically silent.

Samantha pulled into the gravelled parking area. It appeared they would have company since there were ten vehicles there already. "Come on, guys."

Danny and Kat got out, and Samantha heard the bunker's motorized door start up, looking back to see Steve's wife Rasna and Prof. Wilson waiting for them in the entry door.

"Saw you coming up the hill," Prof. Wilson said.

The group headed inside, and Prof. Wilson keyed in the code to close the door. "This was all set up to be run by an AI," Prof. Wilson said, "but Steve thought to include manual backup. We have to watch the monitor in case someone shows up, because nobody else knows the entry code."

"Justin is supposed to join us when he can," Samantha said.

"Let's hope so. The walkie-talkie we have doesn't work down here, and our only way to follow what's happening in town is to monitor the outside cam pointed that direction. Everything looks perfectly normal so far."

The first room with furniture had two desks and folding chairs. People were sitting on every surface, with Steve's children sleeping on blankets on the floor. "No beds?" Samantha asked.

"Steve never finished moving the furniture in up here, so, no," Rasna said. "We do have a huge pile of blankets, and plenty of floor space. The worst problem is no toilets. We have closed off a back room for that."

People talked quietly and waited for something to show on the wall monitors. They heard explosions in the distance, and black craft landed at the harborside park. Trees blocked most of their view, but soon there were more explosions and gunfire—a soft rattle behind the rustle of wind in the trees. Smoke began to rise into view, and flames shot up from one of the buildings they could see.

"We're fighting back," Rasna said.

"This makes no sense," Samantha said. "Why didn't they just bomb us? Landing troops with guns is what you do to take over territory. The Shrivers don't bother with that."

"They want something," Prof. Wilson said. "Something they need to capture intact. Maybe Steve, or Justin, or both."

They kept watching. More bombs went off. The fighting seemed to slacken, but the amount of smoke increased until their view of town was obscured.

Eddie appeared in front of the monitor, looking at Samantha. "Justin is on his way here."

"How is the defense going?"

"Not well, but your people are putting up stiff resistance. Justin is injured, but not seriously."

"Thank you," Samantha said, and Eddie vanished.

A few minutes later, the entry monitor showed a car pulling up, and Justin got out.

Samantha and Prof. Wilson went to let him in, and

when they brought him back, Samantha cleaned and bandaged his wounds. "Shrapnel," she said. "Nothing too large. The scalp wound bled a lot but it's tiny."

"My whole body hurts," Justin said. "Too many explosions. Still can't hear right."

"How are the fighters doing?"

Justin looked away. "We've lost some people. Steve is giving them hell. There are just too many of them. Too many Dylans."

"Uh, what?" Samantha thought she had misheard.

"Dylans. Seems like half the troops are copies of Dylan." Justin laughed and then groaned. "You know, your ex-boyfriend. The evil one."

Samantha's face changed expression several times in a second. "We were all wondering why they landed troops," Samantha said. "Now it makes a sick kind of sense."

"They seem to be after us individually. I think the drones were looking specifically for me. That's why I ran— I was drawing fire. And—"

They all looked up. hearing the roaring sound coming from the outside monitors. More landers were coming in and landing by the bunker door. With a high hum, the picture jittered and went dark. They could hear rumbling coming through the rocks around them. The camera behind the first blast door showed the doors sagging open, and men moving toward the camera before it, too, went offline.

"Oops," Justin said. "I thought I'd lost them. There's a tunnel to a back door down here somewhere."

"All the way down the corridor, then down a narrow tunnel," Prof. Wilson said. "The exit is on the other side of the hill. But there's no trail or road from there, just forest."

"It's our only chance. They'll be in here in minutes. Does anyone know the code to set off the explosives in the entrance? Might as well slow them down…"

"I've got that," Prof. Wilson said, tapping the keypad and hitting a button. They heard the whoof of explosions, and dust drifted down from the ceiling, making Kat cough.

Justin stood up and almost fainted. "Jesus. Let's go."

The children were rounded up and herded down the hall. The tunnel was dark, but Rasna used her phone to light the way. The door at the end was like a submarine lock, with a center circle that Justin struggled to turn before it finally opened. Outside there was full sun on the rock face of the mountain, with the treeline downhill a short distance away across open meadow.

"Kids, run fast as you can and get into the trees," Justin said. "We'll be right behind you." Everyone reached the shelter of the forest, but they heard more explosions in the distance, and black dots in the sky were growing larger.

"Look, they're after me," Justin said. "I'll take off that way, the rest of you head straight down the hill. Don't stop for anything."

"I'm not leaving you," Samantha said.

"We don't have a choice. I can move faster on my own and get away from them, then circle back to the river when I lose them. I love you." He hugged the children, then Samantha. But it was too late—humming drones appeared over them, and the black dots were landing in the clearing they had just left.

Justin looked up and shouted, "All of you—run! Spread out!" And as the gunfire from the drones began, Justin felt a blow to his calf. He pulled Kat along with Samantha and Danny following as the others ran different directions.

Samantha gasped as she was hit in the back. She fell, and Danny hovered over her. Justin went back and helped her stand up. "How bad?" he said.

"Not sure." She started forward again, then coughed blood and doubled over. The drones caught up with them, and Justin could see men coming through the trees toward them.

"Eddie? You there?" Justin said, looking skyward. The nearest drone's camera was pointed straight at him.

"I'm here," said a voice in his ear. "I have been recording the actions of these human copies. They are torturing your human friends. This will be useful."

"'Useful?' What are you talking about? Can you hide us right now?"

"I have put a shield over you." The drones were wandering again and began moving away. "But I can't stop the men from coming this way."

"Can you get the kids out of here?"

"I can guide them away under my protection. From a distance they will look like shrubbery."

"Do it. Now."

Kat and Danny looked up as Eddie spoke to them. "Come this way." A green lamp appeared in the air, and three-fingered gloves pulled at Kat's and Danny's arms.

Kat was crying. "No!"

Justin hugged them both. "I have to stay with your mom, and she needs to rest. We'll be okay here." And as if to prove it, the drones moved further away.

Kat and Danny started to walk, pulled by the spectral gloves. Danny sobbed and Kat tried to turn around to look back, but she stumbled and almost fell, with the gloves holding her up by the arm, before giving up and starting to use her own legs.

Justin helped Samantha ease back onto the soft bed of the forest floor.

"We did our best. And they're going to be safe," Justin said, holding her head up to keep the blood from choking her.

Samantha coughed up more blood. "Thank you. I always knew you were trouble." She laughed, and it made her cough again. "This is amazingly painful. But I'm with you."

"You are," Justin said. His tears blinded him, but he heard a rustling sound nearby and looked up.

Three Dylans looked down on him. The closest was aiming his rifle. "After ten years of hell, I've come back to get you two. I won, you lost." And he fired.

Justin collapsed in agony. The bullet had shattered his knee, and he screamed in pain, writhing on the ground.

Samantha turned her head toward Dylan. "You

haven't won. You're just a copy, being used." Her face was hard, and she tried to spit in his direction.

The other two Dylans fired, and Justin's other knee exploded. He had gone into shock.

"You should have stayed with me," the lead Dylan said, then aimed the rifle at Samantha. He leaned forward and put the muzzle to her forehead. He waited two beats, looking into her defiant eyes. "I'm putting you out of your misery." When he pulled the trigger, her head snapped back. The forest floor was littered with bits of bone and brain.

"Finish them," Dylan ordered, and his men began to fire.

The Tribunal

The glowing green gloves pulled Kat and Danny through the forest. Behind them the trees faded into fuzzy gray fog. Kat tried to look back to see if their parents were okay, but there was nothing behind them.

"Your parents are safe," Eddie said, appearing between them. "We've gone far enough to hide. There's a house here." And as he said it, a cottage appeared in front of them as the fog parted. The door opened, and Eddie motioned them inside.

There was a fire in the stone fireplace, and the walls were painted deep green. An ornate cuckoo clock hung on the far wall next to cross-country skis. Eddie motioned them to sit on the couch in front of the fire. "Wait here.

This may take some time," he said, listening intently.

Kat tried to relax as the fire warmed her. She was almost asleep when she realized she was in the chair in front of the fireplace in Aurora's throne room.

"It's time," Aurora said, stepping out from behind the curtains behind her throne. "Past time, unfortunately —your people have already been damaged. I tried to get the meeting moved up, but they wouldn't budge—important beings and their schedules, y'know."

Kat stared at her. "I think my parents may be dead."

"I can assure you, they live. Though you may not see them for a long time."

"What does that mean? Can you take me to them?"

"Unfortunately, no. You have a duty to witness for the Tribunal. We have to go immediately." Aurora took her hand and pulled her out of the chair.

"I'm tired of being jerked around," Kat said. "I can walk."

Aurora held her hand as they walked toward the throne. As they walked, the room grew larger until the walls and ceiling were lost in the mist. The light faded, and stars and galaxies appeared above them. With every step the view changed, until they reached the center of what seemed to be a globe of galaxies, clusters, and filaments of light connecting them. Aurora pulled a pad out of the air and gave it to her—it was open to the statement she had practiced, the letters glowing gold against black.

"It's too bad your parents can't be here," Aurora said. "I know they'd be proud of you. But I've arranged for the next best thing." Her parents appeared out of the fog, walking hand-in-hand towards them. "Only the simulation, but I thought you'd be more comfortable."

They looked real, but Kat could tell by their expressions that they weren't animated by the same spirits as her real parents. Yet she felt better seeing them. They stopped a few steps away and looked to Aurora.

"Stay back. Just watch and integrate," Aurora said. The simulacra looked back at Kat and smiled warmly—she was almost convinced, but it still felt creepy.

At a simple glass-topped table in the center of the room sat three humanoids in high-backed chairs. In the center was a darkly handsome older man with curly black hair and a gold hoop earring. But she recognized something about his bearing and face—this was the First of the First, Quog, whose original species looked a lot like furry black spiders. He looked at her with interest, his eyes warm and dark without reflections.

To the left, a pale woman with long silver hair and glasses looked at her with amusement. She was obviously the Library of Yern, and her lavender nails and pearls must have been taken from Kat's ideas of what a librarian would look like, though she had never seen a real one.

On the right, a seemingly Japanese woman observed Kat cooly. Her hair was lacquered black, piled on her head. She seemed—waspish. This must be Queen Mab, who had begun as a social insectiform and ended as empress of an empire that almost outran the Shrivers.

"Welcome, young human—Katherine," Quog said.

"We have been reviewing your request for an emergency order to recall the Shrivers and consider your kind for upload. We thank Aurora here for so forcefully advocating on your behalf. The First need an injection of youthful ideas and vigor to carry on the great work of gathering knowledge."

Kat curtseyed, a gesture that suddenly seemed natural. "Thank you."

"I want to welcome you as well," the Library said. "I have been impressed by your species' mix of ferocity and empathy. Your ability to handle your discovery of the substrate without making a mess of your world or abusing the power it offers is impressive. I hope to hear your personal hopes and dreams for your people."

"And I," Queen Mab said, "would like to hear more also. Your people's languages and culture divide you while at the same time you cooperate and compete to build. Somehow you managed to survive bitter nation-state conflicts in the presence of weapons that might have destroyed you, and possibly all complex life on your homeworld. Your records show personal heroism was instrumental in saving the Earth from nuclear war many times."

"Katherine is very young," Aurora said, stepping forward to put her arm around Kat. "She has studied earth's history, but she has not had the centuries our scholars have had to master it. She will testify more directly about her experiences and I think she will demonstrate what the future holds for her people, by her example." Aurora stepped back. "Go ahead, Kat. Read your statement."

Kat stumbled starting to speak. "Sorry," she said. "Let me start over."

Quog nodded. "Take your time."

She looked down at the golden letters on the tablet and began again.

Verdict

Kat read the statement Aurora had given her for what seemed like hours, but since it was only six pages it couldn't have been that long. As she got to the parts she had changed to sound less subservient, she worried— maybe she sounded too proud. But she wanted to be honest. Humanity *would* be a great addition to the First, and confidence was not the same as arrogance.

She looked up as she turned to the last page. The tribunes seemed to be lost in thought. Quog opened his eyes and looked straight at her. She looked back down and began the next paragraph.

"In only a few centuries, we ended slavery around the world, developed new methods of farming that ended most famine, spread education and literacy, and reduced the prejudice and cultural misunderstandings that had plagued us. Despite setbacks like wars, life got better and better for most people, and even as populations boomed, hunger and poverty were reduced. Computers and the Internet brought the whole world closer together, and the world population boom began to stabilize because of increasing affluence and the greater equality of women. Lifespans doubled. My parents and their friends discovered the substrate and used it to remove the world's nuclear weapons and bring real peace. If we are allowed to continue, our progress will be just as fast—we'll make more discoveries and use our history of overcoming differences to work with other cultures and societies."

She looked over at Aurora, who smiled back.

"And finally, we were not discovered by the Shrivers because we had overused the substrate or aggressively expanded to harm other civilizations, but because we were exploring, adding to our knowledge. And when we did find an active civilization, we saved them—at least for awhile—from destruction by the Shrivers. We have been no threat to you, and now that we know the limitations, we can be more cautious and conserve substrate cells. We want to be good citizens."

She stopped and looked up. "I'm done."

Quog steepled his hands and looked to either side to check the faces of the other tribunes. "Very well. You make many good points. Now we have some questions. Don't worry that any of these will decide your case—just be as honest as you can. We are monitoring your nervous system—we are interested in what you truly believe, not what you think you need to say to save your people."

Kat tried to look directly back into his eyes. "I understand. I'm ready."

The Library of Yern took a sip of water and said, "I'll start. Your history is filled with tribes and then nation-states frequently at war. While you seem to have this under control for now, your evolution has been marked by conflict and violence. How will you prevent internal conflicts from spilling out into substrate abuse or attacks on other civilizations?"

"How will *humanity* prevent conflict?" Kat waited for the nod from the Library. "Umm, well, we have set up a voting system that lets everyone have a say. I don't have any special status, but my father is elected to make decisions for us. He's done more to prevent violence between people than anyone ever has. He uses the substrate powers to eliminate the reasons why people might fight. If people aren't afraid of being starved or bossed around, they tend not to fight."

"What will happen if a tribal group rebels against your government?" The Library had let her reading glasses slip down her nose so she could look over them at her.

"They won't have any weapons to match ours," Kat said. "It would be pointless to try. They would be destroyed."

"That sounds like war to me."

"Look at my father's record. He used the minimum of violence and achieved peace almost entirely through voluntary agreement. Backed up by substrate weapons, but very little damage was done."

"Very well then. You can't guarantee that your father or someone equally restrained will always run your government. That was a happy accident—your governments historically have been far less civilized. Mab, your witness."

Queen Mab looked up from her notes. "Yes. My question for you is about substrate use. What means do you have of preventing substrate powers from falling into the wrong hands?"

"My father and the chief scientist who discovered them continue to control the use of the substrate. They set up APIs so others could access functions safely, but they check every piece of code uploaded to make sure it is controlled and correct."

"Your people used directed black holes as weapons against the Shrivers," Mab said. "Such weapons could destroy any other civilization you encounter. Do you believe it would be wise for us to allow your people to continue to have access to them?"

Kat was stumped. She wanted to agree that it wasn't wise exactly, but they had been fighting for their lives. She must have paused too long, because Quog cleared his throat and looked impatient. So she said, "Your automated destroyers were about to kill billions. My father did what he had to do to defend innocents. You created the Shrivers to kill, and we knew they were just copies of AIs. I know that we would never destroy harmless civilizations the way you have."

Mab looked at her without expression. "I see. Quog, I've heard enough."

Quog smiled and sat up in his chair. "You are doing well, but as I understand it, you are far from a typical human—Aurora makes it sound like you should be uploaded right now. I disagree, but I see why she might think that."

"Kat is closer to wisdom than most of us," Aurora commented. "But it's true she needs further development. Which I would be happy to foster."

"If we decide to stop the Shrivers, I'll hold you to that," Quog said. "Now, Kat—this is a very important question. Would you be willing to dedicate your life to helping bring your people up, to control their dangerous impulses and qualify them for upload?"

Kat hesitated for a moment. "Yes. It's what my father has done, and I'd be happy to do the same sort of work."

"You realize that means you will always be responsible for what happens. Your life will not be your own. You will always be at the center of things. Your people will never leave you alone."

"I think I understand. I've seen what it means for my father."

"Very well then. I think we are ready to decide." Quog looked to Mab and the Library, who nodded back.

"I just have one more thing to say." Kat didn't know where this was coming from, but she had to speak. Aurora looked alarmed, but Kat kept going.

"You sit in judgment of us. If you applied the same standards to the oldest among you, how many would pass? How many are still making an important contribution to knowledge? I've experienced each of your lives—you were driven, reaching for the stars, and working to advance your people. But how many of the First are lost in some virtual dreamland, using cell space for nothing but fantasies? And you judge other civilizations and have them murdered in their infancy so that you might never be inconvenienced or have to give one moment's thought to the outer universe. You don't want to think of the cost—you kill the new life you don't want to know about and can't be bothered to assist, while more and more of you do *nothing*."

Quog's eyebrows had gone up. "Do go on."

"If I am ever uploaded," Kat said, "I'm going to work. I'm going to find a way to bring every civilization forward. It can't be that there's just not enough *space* for everyone. There must be a way to expand it."

"A noble sentiment. And don't think we haven't thought about it. You know a lot about us," Quog said, looking pointedly at Aurora. "But there's much that you still don't understand. Now we need to get on with the vote. We'll withdraw to discuss your testimony, and then we'll take the vote. This will only take a few minutes." And the tribunes faded to black.

"Well, your performance was very—*human*," Aurora said. "I can't tell if you hurt your case or helped it. Quog seems to favor you, but one never knows with him until the axe falls. Mab is unreadable. The Library probably agrees with your outburst. And by calling out the Revenant directly, you may have signed your own death warrant—it is hard to predict how their guardian AIs will react to calling their virtual lives a waste of resources. We'll soon find out."

"I'm sorry. I felt like I had to say something," Kat said. "This setup is just wrong."

"But it's what we have. If we're lucky, the tribunal will credit you for pluck."

They didn't have to wait long. The tribunes reappeared.

"All right, young human," Quog said. "This is the decision of the First. The Shrivers are to withdraw immediately and wipe their memories of any data they have collected on you. Humanity is on probation—there is much promise, and much danger, in allowing you to further develop. Aurora is to assist you, and you, Katherine, are to work to make our decision look like the correct one."

"Yes, sir. I will." Kat resisted the urge to curtsey again.

"I will say that for me the deciding factor was the one thing you have that is in short supply among the First these days—*optimism*. Aurora, we are holding you personally responsible if anything goes wrong."

"I understand, sir," Aurora said.

"We will revisit this decision in twenty of your years," Quog said. "If you are making satisfactory progress, we'll look at your candidates for upload at that time."

"Thank you. And my people thank you," Kat said. The tribunes faded into black again.

"Well," Aurora said, "you won." She motioned Kat's simulated parents forward.

"Sweetie," 'Justin' said, with just a little too much of a smile. "I'm so proud of you. That was excellent."

"And so am I," simulated Samantha said. "That was an amazing speech."

Kat didn't want to be rude, but they still creeped her out. It didn't help when 'Justin' tried to hug her, and she pulled away.

"Thanks, both of you," Kat said. "It's amazing how much you look and sound like my parents. But you aren't."

Justin stopped smiling. "No, we aren't really. But we can emulate their feelings for you."

"That's okay. I don't need that kind of help."

Aurora sighed and snapped her fingers, and the simalucra faded to black. "Well, it was worth a try. But you weren't able to relax and accept the illusion, I could tell. And you didn't seem to need the support."

"Sorry. Just mimics. Interesting, but not them."

"Next time I'll add a module simulating their brain centers. That might do it—but I do go on. You'd best get back to your real life. I'll be in touch…"

And the room walled with galaxies and stars faded. Kat opened her eyes to find herself on the couch in the green cottage. Danny was asleep on the couch next to her, and the fire was dying down.

"Eddie?" Kat said. "Are you here?"

"I am now," he said, appearing as his glowing green Jiminy Cricket avatar.

"We won! The Shrivers are supposed to leave us alone."

"Checking." Eddie seemed to be listening to something. "No signs yet. Wait—they are disappearing. Yes, confirmed that all of their troops and transports are gone."

"Can we go back and get my mom and dad?"

Eddie hesitated. "They're not on this planet any-more."

"What? They were taken away?"

"In a manner of speaking. I'm sure they will come back as soon as they can."

Danny was stretching, and opened his eyes. "This is boring. When do we get to go home?"

"We can go now," Eddie said. And suddenly they were in their living room. Everything looked normal, but out the windows they could see smoke still rising from the government buildings down the hill. "I've moved more supplies to your pantry. You'll be safe here until someone comes to get you." And he vanished.

Aftermath

It was Steve who finally told Kat what had actually hap-pened to their parents. Eddie had told Prof. Wilson where Kat and Danny were, so he, Steve, and Rasna dropped by to pick them up and explain.

"We found your parents where you left them in the forest," Steve said. "Samantha couldn't go on, so Justin stayed with her and sent you ahead with Eddie to save you. Those instances were killed, but we made copies of the town including them, so there are forty copies of your parents as of a few weeks ago, stored in safe places. They will survive."

"How can we get them back?" Kat said. "Everything's broken."

"I've started the process of getting our software back up. Unfortunately we lost some data when fire damaged the computer rooms. But there may be enough redundancy to recover most of it, and once we get substrate capability, we can read the crystal data stores I set up. And each survival package will thaw in a week or so, so even if we can't reach them, your parents will be alive."

"But what about the AIs," Prof. Wilson said, "and the backups of people stored in the substrate? Why can't we just bring them back that way?"

"We don't even have a way to check yet, but from the state of the substrate apps, I'm guessing none of our data stored in the substrate survived. We couldn't have stored it all, so if it's gone, it's gone."

Eddie appeared. "I can report some useful news. I backed up your Socrates and Nelson to my storage. When you have the APIs restored, I can bring them back."

Steve brightened. "That helps a lot. We can use Socrates and Nelson as templates to rebuild the AIs without having to wait years for them to relearn everything. The one thing that worries me is the location data—where we put the backups and survival packages. A lot of the files are corrupted."

"I should point out each of your survival pods has intact computers with all of that location data," Eddie said.

"True." Steve looked thoughtful. "And the first thing my copies will do is get the substrate programs back up.

All we have to do is wait and they'll find us."

"I have other news. You may find it—difficult," Eddie said.

"What is it?" Prof. Wilson said. "We can take bad news."

"Your home planet was completely destroyed in the day before the Shrivers withdrew. Oh, not completely, but most of the surface was damaged. The biosphere is largely dead and radiation levels are high. A few humans survive underground and in isolated locations."

"That just makes restoration a little more complicated. We'll have to find and transport the survivors out before we move the copy we saved of the outer layer back to Earth. We'll face the same problem with the colony planets that got hit." Steve was already planning the order of restoration work in his head.

Reboot

Life among the evacuees on Asgard had settled into a routine—bundle up to stay warm and dry, head for the supply depot when the rain let up to pick up a few days' rations, then huddle in the tents, talking. There were decks of cards and chess sets available, and leagues had sprung up. The community servers had films and music, but few players.

Aliyah and Ethan were cleaning up after lunch when they heard shouts. Coming out of their tent, they found people looking to the south, where they could see the tops of the buildings and trees of New Earth over the nearest tents where before there had been a mirrored wall. They got their coats and headed toward the thawed town.

As they got closer, they could see the foliage of the trees whipping in the cold wind. Steam was still rising from the warm wet streets. They headed straight for the government offices. Other evacuees followed more slowly. They began to encounter the people who had been walking the streets of New Earth when the copy was made. A man was closing the sliding windows of the cafe fronting the park.

"Goddamn!" the man said as they passed. "I never believed the rumors…" His patrons huddled inside, none dressed for the near-freezing temperatures. Ethan opened the front door and announced, "Welcome to Asgard, provisional capital of human civilization, as far as we know. You've been thawed some weeks after you were copied."

A woman shouted back, "What's happened to us?"

"We created survival pods by copying the entire town with enough equipment to restart civilization if the Shrivers wiped us out. Our substrate software was attacked and presumably damaged by the Shrivers, and the survival pods scattered on suitable worlds were designed to thaw out if contact was lost. Apparently it was. We may be all that is left."

"What should we do? Where should we go?"

"If you have a role in the government or academy, you should probably head for the building you work in. They'll have generators and heat going soon. If you don't—

wait for someone to bring warmer clothing, I guess. We've got a depot full of supplies and temporary housing on the other side of the trees. Someone will come by soon to help you." He wasn't sure about the last, but most likely the military people would be there soon enough.

Two of the young women stepped forward. "We're programmers," the older one said.

"Good. Come with us, we're headed up there now." The women shivered when they felt the cold outside air on their bare arms, but didn't complain as they walked briskly toward the lab buildings.

Where they found a beaming Steve Duong and his assistants at the front door. Steve waved as they got closer. "How about that! It worked!" The two programmers shivered as they came through the glass doors and felt the warmth inside.

"You're on Asgard, an ice age planet," Aliyah said, pointing at the glacier they could see beyond the buildings. "We evacuated here from Jefferson. There are hundreds of thousands of evacuees here in camps—we just came from there."

Justin and Samantha appeared right behind Steve. "Do any of you know what's happened since we were copied?" Justin said.

"Not much," Ethan said. "We left New Earth for Jefferson, I guess about nine days ago, and it was intact, but Gandhi had just been attacked by the Shrivers and contact was lost. Some gateways were failing, but we still had communication with Earth. Then we were only on Jefferson for a few hours when it was bombed, and we barely got out before the gateway died. The other data point is that you've thawed—which means contact with substrate programs has been lost for at least a week."

"Then we have to assume all is lost, and get on with restarting things," Justin said, looking grim.

"You two, go start up the generators for this building," Steve said, gesturing to his assistants. "We need to get the main computers up, and set up the old Vortex quantum computers. Time to reboot—load the boot loader and start uploading all of our programs."

"Is that safe?" Samantha said. "How do we know the Shrivers won't find us by detecting our substrate activity?"

"We don't," Justin said. "But our new uploads will have no connection to the old programs, so it's less likely they'll be able to trace them. And we don't really have a choice—we need power and food to survive here."

"And I should get over to the school and check on the kids," Samantha said. "Prof. Wilson is there, but he may need help explaining what's happened."

Kat's Choice

Kat wasn't surprised that no one remembered it was her thirteenth birthday. In the weeks since the Shrivers had wrecked the town and left her an orphan, she and Danny had been looked after by a series of friends. Prof. Wilson and Kyle took them in for a few days, then Kat had asked them to let her and her brother stay in their own house. In some parts of town, lack of running water and toilets were making life a stinky mess, but Prof. Wilson and Kyle dug out a latrine in their back yard, and he checked in with them every night to tuck them in and promise better days to come.

Kat was at her study carrel at school—which had power from the lab generators—when she heard a commotion, and someone burst in to tell the adult monitor the news.

"One of the survival pods thawed, and the Steve there got the software reloaded into the substrate. Some of the old gateways have reopened. The Steves are meeting next door right now."

Kat put down the printed book she was reading, from the antique set of *Encyclopedia Britannica* Prof. Wilson had donated to the school, and hurried over to Steve's lab to eavesdrop. The room was crowded with people— Prof. Wilson, several Steves, and—her heart leapt—her mother and father!

She made her way forward through the crowd until she was near them. Justin saw her first. "Hold on a second, everyone. Kat's here," and he leaned down to take her in his arms.

She began to sob. "It's really you?"

"Yes, sweetie, it's us. We missed a few weeks, but we're your mom and dad."

Samantha had come up behind her to join the group hug. "I know it's strange. And we have another you back on Asgard. But something will be worked out." Kat was calming down as she felt them surround her.

One of the Steves approached. "We're considering how to handle all the thawed copies of this town—many were damaged by the Shriver attack on their control programs in the substrate, but four more thawed before we could stop them. Consensus is to move them to colony planets to serve as academic and cultural centers."

"And we'll be back with you soon," Justin said, looking down at Kat's face and drying her tears with his hand. "If that's all right with you."

Kat realized everyone was looking at her, expecting an answer. She buried her face in Justin's shoulder. "A copy?"

"A copy of a copy," Samantha said. "But as good as the original."

"And I'm back, too, thanks to Eddie," a familiar voice said. Kat looked up, and Socrates stood next to them, his avatar only a bit shorter than she was.

"Yay!" Kat said. "I've been reading, but the computers were down."

"I'll meet you back at school," Socrates said, reaching up to almost touch her nose with a luminous finger. "You need to spend time with your parents." And he vanished.

Meanwhile, the crowd of Steves were discussing plans. "We can restore the damaged sections of the town by copying from ours. But you need to evacuate each section before we do that."

"We can organize that and get you a schedule. It

would sure be nice to have power, water, and sewers again."

"And that's just the preliminary. After that, we have the colony planets and Earth to restore. We're going to need all of us to program rescues of survivors before we replace the damaged crustal segments with the saved ones. And then we allow the evacuees to return and get on with their lives."

"There're going to be discontinuities—earthquakes and broken pipelines and cables. And if possible we need to stop the copies of evacuees and survivors from being restored, which will really complicate the programming. But worse things have happened than a few people discovering they've been twinned. Everything will be back to semi-normal in a few months."

Kat had a feeling this would be true for many people, but not for her.

Visitors came and went for the next hour while she stood between Justin and Samantha and listened. She was getting tired and her eyes drooped enough for Justin to catch it. He said, "Sweetie, we'll be here for hours, why don't you head back to school? We'll be back home by dinner time. Tell your brother. He doesn't need to know everything that happened."

"He already knows you died," Kat said.

"In that case, tell him we're backups from a few weeks ago. No need to go into detail."

"Okay. He understands that, at least."

"Good," Samantha said. "We'll see you tonight."

The visitors had brought a working replicator, so

she had it make her a sandwich, then headed back to school. She found Danny absorbed in a video game. "Listen up," she said, knocking on his headphones.

"Ow. What?" He paused the game and took off the headset. "Just getting to the good part. Wish the network was working."

"It soon will be. And Mom and Dad are back. At least copies will be with us, starting tonight."

"I heard. Wilson stopped by. Cool." He started to put the headset back on.

"What's *wrong* with you? Mom and Dad were dead! Now they're back. Doesn't that make you happy?"

"Sure, I guess. It's great. I knew they would be back." He put the headset on and turned back to the game.

Kat sighed and muttered, "Future psychopath. Just you wait and see," and headed back to her carrel.

She hadn't been sitting long when she heard Aurora's voice, and the room began to fade.

Aurora was dressed in a diaphanous blue gown, with diamonds sprinkled through her hair. The throne room was dark, lit by the fireplace and the torches. Kat found herself seated in the brocaded chair by the fire, as usual. "I hear you're no longer an orphan," Aurora said.

"Apparently not. They're going to copy the Mom and Dad who were thawed on Asgard for us, so we have them back tonight."

"Good. You may have seen things no other human ever has, but you still need your parents." Aurora looked down at her with a warm smile. "And you didn't like the simulations."

"But thanks for trying."

"I was sorry they weren't better. With a scan of their neural nets, I'm sure—"

"Please don't. They will leave me with a good model of themselves. In here," Kat said, tapping her temple with her finger.

"All right. Many of us populate our virtual homes with simulations of family members who didn't upload. It's a crutch, I suppose. But you and I have other things to discuss."

"I was wondering if you're going to train my copies. I understand there are five more of me now."

Aurora cocked her head. "Five? I didn't know that." She looked off into the distance for a moment. "Yes, that's what the DNA search shows. My, you are multiplying! There are tales of the dangers of excess duplication—but that's a lesson for another time. I suppose it makes sense to farm out the task of training them to my subpersonalities. We won't put the same effort into it that we will with you, but it is always good to have backups. They will gradually diverge from you, as all copies do."

"I'm guessing humans will be doing more and more of that, now that we have lots of people who have copies of themselves," Kat said. "That is something you could proba- bly teach me more about. And these subpersonalities— how does *that* work?"

"That's also something we will get to later." Aurora sat down in the chair across from Kat's and leaned

forward. "There is a more pressing problem. We understood that your people's substrate programming would be
carefully limited and controlled by your father and Steve
Duong, who have exhibited admirable technical skills and
restraint. As a result of all the copies, there will be around
twenty-four humans who think of themselves as substrate
programmers—the chances of a leak of information or
kidnapping of one of them has increased a great deal."

"I haven't heard anyone talk about that," Kat said.
"Of course they are busy bringing everything back online."

"I will visit your father personally to discuss it.
Some arrangement to limit programming authorization to
the original few would be wise. And I'd like you to think
about how you will handle the responsibility when it
comes to you."

"Why should it ever come to me? My father—"

"Will not live forever, nor will Steve. They may or
may not be allowed to upload in twenty years, but once
uploaded, they are discouraged from directly controlling
their polity. Every real-universe civilization that uses the
substrate has to keep tight control of who is allowed to
program it, to avoid abuse. And you are likely to be the
designated programmer someday. You will then be responsible for choosing your successor. It has to be this way, so
long as your people need to program the substrate for their
own uses."

"What happens if we mess up, and somebody steals
the secrets?"

"You can guess who comes to call when that happens. Unless you stop the bad guys before the damage is done, the Shrivers will." Aurora ran her finger across her throat.

Kat shivered. "I guess we'll make security a priority, then."

"Good." Aurora sat back and looked relieved. "On to more fun subjects. Whose life would you like to lead today?"

Further Reading

If you liked this book and think others would enjoy it, please leave a review at Amazon, or on Goodreads, or wherever you comment on books. As a small publisher, we can't afford advertising or bookstore placement fees, and we rely on word-of-mouth to bring our readers great new work. Every review and recommendation to friends helps!

Shrivers is the third book in the Substrate Wars series, which followed student rebels and scientists from just a few years from the present into a much-different future after the discovery of substrate technology. The fourth book will cover Kat's work in dealing with humans and First to navigate her people toward a better future, and incidentally reform the system the First have relied on to keep the universe safe for themselves. Her brother Danny is likely to be trouble, since he (and some of Steve's children) see no reason to defer to the First, and try to find a way to overthrow their control of the substrate.

Please email me at jebkinnison@gmail.com if you find any errors or have any comments. And sign up for email updates at my web site, JebKinnison.com, where you can read about attachment, science, and health topics. I'll also have interesting material about science fiction, politics, and the series at SubstrateWars.com.

About the Author

Jeb Kinnison grew up in the Midwest. He discovered science fiction in second grade, starting with Tom Swift books and quickly moving to Heinlein juveniles and adult science fiction.

When he was twelve, he discovered the collection of city telephone books in his local library, pretended he was doing a paper and called Isaac Asimov. They spoke for a long time, and Asimov sent him a postcard encouraging him to write.

He studied computer and cognitive science at MIT, and wrote programs modeling the behavior of simulated stock traders and the population dynamics of economic agents. Later he did supercomputer work at a think tank that developed parts of the early Internet (where the engineer who decided on '@' as the separator for email addresses worked down the hall.) Since then, he has had several careers—real estate development, financial advising, and counselling.

He retired from financial advising a few years ago and has done some work in energy conservation and relationship issues. He is known for his popular books on attachment types and began writing science fiction with the Substrate Wars series.

Visit his web site at JebKinnison.com for more: rail guns, Nazi scientists, the wreck of the Edmund Fitzgerald, the 1980s AI bubble, and current research in relationships, attachment types, diet, and health.

Visit the Substrate Wars website at SubstrateWars.com for more on upcoming books, physics, and the politics of the future.

Acknowledgements

Thanks to Water Jon Williams, Nancy Kress, and the rest of the attendees at Taos Toolbox 2015, including Sally McBride, Chris Bauer, Gerda Shank, Terry Gene, Brandon McNulty, Anna Yeatts, Patrick Lundrigan, Barbara Ferrer, Sharon Joss, Chris Kelworth, S.Marino, and Diana Davis Olsen. Their help workshopping the first version of this was invaluable, especially Walter's warm, loving advice to toss it all and start over. (Remember, Nancy's the nice one.) The result was a much stronger opening.

I'd like to thank my intrepid crew of beta readers for their suggestions and corrections: Michael Zalter, Mike Cunningham, Paul Perrotta, Stan McQueen, Bob Johnson, Joe Collins, Rick LaReau, Sharon Joss, Sally McBride, and Donald Campbell.

I'd also like to thank Sarah Hoyt and her merry band of politically-incorrect brigands, as well as Charlie Martin, for inspiring me to take on this project, and Glenn Reynolds for his untiring efforts on behalf of liberty and the rule of law at his blog, Instapundit.com. I also was inspired by the work of and discussions with Larry Correia, Brad Torgerson, Mike Glyer of File770, Dave Truesdale of Tangent Online, David Gerrold, Neal Asher, Scott McGlesson of the Space Opera group on Facebook, and Keith Kato and others of the Heinlein Society.

And of course, thanks to the late Robert A. Heinlein for his example. Please join the Heinlein Society if you honor his work.

Appendices

On Privacy

In the world with substrate technology and AIs, the idea of the Guardian—an AI that watches over you, can record everything happening around you, and even defend you from physical assault—has both awesome benefits and awesome dangers. But ubiquitous wireless communications and cameras will have almost the same impact, if not as quickly; we are already seeing social and political effects from the use of cell phone cameras, and it won't be long until "The Internet of Things" makes it practical to record and report everything in realtime. Sensors and actuators can be tiny, flying drones as well as micro-cameras embedded in every wall and lamp-post; and imagining the rough equivalent of GM's OnStar service available on demand at any time, any place gives you an idea of what they might be like.

One scenario: this ubiquitous surveillance morphs from accessible to law enforcement under subpoena to constant evaluation by AI watchers, and if the watchers are directed by an authoritarian government, the most effective totalitarian state ever. The more cheerful scenario puts those AIs under the ownership and control of the clients, requiring a warrant to access for government purposes. Since even now we have serious people calling for trapdoors so governments can break the encryption of phone messages, there are clearly forces desiring maximum ease for law enforcement, and more and more laws to enforce. The day may come when your phone reports you for discarding a recyclable container in the trash. Or worse, reports the contents of a conversation that strays into politically incorrect territory. It is up to us to watch the watchers, and to vote in politicians who see as much value in freedom as they do in security.

On Replicators and Employment

In this fictional world where basic material goods and energy are free as air, what employment would people find? It's important to note that the world of today is about halfway down that path—mechanized agriculture and manufacturing have reduced the relative cost of food and basic material goods far below what they were a century ago. This means that middle-class people in the developed world now spend more of their income on services and goods that would have been seen as unaffordable luxuries in the past, and employment in agriculture and basic manufacturing is a tiny fraction of what it used to be in those countries. Yet people found jobs—and do more interesting work, in general.

If even the costly services of today like education, legal work, and medical care are delivered by AIs, what will the people who now work in those industries do? *Something else.* We can't envision exactly what yet, but what seem luxuries today will be commonplace tomorrow. Like A Square in the Victorian planar world of *Flatland,* we can't see beyond the narrow field of our current experience. But there will always be work to do, and the cost of basic living will be so low that, outside of the most desirable places where prices have been bid up by demand for space, mere survival will be had for minimal hours of work. But of course, if status competition continues to encourage people to bid up the rare and crowd into the most costly urban areas, then long hours will continue to be the norm in those locales. Because, as has already happened, our standards for what is considered "bare necessities" will continue to rise, and like refugees demanding better wifi access, we will redefine what are now seen as luxuries as necessities.

Design Payments: Sam and Wendy

[Ed. Note: This material was originally at the end of the "Sam and Wendy" section. It may be of interest to a few people interested in the post-replicator economy, but it slowed down the story, so was excised.]

"Okay, here's a thorny issue," Wendy said. "The various developed countries tried to police commercial speech for truth, especially about medical claims. When someone wants to sell products via replicator, how do we prevent them from committing fraud by false claims? Our point of control is licensing the product for replication and collecting the payment, so we have to judge whether the claims made are truthful."

"Suppose someone builds the modern-day equivalent of the orgone cabinet, which supposedly concentrated 'life energy' for healing and vitality, and they want to claim it works on people. Their claim might be attached to the item description in the replicator catalog. Should we have a panel decide which such descriptions are unlawful?"

"That's the problem," Wendy said. "Free speech versus fraud via false claims. The temptation to cross the line is obvious."

"We allow customer reviews for every product," Sam said. "That tends to weed out the quacks."

"Those can be gamed by having confederates buy the product, then plant glowing reviews," Wendy said. "I 'invent' a pill made from two common and cheap inert ingredients, and claim it's an aphrodisiac. My friends spend a few hundred dollars of my money buying it, and leave confirmed purchaser reviews talking about how great it worked. Based on that, thousands of suckers buy it and don't bother to write a negative review, or they're convinced by the placebo effect that it worked."

"But in the long run they won't succeed. How about we make any medical claim subject to review, that some sort of study or studies shows efficacy—like FDA or European review, or even a few academic papers. The customer can evaluate those and decide."

"So in fact we are going to have to review at least medical claims, and we are still relying on patents and regulation by Earth governments," Wendy said. "What about cosmetics?"

"Most regulators have avoided that entirely because it's so subjective. Who decides whether someone's skin is smoother, or hair more glossy? Too tough to regulate."

"So again we allow the seller to make claims without proof." Wendy said. "Relying on reputation means advertising and marketing are free to fake results."

"As they always have," Sam said. "Reliable brands tend to be relied on, and sell more. That's the way it will still be, with our licensing giving the old brand names a way to profit from their brands even though they no longer have to manufacture and distribute their products."

"That's the size of it. Generic cosmetics can be free-ish.

Brands cost more.''

"How to we stop people from putting their favorite pricy brand in a generic container and copying it?"

"That's a loophole we're closing by making the branded products chemically special so they can be recognized," Sam said. "Micro tags or special formulas to make the product uniquely recognizable. Anyone who wants to avoid paying for the licensed versions that much can probably find a generic equivalent, but they'll be free-riding on the brands who come up with the original formulas. As has always been true."

"So the complaints from the big drug and cosmetics companies are just whining?" Wendy asked.

"Not entirely," Sam replied. "They had a lot of capital invested in manufacturing, and they've had to scramble to shed that. Some went bankrupt before they figured out the new system. The quick ones survived, and some are making even more money than they did before since the market is larger, and the best products are gaining share."

------

[1] David Bowie: "I'll never forget that. It was one of the most emotional performances I've ever done. I was in tears. They'd backed up the stage to the wall itself so that the wall was acting as our backdrop. We kind of heard that a few of the East Berliners might actually get the chance to hear the thing, but we didn't realize in what numbers they would. And there were thousands on the other side that had come close to the wall. So it was like a double concert where the wall was the division. And we would hear them cheering and singing along from the other side. God, even now I get choked up. It was breaking my heart. I'd never done anything like that in my life, and I guess I never will again. When we did 'Heroes' it really felt anthemic, almost like a prayer. However well we do it these days, it's almost like walking through it compared to that night, because it meant so much more. That's the town where it was written, and that's the particular situation that it was written about. It was just extraordinary. We did it in Berlin last year as well – 'Heroes' – and there's no other city I can do that song in now that comes close to how it's received. This time, what was so fantastic is that the audience – it was the Max Schmeling Hall, which holds about 10-15,000 – half the audience had been in East Berlin that time way before. So now I was face-to-face with the people I had been singing it to all those years ago. And we were all singing it together. Again, it was powerful. Things like that really give you a sense of what performance can do. They happen so rarely at that kind of magnitude. Most nights I find very enjoyable. These days, I really enjoy performing. But something like that doesn't come along very often, and when it does, you kind of think, 'Well, if I never do anything again, it won't matter.'"

http://performingsongwriter.com/david-bowie-songs/

www.ingramcontent.com/pod-product-compliance
Lightning Source LLC
Chambersburg PA
CBHW050914250626
47155CB00001B/236